Praise For Laura Childs'
Bestselling Tea Shop Mysteries

***Featured Selection of the Mystery Book Club
"Highly recommended" by the Ladies' Tea Guild***

"You'll be starved by the end and ready to try out the recipes in the back of the book...enjoy!"
—*The Charlotte Observer*

"A page-turner."
—*St. Paul Pioneer Press*

"The perfect series for tea and mystery lovers."
—*The Tea Caddy*

"Tea lovers, mystery lovers, [this] is for you. Just the right blend of cozy fun and clever plotting."
—Susan Wittig Albert, bestselling author of *Bleeding Hearts*

"Delightful!"
—*Tea A Magazine*

"Engages the audience from the start...Laura Childs provides the right combination between tidbits on tea and an amateur sleuth cozy."
—*Midwest Book Review*

D0038440

Tea Shop Mysteries by Laura Childs

DEATH BY DARJEELING
GUNPOWDER GREEN
SHADES OF EARL GREY
THE ENGLISH BREAKFAST MURDER
THE JASMINE MOON MURDER
CHAMOMILE MOURNING

Scrapbooking Mysteries by Laura Childs

KEEPSAKE CRIMES
PHOTO FINISHED
BOUND FOR MURDER

CHAMOMILE MOURNING

Tea Shop Mystery #6

LAURA CHILDS

BERKLEY PRIME CRIME, NEW YORK

THE BERKLEY PUBLISHING GROUP
Published by the Penguin Group
Penguin Group (USA) Inc.
375 Hudson Street, New York, New York 10014, USA
Penguin Group (Canada), 90 Eglinton Avenue East, Suite 700, Toronto, Ontario M4P 2Y3, Canada
(a division of Pearson Penguin Canada Inc.)
Penguin Books Ltd., 80 Strand, London WC2R 0RL, England
Penguin Group Ireland, 25 St. Stephen's Green, Dublin 2, Ireland (a division of Penguin Books Ltd.)
Penguin Group (Australia), 250 Camberwell Road, Camberwell, Victoria 3124, Australia
(a division of Pearson Australia Group Pty. Ltd.)
Penguin Books India Pvt. Ltd., 11 Community Centre, Panchsheel Park, New Delhi—110 017, India
Penguin Group (NZ), Cnr. Airborne and Rosedale Roads, Albany, Auckland 1310, New Zealand
(a division of Pearson New Zealand Ltd.)
Penguin Books (South Africa) (Pty.) Ltd., 24 Sturdee Avenue, Rosebank, Johannesburg 2196,
South Africa

Penguin Books Ltd., Registered Offices: 80 Strand, London WC2R 0RL, England

This is a work of fiction. Names, characters, places, and incidents either are the product of the author's imagination or are used fictitiously, and any resemblance to actual persons, living or dead, business establishments, events, or locales is entirely coincidental. The publisher does not have any control over and does not assume any responsibility for author or third-party websites or their content.

CHAMOMILE MOURNING

A Berkley Prime Crime Book / published by arrangement with the author

PRINTING HISTORY
Berkley Prime Crime hardcover edition / May 2005
Berkley Prime Crime mass-market edition / March 2006

Copyright © 2005 by Gerry Schmitt.
Cover art by Stephanie Henderson.
Cover design by Lesley Worrell.

ISBN: 0-425-20618-1

BERKLEY® PRIME CRIME
Berkley Prime Crime Books are published by The Berkley Publishing Group,
a division of Penguin Group (USA) Inc.,
375 Hudson Street, New York, New York 10014.
The name BERKLEY PRIME CRIME and the BERKLEY PRIME CRIME design
are trademarks belonging to Penguin Group (USA) Inc.

PRINTED IN THE UNITED STATES OF AMERICA

10 9 8 7 6 5 4 3 2 1

ACKNOWLEDGMENTS

My thanks go out to some very special people: Samantha, my editor, who helps make my books ever more readable; my agent, Sam Pinkus, who has made all the difference in the world for me; all the extremely talented folks in publicity, design, editing, and sales at Berkley Prime Crime; my sister, Jennie, who encourages me; my husband, Bob, who has always believed in me; all my friends who actually go out and *buy* my books; all the wonderful booksellers and mystery bookstores who carry my books (thank you, thank you, thank you!); all the delightful tea shop owners who also carry my books and continue to foster the gentle art of tea; all the reviewers, writers, and columnists who have written such kind words; all the tea and mystery aficionados who continue to e-mail me with personal messages and good wishes. Thanks to you all!

This book is dedicated to Mom.
Sure do miss you.

1

❧

Since the weatherman at Channel 8 had predicted a glorious evening, that's exactly what Theodosia Browning was expecting. Temperature in the mid-seventies, light breeze off Charleston Harbor, threads of wispy pink clouds etched against deepening azure-blue skies.

But was the weather cooperating? Had that upbeat forecast been remotely accurate?

"Not in this universe," muttered Theodosia as she grabbed for a Crown Dorset teapot that threatened to go tumbling off, Wizard-of-Oz-style, into the nearby garden. Safely tucking the teapot into a wicker hamper, Theodosia flashed another quick glance at surly, dark clouds that roiled overhead. It was just her luck, she noted, that gigantic raindrops were beginning to spatter down upon her elegantly set tea table.

"We'll have to move everything inside immediately," cried Drayton as Theodosia struggled against the building wind, trying to salvage her cake and tea sandwiches by draping them with plastic wrap.

"It almost feels like a hurricane," replied Theodosia, her voice rising to compensate for the noise of the storm. "Even though it's a little early for hurricane season. Oh, good heavens!" she cried, as a string of lights came swinging toward her. "Even the twinkle lights are blowing out of the trees." Theodosia's mirthful blue eyes and normally placid face had taken on a harried, worried look, and her auburn hair, always full to begin with, billowed out from under her straw hat. Usually the picture of high enthusiasm tempered by Southern grace, Theodosia's good humor was being sorely tested tonight.

Impeccably attired in a wheat-colored linen jacket, navy slacks, starched white shirt, and trademark bow tie, Drayton Conneley, Theodosia's sixty-something master tea blender, also had disappointment written on his grizzled face. He dashed about frantically, struggling to repack silver candlesticks, creamers, and sugar bowls.

This first-ever Poet's Tea at the Heritage Society had been Drayton's brainchild, a way for the organization to participate in Spoleto, Charleston's beloved arts and music festival. And now this sudden spate of horrible weather that had blown in off the mercurial Atlantic was threatening to ruin tonight's festivities. At least the outdoor portion, anyway.

Theodosia clapped a hand atop her floppy broad-brimmed hat as the ever-increasing winds swooped and swirled and threatened to send it flying, too. "Some garden party," she cried as she tried to rescue crisp linens that were turning soggy and a collection of Spode and Limoge teacups that were slowly filling with rain. "In ten minutes flat we went from brewing tea to a brewing storm."

"Grab this, will you?" cried Drayton as he thrust a silver platter laden with tea sandwiches into her hands. "Haley and I are just going to drag the entire table inside."

Theodosia Browning scampered for the safety of the Heritage Society's limestone building and joined the crowd that had taken refuge in its large cypress-paneled gallery. A few guests were already seated and waiting for the poetry readings to begin. But a good-sized group of die-hards milled about, obviously disappointed. They'd come dressed for a garden party and now that event looked like a total washout.

"We're scheduled to begin the poetry readings in ten minutes," hissed Timothy Neville. The silver-haired patriarch of the Heritage Society stood at Theodosia's elbow and favored her with his famously stern gaze. "With this abrupt change in plans, the last thing we want is for our guests to get restless."

Daubing a linen hanky to her rain-streaked face, Theodosia nodded in agreement. "Just give us a few minutes to rearrange things at the back of the room." Her bright eyes roved about the great hall, taking in the u-shaped balcony that served as a kind of choir loft overhead, and confirmed her snap decision. *Yes*, she thought, *the best place to set up the tea table is directly behind the chairs. The little kitchen's back there and we'll be out of the way, but still accessible.* "We'll start serving as soon as the program's finished," she promised Timothy.

Timothy splayed out all ten fingers. "Ten minutes," he

3

told her again. "You'll have everything in place by then?" His raspy voice carried a distinct edge. Timothy was more advanced in years than he appeared, just past eighty now, and didn't always cope gracefully with stress.

"No problem," Theodosia assured him. She spun on her heels and swooped toward the double doors, pressing them open so Drayton and Haley Parker could gently edge their way in. "Watch your fingers," she cautioned her two assistants as they struggled with the sturdy wooden table. "This doorway's awfully narrow." Theodosia watched nervously as the cake tottered and stacks of teacups rattled precariously, but finally they maneuvered the table inside.

"This weather is insane," grumped Drayton, as he brushed dampness from his jacket. "All our guests came dressed in their summer finery and now this bad cloud has everyone looking bedraggled."

"Come on, Drayton," said Theodosia, helping them carry the table to the back of the room. "We've haven't got much time. Timothy is chomping at the bit to start the program."

But Drayton seemed to be relishing his cranky mood. "Oh, for heaven's sake," he said, frowning and pointing toward their cake. "Some of the frosting's melted away. Look at those divots!"

"Someone left the cake out in the rain," quipped Haley as she pushed her stick-straight blond hair behind her ears and flashed a mischievous, lopsided grin.

Theodosia couldn't help but giggle. A slightly damaged cake was no laughing matter, but Haley's quirky comment appealed to her sense of the absurd. Unfortunately, Drayton didn't seem to be taking any of this in stride.

"Such a pity," he lamented, shaking his head and adjusting his bow tie for the umpteenth time. "Our newly renovated patio would have been such an ideal venue."

"We'll be fine," said Theodosia, trying to remain positive while knowing full well that Drayton was heartsick. The newly installed patio set amidst the Heritage Society's formal gardens featured a lovely, cascading waterfall and fish pond, patio stones formed from the distinctive red-yellow clay found in South Carolina's Piedmont region, and stands of Japanese maples and Italian cypress trees. The patio area was further highlighted by wrought-iron benches, large terra-cotta urns stuffed with palmetto trees, and giant boulders trucked in from the picturesque Chattooga River region, where the movie *Deliverance* was filmed.

The plan had been to seat all the guests in the Heritage Society's great hall for the poetry reading, then, in a final grand gesture, throw open the three sets of side doors to reveal the new patio and invite everyone outside for a sophisticated soiree under the stars. A relaxing, informal party where guests would be lulled by warm weather, a string quartet, and, of course, flutes of champagne, dainty teacups of excellent South Carolina black tea, tasty tea sandwiches, and slivers of sweet almond cake.

And now that simply wasn't going to happen. The agenda had changed big time.

But Theodosia was a small business owner. Proprietor of the Indigo Tea Shop and a fledgling entrepreneur. Which meant she'd long since learned how to resuscitate disastrous situations, change proverbial horses in midstream, and, in general, fake it. Recovery was her stock in trade, whether it meant brewing pots of Darjeeling and Assam for last-minute customers, staging impromptu tea tastings, or sweet-talking traditionally tough tea vendors into emergency overnight shipments. The real trick, of course, was flexibility. Adaptive behavior scientists tell us we can all learn, though some of us seem to learn at very different rates.

It had been almost three years since Theodosia quit her job in the dog-eat-dog world of advertising and launched the Indigo Tea Shop. Converting a dusty little space on Church Street into a cozy tearoom where the world's finest loose leaf teas were brewed and served alongside light lunches, tea savories, and luscious desserts worthy of a Parisian *patisserie*. It had been a monumental struggle, this birthing of a small business, but Theodosia had triumphed. Her flair for marketing and fearless risk taking, Drayton's innate charm and vast tea knowledge, and Haley's youthful exuberance and skill in the kitchen had won out. Their formidable talent, forceful personalities, and *joie de vie* were the glue that held it all together. In no time at all, the Indigo Tea Shop quickly earned its rightful place among the elegant tapestry of quaint shops, historic homes, charming courtyard gardens, and cozy B and B's that made up Charleston's historic district.

Theodosia glanced up, surprised to find a tall, hawkish-looking man staring intently at her.

"I'm sorry," she said as she gazed into the man's dark eyes. "We're not set up to serve yet." She gave a slightly helpless shrug. "Obviously the rain caused a few delays. But once the poetry reading—"

"I require a word with Drayton," interrupted the man. He seemed both aloof and oblivious to the furor of cup wiping and table straightening they were frantically engaged in. "I'm Jester Moody," he added, enunciating carefully, as though his name carried a great deal of importance.

The art dealer, Theodosia thought to herself, suddenly focusing on this tall, dark-haired man who fairly crackled with intensity. She'd heard about Jester Moody. Slightly enigmatic, recently awarded some special honor by the People's Republic of China, Jester was a high-end dealer who specialized in Asian antiquities. In a town where most antique dealers focused on oil paintings, furniture, collectible porcelains, and estate jewelry, Jester Moody dealt in rare Shang Dynasty bronzes, Han Dynasty ceramics, and Ming vases. At least that's what was on display in the glittering front window of Passports, his small jewel box of a shop down on King Street.

"Jester!" exclaimed Drayton, as he pushed his way through the swinging door that led from the Heritage Society's small kitchen. "Sorry, but we're not serving yet."

"Forget the tea," Jester Moody snapped. "My interest here is strictly business."

From out of nowhere Drayton produced a white tea towel and proceeded to wipe a seemingly invisible speck of dust from inside a teacup. "Just what is it you want, Jester?" he asked. Now *his* tone had assumed a harder edge.

"I understand the committee chairman has finalized the list," said Jester Moody as he focused piercing eyes on Drayton, "for next Saturday's auction."

"I believe so," Drayton responded lightly. The Heritage

Society's Spring Art Auction was one week away and so many local galleries had offered to donate works that Roger Crispin, the chairman of the auction committee, had struggled mightily to finalize the list. Much as the Heritage Society greatly appreciated the generous donations of sculptures, paintings, and antiques, they didn't want to overwhelm their auction attendees with a barrage of objects either. So, after considerable deliberation, they'd decided to accept only fifty items. The very best fifty items.

"But I haven't been contacted yet," continued Jester through clenched teeth.

"My apologies," said Drayton, "that the notification process has come right down to the wire. I understand from Roger there are only a few galleries who haven't been contacted yet. And they'll be receiving word soon, certainly by tomorrow night's board meeting."

"But some galleries were turned down?" persisted Jester, hanging on to the subject like a rat terrier to a bone.

Drayton let loose an audible sigh. "As I understand it, yes. I know Roger Crispin had concerns with a few pieces."

"Tell me," snarled Jester. "Did that effete snob have *issues* with my Chinese sword?" Jester's voice dripped with venom, his face a dark cloud. "Not that *he'd* notice, but it's a spectacular piece. Early Warring States to be exact."

"Roger didn't mention any specific pieces," said Drayton, who was beginning to look visibly tired from this little go-round with Jester. "And I think you should hold on until tomorrow to see if your Chinese sword is included."

Jester Moody continued to glower at Drayton. "This is important to me, Drayton," he snarled. "This Spring Auction is a major event! A once-a-year chance to showcase a piece in front of important collectors. For heaven's sake, man, the *Post and Courier* will probably even do a feature!" And with that, Jester Moody whirled suddenly and stalked off, a dark blur melting into the crowd.

"Jester, please," Drayton called after him. "Be reasonable . . ."

"Well isn't *he* a barrel of laughs," declared Haley Parker once Jester Moody was out of earshot. "I just adore a man who comes cowboying in, trying to strong-arm everyone."

Drayton shook his head. "He's normally a fairly decent fellow."

"Uh huh," smirked Haley. "I'll just bet he is."

"Your cake's lookin' a little disheveled," drawled a leisurely female voice. "As does your hat, Theo dawlin'."

"Hello, Delaine," said Theodosia, smiling at her friend's slightly left-handed greeting. Delaine Dish was outspoken, brash, and always opinionated. She was also the proprietor of Cotton Duck, one of Charleston's premiere boutiques specializing in elegant silks, filmy cottons, and rich velvets. Which pretty much guaranteed that Delaine was always beautifully dressed, amazingly coifed, and accessorized to the max. And tonight was no exception. Delaine looked stunning and stylish in a plunging black sheath dress edged with black lace. Coils of highly polished eighteen-karat gold wound around her slender wrists, and her sleek dark hair was pulled under a jaunty bowler-style hat that set off her heart-shaped face to perfection.

"Do you see that lovely man over there?" Delaine asked Theodosia in her best throaty purr.

Theodosia's mouth twitched slightly. Delaine was obviously in prowl mode tonight. "Mm hm," replied Theodosia, glancing toward the front of the hall where a gaggle of good-looking men seemed to be milling about. Her eyes searched the crowd for one man in particular. Her man. *Ah, there he is. Jory Davis. Looking very handsome and dapper as he helped welcome guests to the Poet's Tea.*

Jory was the man Theodosia spent most of her waking moments with these days. When Jory wasn't busy lawyering and she wasn't busy serving tea, that is.

As if reading her mind, Jory suddenly turned toward the back of the hall, caught sight of Theodosia, and gave a wave. Pleased, she lifted a hand and waved back, noting that his curly brown hair and square-jawed, slightly rugged looks never failed to set her heart pounding.

"No, no," said Delaine, frantically trying to redirect Theodosia's gaze. "*That* one. The fellow with the medal pinned to his lapel. That's Jester Moody. Interesting man, no?"

Theodosia was tempted to answer with a resounding *no*. Instead she mustered up a dollop of restraint and replied, "We've only met briefly, Delaine." Giving Jester the benefit of the doubt, Theodosia figured she might be a little nuts, too, if she was waiting to see if the Heritage Society would be showcasing her art in what was one of the premier fundraising events of the year. Business was tough these days, and Theodosia was acutely aware of how critical it was to garner every bit of publicity and media attention possible. *And* get your merchandise featured in front of customers who were big-time spenders and collectors.

But Delaine was still gazing at Jester Moody with a

dreamy look on her face. "I'm going to date him," she declared. She said it with fervent, passionate zeal as though she'd just announced, "I'm going to conquer France." And she said it with great finality, as though it were a done deal.

"Are you serious?" asked Theodosia, stunned by Delaine's pronouncement. *The rather mercurial Delaine Dish dating the sharp-tongued Jester Moody? Never happen.* "You know," began Theodosia, "Jester was just over here, badgering Drayton about—"

"Hey, Delaine," sang out Haley as she emerged from the kitchen carrying a silver three-tiered tray that showcased a dizzying array of chocolate truffles. "Great hat."

One of Delaine's hands fluttered to her hat even as her eyes remained on her prey. "Like it, dear? Gracie Venable over at Bow Geste created it exclusively for me. Of course, Gracie's not *officially* open yet, won't be for another five days, but I talked her into doing a *custom* order."

Bow Geste was a new millinery shop just down the block from the Indigo Tea Shop. Theodosia had recently established a friendly, bantering acquaintance with the shop's owner, Gracie Venable. Gracie had dashed in more than a few times over the past couple weeks to chatter about her grand opening plans and grab a cup of tea for takeout. Theodosia wasn't sure just how profitable a millinery shop was going to be, but Gracie was bubbling over with enthusiasm and obviously intended to give it her very best shot. And, Theodosia had to admit, the enormous resurgence in tea shops, tea parties, and special event teas seemed to have ushered in a whole new era where women were, once again, happily sporting white gloves and beautifully decorated hats.

Haley's eyes danced merrily as she regarded Delaine's hat, a black straw bowler with a froth of flowers bunched on one side. "Gracie told me she'd been working on a hat for you."

"Did she now?" said Delaine in a disinterested tone. Her eyes were still lasered on Jester Moody.

"You know, Delaine," said Haley, "I helped write the business plan for Gracie's new shop." There was pride in Haley's voice.

Haley's statement finally managed to capture Delaine's attention. "You?" she said, her nostrils flaring delicately as she regarded Haley as one might confront a science project. "I thought you were a *baker* by trade."

"Well, I am," said Haley, slightly unsure of herself now. "But I'm a part-time college student, too. Helping Gracie with her business plan was one of the final requirements for my business internship."

"Haley's studying business administration," explained Drayton as he joined them, carrying another tray lined with sparkling teacups. "She'll probably end up as a hard-charging CEO for some *Fortune* 500 company. With an enormous salary and stock options to boot."

"Well, don't give up your day job just yet," was Delaine's parting shot to Haley as she scurried off.

Haley looked stung. "Delaine *never* gives me any credit," she complained. "She treats me like a kid. A *nobody*."

Drayton peered at Haley over tortoiseshell half-glasses that gave him the look of a learned owl. "Be serious," he told her. "In the scheme of things, does it really matter? You know you're a smart, talented young woman. Theo and I value you enormously."

Theodosia slung an arm around Haley's shoulder in a gesture of support. "Delaine means well," she told her young helper. "But she often falls short in the diplomacy department."

"Her taste can be a little questionable, too," said Drayton in a loud whisper. "If you ask me, I'd say that dress is completely over the top. I believe Delaine's confused black-tie with black widow spider."

"Oh, Drayton," laughed Haley, bouncing back to her usual good humor. "If you had your way we'd all be parading around in corsets and button boots."

Drayton rocked back on his heels. "Don't knock tradition, young lady," he said in a serious, thoughtful tone. "I certainly don't advocate a return to the eighteenth century, but there *was* a time when genteel people displayed intelligence and taste in their mode of dress." He sniffed. "Nowadays, people go out to dinner wearing Bermuda shorts and trucker caps!" He shook his head in disbelief. "Can you believe it? Trucker caps!"

"The real problem," said Haley, squinting at the cake that sat center stage on their tea table, "is how are we going to perk up Theodosia's cake?" She poked a finger at one of the bare spots and wrinkled her nose. "Figure out how to camouflage those melty spots."

Theodosia had long been content to be the brewer of tea, greeter of customers, and master planner of events. But this afternoon she'd actually stepped out of character for a few hours and barricaded herself in the Indigo Tea Shop's tiny kitchen to bake an almond cake for tonight. Six layers of almond cake to be exact. Haley had coached her on the recipe, slipping in an extra egg or two, and helped with the butter cream frosting. But Theodosia had definitely honchoed the baking of the cake. And now, although the cake would still *taste* delicious, there were a few surface dimples and bare spots, casualties of the rain.

"You worked so hard on this," continued Haley, as she assessed the cake. "We've got to come up with a plan to salvage its former grandeur!" She scrunched up her face and thought for a moment. "Maybe if I ran back to the tea shop and whipped up another batch of frosting? We could throw on some well-placed squiggles and swirls."

"Squiggles would probably work like a charm, but I've got another idea," said Theodosia. She snatched a bouquet of blush-pink tea roses from a crystal vase at the end of the table. "Let's try a little freestyle decoration." Snapping a stem off one of the roses, she stuck the flower onto the side of the cake.

Haley nodded her approval as Theodosia continued to plant a line of blossoms in a graceful s-curve. In no time at all the parts that had resembled the moon's surface were skillfully hidden.

"Fantastic," declared Haley. "Now your cake looks even more fancy and festive. Much better than just frosting alone, I think. *Gâteau aux amandes.* Doesn't that sound classier than just calling it almond cake?" Haley suddenly raised an arm in an exuberant wave. "Hey, Gracie! Over here!"

Gracie Venable, proprietor of the soon-to-be-opened Bow Geste, came plowing through the crowd. With her mop of curly blond hair, green eyes, and short button nose, she looked every inch a *Gracie*.

"What's this?" asked Haley as Gracie thrust a round hatbox into her hands.

"Just my way of saying thanks," said Gracie. "For all your help with the business plan." She smiled at Theodosia and the newly refurbished cake. "Nice cake. I love that you incorporated roses into the decor." She winked. "You just might have a future as a hat decorator, too."

"I love it!" squealed Haley, as she pawed open the hatbox and plopped a white straw hat strewn with yellow daisies on her head. "It's gorgeous!" She spun toward Theodosia. "How do I look?"

"Adorable," pronounced Theodosia. "Like you should be languidly sprawled in an antique wicker chair amidst one of Charleston's gorgeous courtyard gardens, posing for an oil painting."

"Drayton?" asked Haley, trying for another opinion. Standing off to the side, frowning and mumbling to himself, Drayton was rehearsing the poem he was scheduled to read later in the program.

"Charming," he muttered, his eyes still darting across his book page.

"You didn't even look at it!" howled Haley.

Drayton glanced up and favored Haley with a perfunctory inspection. "Ah yes, quite lovely. Happy now?"

"Yes!" cried Haley.

"You," Gracie said to Theodosia, "will be receiving a hat as well. As soon as I find a spare fifteen minutes to breathe!"

"Not necessary," protested Theodosia. "You've got more important things to do."

"Are you kidding?" cried Gracie. "Honey, after all those

free scones and complimentary cups of tea, I owe you big time!"

"You're our neighbor now," Theodosia assured her. "Part of the Church Street retail gang." Theodosia knew it was important for all the small businesses that lined Church Street—including her own tea shop, Pinckney's Gift Shop, the Chowder House, and the Antiquarian Booksellers—to stick together. For moral support as well as from a business point of view. *What was it Benjamin Franklin had espoused to his fellow revolutionaries? Something to the effect that we'd better hang together or we shall all hang separately.*

But Gracie was adamant about creating a special hat for Theodosia. "What's your favorite flower?" she probed. "Roses? Lilies?"

"Crepe myrtle," said Theodosia, thinking about the twisting vines that grew out at Cane Ridge, the old rice plantation where her parents were buried. "And dogwood."

"You got it, sweetie!" exclaimed Gracie as she blew a series of air kisses at Theodosia and Haley, then dashed off.

"Don't you just love her?" asked Haley. "She's like the perfect sister you always wanted."

Theodosia, who'd been an only child, who'd lost her mother when she was just six, her father when she was in college, nodded in agreement. There had been times in her life when she'd have given her left arm for *any* sister, not just a perfect one.

"Time to look sharp," said Drayton, snapping his book closed. Even though he was scheduled to be the last person to read tonight, Drayton always prided himself on being well-prepared. As Haley often joked, Drayton was a prudent man. The kind of man who wore a belt *and* suspenders.

"Roger Crispin's all set to run the slide show?" Theodosia asked Drayton. She had helped put together some special background effects that would be projected on a screen behind Drayton when he did his poetry reading. And Roger Crispin, the managing partner at Crispin and Weller Auction House and one of Drayton's fellow board members, had been tapped to man the projector.

"Roger should be standing by upstairs," replied Drayton. "We did a quick run-through an hour ago, before anyone arrived, and everything went smoothly."

"Roger's not upstairs," said Haley, glancing into the crowd. "He's been running around schmoozing people like crazy. And now he's over there, talking to Gracie."

"Good grief," exclaimed a flustered Drayton. "Here I thought we were all set to go."

"What a control freak," laughed Haley.

But just as Drayton was about to rush over, Gracie placed a hand on Roger Crispin's arm and the two of them bent their heads together in a conspiratorial gesture. A split second later, Timothy Neville stepped to the podium and his voice boomed out across the hall.

Looking larger than life for such a wiry little man, Timothy welcomed the audience to the Heritage Society's first ever Poet's Tea. As if on cue, Roger Crispin and Gracie parted company and Roger dashed across the room and disappeared up the side stairway that led to the balcony.

After a round of applause for his short but rousing welcoming speech, Timothy quickly introduced the program's first reader. Sheldon Tibbets, who wrote the arts column for the *Post and Courier*, was going to read *Angel of the Church*, by William Gilmore Simms, one of South Carolina's former poet laureates.

Still trying to adjust to the change in plans, Theodosia remained standing behind the tea table, fussing with the final arrangement. Drayton scurried up front while Haley wandered off to take a seat in the audience.

As Theodosia listened to the soothing, uplifting words written by Simms, she suddenly had an urge for a cup of tea.

Slipping into the small kitchen, Theodosia poured a cup of freshly brewed Egyptian chamomile. Mild and naturally sweet, with a slight apple flavor, chamomile was a delightful tea. Taking a sip, Theodosia breathed a sigh of sublime contentment. Truly, there was nothing more rewarding than a good cup of tea. It nourished the spirit, soothed jangled nerves, let you savor a quiet moment.

Then she suddenly wondered . . . should she take a cup of tea up to Roger Crispin?

Should I? Well, why not? He's a friend of Drayton's and the poor man is stuck up there all by himself. In fact, he's probably huddled in back at that old desk where they keep all the audio-video gear.

The rear staircase just to the left of the kitchen was steep and dark. Not the kind of place a woman in a frilly summer dress, straw hat, and high heels should be trying to maneuver. Especially when she was balancing a steaming cup of hot tea. But Roger Crispin was up there in the balcony, or peanut gallery, as Drayton always called it, being a hardworking volunteer and running the projector. So Theodosia figured he certainly deserved a little consideration.

"Mr. Crispin?" Theodosia called in a low whisper when she was a few steps from the top. "It's Theodosia Browning. I brought you a cup of tea."

She stopped, blinked, searched the darkness. "Mr. Crispin?" she called again, her voice suddenly not as confident as before.

There was a rustle in the corner and, as Theodosia's eyes slowly became accustomed to the dark, she saw that Roger Crispin was hunched at a small desk, whispering into his cell phone. AV equipment was stacked on shelves behind him, a thick black cord ran to the projector that sat perched on a shelf at the front of the balcony.

No wonder Roger didn't hear me.

When Roger Crispin looked up and saw her coming, he smiled and nodded with a look of appreciation. Then, still on the phone, he hastily cleared away a spot on the table for Theodosia to place the teacup.

Thank you, he mouthed silently.

You're welcome, she mouthed back.

Roger's a real sport, Theodosia told herself as she descended the narrow stairway, taking care to be as quiet as possible. *Here he is, squatting upstairs in a dusty balcony, running the slide projector for Drayton when he could have remained downstairs, hobnobbing with the rest of the guests and drumming up business for his auction house. Nice guy.*

The second reading, a poem by Archibald Rutledge, was well under way by the time Theodosia got back downstairs. Busying herself in the kitchen, Theodosia readied the fancy

Sevres, Spode, and Fitz and Floyd teapots they'd brought along and measured out additional scoops of chamomile, Formosan Oolong, and Assam tea. Then, after another twenty minutes or so, confident that everything was prepped and ready, Theodosia emerged to find it was Drayton's turn at the podium. Time for the grand finale.

Taking his position in front of the large movie screen that had been hastily set up just for him, Drayton paused dramatically. One of the volunteers up front rotated the dimmer switch and the room slowly sank into darkness just as the first slide, a sepia-toned engraving of Charleston Harbor, flashed on the oversized screen behind him.

There was a ripple of applause, a few hushed murmurs, then the crowd fell silent. Their attention was riveted on this dramatically offbeat final presentation.

As a tribute to his beloved city of Charleston, Drayton had chosen to recite Edgar Allen Poe's poem, *Annabel Lee*. The ill-fated yet enormously talented Poe had spent a year in Charleston and, as his biographers all seem to agree, had been deeply moved by the storm-tossed seas, lonely windswept shoreline, and highly atmospheric landscape. Poe had been stationed at Fort Moultrie on Sullivan's Island from November of 1827 to December of the following year. And it was a long-accepted notion that Poe's residence in the Charleston area had inspired his poem, *Annabel Lee*. In fact, "a kingdom by the sea" was Poe's lyrical reference to the city of Charleston.

In creating the slide show for Drayton's reading, Theodosia had drawn upon her old advertising and marketing skills and put together a series of photos, newspaper clippings, seascape paintings, and slides from the Heritage Society's archives. All had been carefully chosen to help illustrate Poe's poem as well as convey the highly charged atmosphere that had existed in Charleston some one hundred and eighty years ago.

As the slides flashed by at a fast-paced tempo, the audience's complete and rapt attention was focused on Drayton as he launched into his heartfelt reading of Poe's wildly romantic, yet sorrowful poem:

> It was many and many a year ago,
>   In a kingdom by the sea
> That a maiden there lived whom you may know
>   By the name of Annabel Lee;

Drayton's voice was well-modulated, his oratorical prowess honed from countless speeches and readings. Theodosia felt chills run down her spine as she stood alone in the back of the great hall, listening to Drayton utter those mournful words. The dramatic, highly atmospheric visuals she had chosen continued to flash on the enormous screen behind Drayton, adding extra dimension to his reading.

Ominously, almost perfectly, just as Drayton arrived at the emotion-laden midpoint of the poem, the heavens seemed to open up. Torrential rains pounded down upon the roof of the Heritage Society. Deep rumbles of surround-sound thunder shook the wooden rafters. Lightning bolts shot through the skies, winking in through the great hall's clerestory windows.

What perfect theatrical sound effects, marveled Theodosia. *Along with a light show from the heavens!*

Yes!—that was the reason (as all men know,
    In this kingdom by the sea)
That the wind came out of the cloud by night,
    Chilling and killing my Annabel Lee.

Rain continued to pelt the windows as Drayton held sway over his audience as he read verse after verse. Then Drayton launched into the final stanza. Lifting his head from the small leather book clutched in his gnarled hands, Drayton let his voice soar with heartfelt emotion, delivering the final lines he'd committed to memory:

And so, all the night-tide, I lie down by the side
Of my darling—my darling—my life and my bride,
    In the sepulcher there by the sea—
    In her tomb by the sounding sea.

A sharp crack of thunder echoed from above. And, as if on cue, another sound rang out. A loud *pop*.

Theodosia jumped at the explosion that sounded above her, then the rest of the audience reacted a split-second later. The ripple of applause that had begun to swell died out immediately.

Was it a sound effect? Theodosia suddenly wondered as she heard a faint sound of footsteps overhead. *Or is this for real?*

Nervous and flustered, a final slide of Edgar Allan Poe projected behind him, Drayton put a hand to his eyes and peered up into the balcony.

And then, as if to answer the question in everyone's mind, a fluttering shadow suddenly appeared directly in front of Poe's twenty-foot-high image. A body falling from the balcony!

Theodosia watched in disbelief as the body seemed almost to descend in slow motion. Cartwheeling downward, arms and legs akimbo. Where one would expect a blood-curdling scream, there was only a strange *hiss,* like air escaping a dying balloon.

And then all action seemed to speed up before Theodosia's eyes, like film footage suddenly switching from slow-mo to fast forward. The audience rose, almost turning in concert, and emitted a collective *ooh*. And finally, finally, Jory Davis had the presence of mind to race to a light switch up front and throw on the overhead lights, just as the flailing body of Roger Crispin slammed down on top of Theodosia's cake with a terrible, bone-shattering *thud*!

2

Water burbled, tea kettles chirped, and the intoxicating aroma of fresh-baked muffins and scones filled the air of the Indigo Tea Shop. Tiny white candles flickered in glass tea warmers, silver spoons were laid out, linen napkins were folded just so on all the tables.

Even though Theodosia, Drayton, and Haley were hard at work this Monday morning, they were still stunned by the events of the night before. Drayton, in particular, seemed subdued as he measured out spoonfuls of Nilgiri tea into a blue willow-pattern teapot.

"What a disaster," he moaned. "Timothy Neville is absolutely beside himself with worry. Here he's just returned from England to host the first of several major events at the

Heritage Society, and what happens? Roger Crispin, poor soul, is shot to death! Execution style at that!"

"Was it really execution style?" shivered Haley. "That sounds so mafioso."

"I wouldn't characterize it as a mob hit," said Theodosia, "but Roger Crispin must have been shot at fairly close range. The police kept mumbling terms like shell casings and powder burns."

"What I can't figure out," said Drayton, "is how Roger's assailant got away so fast."

"I'm not sure he did get completely away," said Theodosia. "There are three stairways that lead down from that balcony. Two in front and one in back where I was standing. Whoever shot Roger could have slipped down any one of them and just faded into the crowd."

"You didn't see anyone on the back stairs?" asked Drayton.

Theodosia shook her head. "Nope. But like I told the police last night, I was in and out of the kitchen during the poetry readings. And I wasn't exactly watching for someone, either."

"Poor Roger," said Haley, shaking her head. "Do we know if there's a Mrs. Crispin?"

"Absolutely there is," replied Theodosia. "In fact, Delaine's mentioned her on more than one occasion. I guess she must be one of her more important customers at Cotton Duck."

Drayton draped a long white apron around his neck, tied it in back, then rolled his sleeves up. "Timothy is insisting that everyone attend the board meeting tonight. He's bringing in the Heritage Society's attorney and he wants to make sure everyone's on the same page."

"Sounds like he's trying to cook up an alibi or something," mused Haley.

"Absolutely not," said Drayton. "Alibis are the provenance of *guilty* parties. Timothy's tactics merely represent sound business practice. It's always beneficial to get your ducks in a row."

"I take it you'll be attending," said Theodosia.

"Absolutely," said Drayton. He nodded at her. "You should come along, too." His gaze shifted to Haley. "Maybe you, too, Haley. After all, you were in attendance last night, as well."

"No way," said Haley. "Last night's events were upsetting enough, what with the police, the medical examiner, and the crime scene team. Here I was, shaking in my boots, trying to pack up all our teacups and stuff, and those weird crime scene guys were helping themselves to tea sandwiches while they chatted about blood-spatter patterns. Very nasty."

"Did I hear that one of those men actually tried to hit on you?" asked Theodosia.

Haley nodded, unhappily. "The short, obnoxious guy. George." She rolled her expressive eyes skyward. "Why is it always the short, obnoxious guy?"

"One of the laws of nature," suggested Theodosia.

"So you see why I don't want to get any more involved?" Haley told Drayton. "Why I don't think *any* of us should get unduly involved?"

"Don't be absurd," snorted Drayton. "None of us have any intention of getting involved. Aside from conveying our sympathies to the family and cooperating with the ongoing police investigation."

* * *

"*You know who* hasn't been in yet this morning?" asked Haley. She was hunkered down in the tiny kitchen at the back of the tea shop. Theodosia hovered nearby, tray in hand, ready to ferry fresh-baked biscuits to their waiting customers. Drayton was out front covering the tearoom. As he poured refills, he freely dispensed bits of tea lore to interested parties who were willing to listen.

"Who?" asked Theodosia. The dozen or so antique wooden tables were completely filled for morning tea and she was already thinking ahead to lunch. They had reservations from two fairly large groups and she was pretty sure Drayton was supposed to conduct a tea tasting midafternoon.

"Gracie Venable hasn't stopped by for her morning cuppa," said Haley as she fussed with tiny champagne grapes and chopped cashews for her chicken salad.

"You're right," said Theodosia. Grabbing a stack of small blue and white plates from the shelf, she dealt them out onto the counter. Five tables of customers were sipping fresh-brewed tea, eagerly waiting for more of Haley's biscuits to emerge from the oven. "Gracie's been a regular here every morning for the past couple weeks."

"Wonder where she is," said Haley, pulling on her oven mitts.

"Probably just jammed up," replied Theodosia. "She's supposed to pull off her grand opening this Friday. And the last time I went by Bow Geste the display racks hadn't even arrived."

"Gracie's been in a dither over setting up her workshop,

too," said Haley. "Designing custom hats requires some very specialized materials. She's ordered Mechlin lace from France, silk and *mousseline* ribbon from Belgium, and silk flowers from Thailand. To say nothing of the boxes of straw hats she's got coming from Panama and Costa Rica."

Theodosia thought about Delaine's adorable little straw bowler and wondered what strings Delaine had pulled to get Gracie to drop everything and create that hat. Especially when poor Gracie was still locked in the throes of setting up shop. Probably, Theodosia decided, Delaine had simply bullied and cajoled her. Like she did everyone else when Delaine had her own personal agenda cooking.

Pulling open the oven door, Haley grabbed two pans of strawberry biscuits. Golden and deliciously plump, their heavenly aroma immediately filled the tiny kitchen. "Maybe I'll take a cup of tea down to Gracie," said Haley. "Say thank-you again for making me that great hat." She slid two pans of popovers into the oven, squinted at her wristwatch, then carefully set the timer. Haley was an absolute stickler when it came to timing. In her kitchen there was no guesstimating, no flying by the seat of your pants. And, of course, no cracking the oven door for a quick peek. Drayton joked that Haley had the personality of a Swiss watchmaker. Precise, demanding, just this side of compulsive.

"Tell you what," said Theodosia, "you're still fussing with your chicken salad. So why don't I get these biscuits out to our guests, then run a cup of tea down to Gracie. In fact I might even dash upstairs and grab Earl Grey for a quick walk. He adores every little chance he gets to stretch his legs."

Earl Grey, the dog Theodosia had dubbed her "purebred Dalbrador," lived above the tea shop with her. Theodosia had found Earl Grey as a pup, huddled in the alley, shivering and half-starved. Her heart had immediately gone out to the bedraggled little guy and she'd taken him in—no questions asked. She'd fussed over him, nursed him back to health, named him, and loved him with all her heart. Though Drayton had looked askance at the notion of a mixed-breed dog, his distinctly mottled coat had instantly won Theodosia over and earned him the distinguished name Earl Grey. Now, Earl Grey had matured into an elegant, graceful dog. Gentle in nature, but still playful and full of spunk. A dog who had sailed through therapy dog training and easily earned his Therapy Dog International accreditation. Now Earl Grey was a regular and welcome guest at the O'Doud Senior Home and several children's hospitals in the area. With his suedelike paws, fine-boned head, and limpid brown eyes, Earl Grey captured hearts even as he spread joy to those who were convalescing.

To Theodosia, Earl Grey was a friend, jogging companion, and trusted confidante. In short, the perfect roommate, since he was quiet, well mannered, and refrained from putting his big paws on the coffee table.

Haley grabbed two fresh-baked biscuits and popped them into a small white bakery bag. "Here, take Gracie a couple of these." She hesitated, then tossed in another biscuit for good measure. "And be sure to thank her for the hat. Tell her I'm lovin' it!"

* * *

But when Theodosia arrived at Bow Geste a few minutes later, she was in for a major surprise. A black and white squad car and a wine-colored Crown Victoria were angled haphazardly into the NO PARKING spot directly in front of Gracie's shop.

What's all this about? Theodosia wondered as she looped Earl Grey's leash around a lamppost and tied a quick half hitch. She pressed her nose to the front window where newly painted gold lettering spelled out BOW GESTE—HATS, ACCESSORIES, CUSTOM MILLINERY. Shading her eyes from the sun's glare, peering through what was certainly a newly installed display of summer hats, Theodosia spotted Gracie standing at the rear of her shop. Gesturing expansively, wearing a look that Theodosia registered as mild panic, Gracie seemed engaged in a heated discussion with two men.

Gracie in a heated confrontation with the police? Hmm.

That was good enough for Theodosia. Ferocious curiosity and a penchant for rushing to the aid of people who were under fire made Theodosia push open the front door and boldly plow her way into the shop.

And what a shop it had suddenly become! A blossom of inventory had seemingly sprung up overnight. Summer hats with silk flowers and sprightly sprigs of greenery perched like exotic butterflies atop sleek black velvet mannequin heads. Wide-brimmed hats with long ribbon streamers hung from brass hat racks. Smaller cloche hats with ribbon rosettes and poufs of feathers were tucked into cubes of glass shelving. Bow Geste had suddenly materialized into a bona fide millinery shop!

Canted mirrors hung everywhere, reflecting the miniature

landscapes of each hat again and again. Dazzling arrays of feather boas, fluttering scarves, beaded handbags, and long, opera-length strands of pearls hung on a side wall. The overall impression was of riotous color and highly exotic flora and fauna. As though a tropical greenhouse stuffed with exquisite foliage had magically merged with the most marvelous accessories store.

Theodosia grinned. She couldn't help herself. The shop just looked so wonderfully enticing. So with a big smile still plastered across her face, Theodosia sauntered over to Gracie Venable. "Hi Gracie," she began, choosing to ignore the young man in the slightly strange seersucker suit who was planted next to Gracie, pen and spiral notebook in hand. "Your shop looks spectacular."

Gracie's green eyes darted from Theodosia to the man who stood facing her. "Thanks," she told Theodosia. Her voice had a high, jittery edge to it and she looked a little nervous. She clutched a sheaf of papers in her hands.

"Miss Browning," boomed a low voice. "Turning up yet again like the proverbial bad penny."

It took a split-second for the voice to register. And then Theodosia thought: *Tidwell. I should have known.*

As Theodosia turned to greet him, Detective Burt Tidwell emerged from the back room and took his place beside the younger seersucker-suited man, who she assumed was some sort of detective-in-training.

"Hello, Detective Tidwell," said Theodosia. "Out shopping for a new Panama hat? Just dropped by for a fitting?" She glanced at the papers in Gracie's hand and decided they looked suspiciously like a lease agreement.

Tidwell's bullet-shaped head swiveled toward Theodosia and his furry caterpillarlike eyebrows pulled themselves into twin arcs of surprise. Intelligent dark eyes burned into her as his large, rather bulbous body seemed to spasm, then, instead, vented an enormous sigh. A sigh that clearly said *oh please*. "We're in the process of questioning a *witness* here, Miss Browning," said Tidwell, pursing his lips in a further show of vexation.

"A witness?" she said.

Tidwell continued to frown. "Regarding Roger Crispin's rather untimely death last night," he told her. Then added, "You need not play coy, Miss Browning. I know you were there."

"How interesting that you're suddenly involved," said Theodosia. "As of last night, I don't believe you were assigned to this case."

"I've been asked to intercede," said Tidwell in a low growl.

Theodosia gazed intently at Tidwell, looking for a sign, any sign at all, that this was just a quick, impromptu meeting. A mere formality that had to take place given the terrible events of last evening. Tidwell gave her nothing.

"Well, it's lovely to see you," Theodosia enthused, suddenly turning on the faucet and letting her best Southern charm spill forth. Cocking her head toward the young man in the horrible seersucker suit, she asked, "Who's your young assistant? I probably brushed shoulders with him last night, but in the ensuing furor we were never properly introduced."

Cowed by this sudden outpouring of gracious manners and female etiquette, the fellow in the seersucker suit had no alternative but to scramble and offer his hand. And bestow upon Theodosia a pained and somewhat lopsided smile. "I'm Detective Neil Beaderman," he told her. "Pleased to make your acquaintance, ma'am."

Looming beside him, Tidwell rolled his eyes.

There's one point scored, decided Theodosia.

"You must be newly promoted," said Theodosia, continuing to ooze what she hoped was Scarlet O'Hara–type charm.

"I'm a new hire, yes ma'am," Detective Beaderman answered. A smile had broken out on his broad face in spite of himself.

"A new hire," murmured Theodosia, as though it were the most marvelous news she'd ever heard. "How lovely for you. How exciting!"

"Hrmph," muttered Tidwell.

"Detectives Tidwell and Beaderman were just finishing up their questions," said Gracie, seeming to draw courage from Theodosia's upbeat, breezy approach.

"I take it they had questions concerning your lease, too?" asked Theodosia.

Gracie nodded. "Yes."

"Aren't we perceptive," murmured Tidwell.

"I'm sure these fine gentlemen will also be interviewing *dozens* of other witnesses," continued Theodosia.

"Did you know Roger Crispin well?" Detective Beaderman asked Theodosia. He suddenly seemed to realize he was supposed to be tending to business. And that he'd somehow drifted off or been drawn off the subject at hand.

"No, not really," said Theodosia.

Tidwell tugged at a jacket that made no pretense of

covering the ballooning expanse of his stomach. "Yet you ventured into the dark recess of the upstairs balcony to take the man a cup of tea."

"Just being polite," murmured Theodosia.

"I find it most interesting," said Tidwell, a slight smile finally insinuating itself on his broad face. "That the last two people to see Roger Crispin alive are standing right before me."

3

"*It was the* silliest thing I've ever seen," Theodosia told Drayton and Haley, standing at the counter, trying to control her voice so as not to upset their luncheon customers. "Two police officers in black leather jackets were posted outside Gracie's marvelously frilly little shop. And inside Tidwell and this Beaderman fellow were firing questions willy-nilly at Gracie. Asking specific questions about Roger Crispin!" Theodosia put a hand up to still her beating heart. After she'd been unceremoniously asked to leave, she'd dashed back to the Indigo Tea Shop, stashed Earl Grey upstairs, then rushed back down.

"What are they *thinking*?" hissed Drayton. "What on earth would cause the police to question Gracie Venable? The lady's a *hatmaker,* for goodness sake."

"Because she was a witness," said Haley. "They're probably talking to lots of people."

Theodosia hesitated a moment, then decided to plunge ahead. "Curiously enough, there's an even stronger connection," she told them. "A business connection."

"What?" asked Haley, frowning. "How so?"

"From what I was able to gather," said Theodosia, "before Tidwell basically kicked me out . . . Roger Crispin is Gracie's landlord." Her eyes roved over the tea shop crowd. "*Was* Gracie's landlord," she amended. "And the two of them were apparently involved in some minor dispute over the lease."

Drayton nudged Haley and pointed to the small table by the fireplace. "Refill," he murmured.

Haley grabbed a full teapot and reluctantly scurried off.

"That doesn't surprise me," continued Drayton. "I know that Roger owned a fair amount of commercial real estate. A couple buildings farther down Church Street and one over on East Bay Street. Additionally, Crispin and Weller were involved in their fair share of disputes." He sighed. "Pretty much comes with the territory."

"Are we talking real estate disputes or problems at the auction house?" asked Theodosia.

"I don't know about real estate issues," said Drayton. "But there have always been problems at Crispin and Weller. Auction houses simply breed contention. And Roger was a hard-nosed businessman, so I'm sure he made more than his share of enemies."

"Why would that be?" asked Theodosia.

"Realize," said Drayton, "that people who put their art or

antiques up for auction are *never* happy with the final price that their goods fetch. They always think their paintings or antique furniture are worth millions! Plus most sellers absolutely detest paying any sort of dealer commission. They're always trying to wiggle or deal their way out of it."

"Gracie must be absolutely terrified," said Haley, returning to the counter with an empty teapot.

"She didn't look happy," admitted Theodosia.

"And what rotten timing," exclaimed Haley. "Her shop is supposed to open in a matter of days!" She thought for a moment. "Can't you talk to Tidwell?" Haley asked. "Tell him he's suspicious of the wrong person?"

"Tidwell's apparently under orders from above," said Theodosia. "Even though he's been promoted to chief of detectives, he's still overseeing this particular investigation."

"I still think they're wasting their time," said Haley, as she stepped behind the counter and held out the teapot to Drayton. "More please."

"Hold on a minute," said Drayton, as he continued to ladle tea leaves into a fancy blue and white porcelain teapot, then slowly poured in hot water. "Let me get my Mai Jiang brewing." This was a new tea he was serving today, a green tea from China with a marvelous aroma. Very light and fresh. "You sound like you're working up to something, Haley," Drayton said finally.

Haley was having trouble containing herself. "Yes, I am working up to something," she snapped. "I think we need to really pull together and give Gracie some help."

Throwing her a look of supreme vexation, Drayton said, "As I recall, *you* were the one admonishing us *not* to get caught up in anything. You were the one spouting your own personal Monroe Doctrine of noninvolvement."

Haley poked her hair behind her ears and frowned at him. "That was *before*. I didn't know Gracie was going to turn up as some sort of suspect, for crying out loud."

"She's not a suspect," said Theodosia. "She's a witness. Big difference."

Haley's gaze shifted from Drayton to Theodosia. "Still, Gracie needs our help. After all, she's a small business, just like we are. Getting questioned by police can shake you up, throw you off course."

Theodosia nodded slowly. Haley had a point.

"You feel a responsibility to her?" Drayton asked Haley.

"Yes, I do," answered Haley. She placed her hands flat on the counter and sucked in a deep breath. "Gracie's a really nice person, a good person. She's gambled almost everything she has to open this shop. Borrowed money, took out loans, maxed out her Visa card."

"You know this because you worked on her business plan?" said Theodosia.

Haley nodded quickly. "Exactly. Gracie was required to do a fair amount of disclosure before our business class could take her on as a project. Open the kimono, so to speak."

"Okay," said Theodosia, "point well taken. But let's save the rest of this discussion for after lunch."

Haley nodded, happy that Theodosia seemed to be giving it her careful consideration. "Sure."

"This tea's brewed," announced Drayton. "Now let's see what our customers think."

While Theodosia scampered about serving lunch, she

mulled over Haley's words. So Gracie Venable had put all her savings into inventory. She could certainly identify with that. Once Theodosia had committed to opening the Indigo Tea Shop, she, too, had laid out a small fortune, pretty much every penny she had, to buy her inventory of tea. She'd wanted only the best, of course. Tiny, black leaf Keemuns; bold Formosan oolongs; Darjeelings, the champagne of teas from India; as well as smoky Lapsang Souchong tea; lush Rooibos from Africa; and wonderful flavored teas such as black currant, peach, and rose hips.

Amazingly, tea could cost as much as one hundred dollars a pound. So dollars had been tight as Theodosia began putting together her tea offerings. And then, of course, she'd had to lure Drayton away from his job as a hotel catering manager. Drayton had worked in the hospitality industry for years, but lurking in his background were his twenty years spent growing up in Canton, where his parents were missionaries; his degree from Johnson and Wales University, the area's prestigious culinary institute; and his stint as tea buyer at Croft and Squire Tea Ltd. in London, where he'd commuted almost weekly to the great tea auctions in Amsterdam.

Yes, Theodosia decided, setting up a business was brutal. You needed money, fortitude, great assistants, and more money.

"*So what's it* gonna be?" Haley asked Theodosia and Drayton once their luncheon service was concluded and only two tables of customers remained. "Are we gonna stick our necks out or what?"

But Drayton was still advocating a wait-and-see policy. "I say let the police sort this out," he advised Haley. "What on earth can we do? We're merely standing on the sidelines."

Haley squirmed. It was not what she wanted to hear.

"We're not exactly on the sidelines," said Theodosia. "If the police are going to interview witnesses, they're probably going to come calling on us."

"You think so?" asked Haley. "I thought the few questions they asked last night was gonna be it."

"Oh, they'll want to talk with Theodosia for sure," said Drayton. He glanced over toward the two tables of customers that were left and lowered his voice. "After all, Theo went upstairs. She carried a cup of tea up to Roger Crispin."

Haley's eyes widened in surprise. "You did? Really? Right before the poor guy got shot? Good lord. Did you see anything up there?"

"Not a thing," replied Theodosia. Her mind had traveled back to the events of last night more than a few times today. And she always came up with the same sequence of events, the same general impression. She'd been focused on negotiating her way up the narrow stairway in her high heels while balancing a cup of hot tea. Her only vivid recollection was that of her hat brim brushing the sides of the narrow staircase. At the time, the feeling or impression or whatever the heck it had been was keenly reminiscent of climbing the narrow attic stairway at her Aunt Libby's house.

"Too bad you didn't see, like, a clue or something," said Haley.

Drayton raised a single eyebrow and held it. Let it quiver, in fact, in his inimitable, maddening way. "You thought perhaps we would blow the lid off this case in one fell swoop?"

"You never know," sighed Haley.

"Youthful yearnings and wishful thinking," Drayton announced briskly, pulling his apron off and giving his vest a good tug. "It's almost two o'clock and I have a tea tasting scheduled for two-thirty. At which time I shall dole out multiple small cups of Bancha, Gyokura, and Sencha tea, extolling on the delightful toasty flavors as well as the phytochemical virtues of green tea." The bell above the front door tinkled suddenly, causing Drayton's brows to knit together. "Oh, drat," he muttered. "Please tell me my dear ladies aren't early."

They all turned to look.

Gracie Venable stood in the doorway. Wide-eyed and a little breathless, there was obviously something on her mind.

"Hey," called Haley, sounding surprised.

"Hey," Gracie called back. Her eyes slid over to Theodosia. "You," she said, "are totally awesome. That pushy little detective in the bad suit is convinced you have a law degree."

"She almost does," chirped Haley. "At least she's dating someone who does."

"Well, your boss intimidated the bejeebers out of a couple detectives," Gracie told Haley.

"Oh, I don't think so," protested Theodosia.

"Good," replied Haley. "Glad to hear it." She was almost giddy that Gracie had shown up.

"Can we talk?" Gracie asked them.

"Sure," said Theodosia. She moved over to one of the

tables, slid a chair out, and glanced at Drayton. "Drayton, I think we're going to need a strong pot of tea."

He nodded. "One pot of Yunnan coming right up."

Gracie Venable put on a good game face, but underneath it all she was obviously badly shaken.

"The police are nosing around because of the lease," Gracie explained. "Roger Crispin drew up a three-year lease, but I never actually got around to signing it." She shrugged. "There were still a couple fine points to be hammered out."

"Roger Crispin let you occupy your space before the lease was signed?" asked Theodosia. She was amazed. No, she was more on the order of stunned. In business, hopscotching protocol and making an assumption that the lease was a done deal was a major no-no. You always dotted the i's and crossed your t's on any contract. At least she did anyway. It was the fiscally smart thing to do.

"Jumping the gun like that was a huge mistake, I'll admit," said Gracie, looking chastised. "But I was in a blind panic to get my merchandise moved in and set up. So I pushed Roger Crispin until he finally said okay." Gracie shrugged again. "Over the last week or so we'd worked out all the piddley little details so the lease was virtually a slam dunk. We were even supposed to meet at Roger's office tonight so I could sign the darned thing."

"Did you share those details with the police?" asked Drayton.

"You mean did I tell them I had every intention of signing the lease?" asked Gracie. "Yes, of course I told them that." She picked up her teacup and gave Drayton a somewhat challenging look. "Did I tell them we'd planned to do it this evening? No, I didn't specifically mention that time frame."

"Hmm," said Drayton in his stilted way. Which caused Gracie's gaze to falter as she squirmed slightly in her chair.

"Okay, maybe I *should* have been more explicit," admitted Gracie. "But those detectives kept hammering away at me until I was completely rattled." Her eyes darted about nervously. "All those rapid-fire questions. It felt like the Spanish Inquisition!"

"I'm sure it did," said Theodosia. She knew it was never fun to be in the hot seat. And it must be even more difficult to be on the receiving end of questions from a pack of investigators. Especially when they were snapping and chasing their tails like a pack of voracious hounds, looking hard for someone to nail.

"We've been talking among the three of us," said Haley. "And, on the plus side, we want you to know that we're willing to help you any way we can."

Gracie's eyes grew brighter and she blinked back tears. "Wow, thanks for the vote of confidence. I could sure use a few allies right about now." She gulped a swallow of tea to steady herself. "And if you know any women who are good candidates for part-time help it'd be great. I'm absolutely drowning in details."

"Maybe I could help out in your shop after I'm finished here," volunteered Haley. "And I could bake some scones and lemon bars for your grand opening party . . ." Haley's voice trailed off and she glanced nervously at Theodosia, who was, of course, nodding yes.

"We'd all be happy to pitch in," offered Theodosia. "Help you merchandise your shop, serve tea and desserts, whatever you need."

"There's a meeting at the Heritage Society tonight," volunteered Drayton, not wanting to be left out of their feel-good circle. "Theodosia and I are planning to attend. Maybe we can ferret out a little more information about what's going on."

Gracie grasped Drayton's hand with both of hers. Now the tears were really flowing down her cheeks. "Thank you," she told him. "Thank you so very much."

"Drayton folded like a cheap tent," commented Haley once Gracie had departed.

Indignant, Drayton set a Brown Betty teapot down, harder than usual, on one of the scarred wooden tables. "I'd hardly categorize my kindly behavior as folding," he replied.

"What would you call it?" asked Haley. Even though they were dear friends and colleagues, Haley liked nothing better than to bait Drayton mercilessly.

"I'd call it benevolence," said Drayton, rubbing a hand against his chin. "You know I can't bear to see anyone in distress."

"Face it," said Haley. "You can't resist a *damsel* in distress. You're a Southern gentleman through and through, even if you do pretend to be the world's biggest curmudgeon."

"I'll have you know that just this morning several women told me I was absolutely charming," sniffed Drayton just as the telephone shrilled. He reached for the phone, then put a hand up to cover his other ear so he could listen intently.

"Now you've done it," said Theodosia. "Drayton's nose is really out of joint."

"Watch how fast he gets over it," replied Haley.

Drayton passed the phone to Theodosia. "For you," he told her.

"Hello?" said Theodosia.

"Theo," said Jory Davis. "How are you? I mean, after last night?"

Theodosia brushed at her eyes. "A little tired. Jittery."

"I think we're all feeling a little of that," said Jory. "What an awful tragedy. I take it Drayton was close to Roger Crispin?"

Theodosia gazed across the room to where Drayton was chatting with their only table of customers. "Fairly close," she replied.

"Listen," said Jory, sounding excited. "I've got something really important I want to talk to you about. Can I come by tonight?"

"Sure," said Theodosia. "Oh, wait. No. I promised Drayton I'd go to the board meeting with him. At the Heritage Society."

"Okay," said Jory. "How about tomorrow then?"

"Works for me," said Theodosia.

As she hung up the phone, she wondered what it was Jory wanted to talk about. An upcoming charity event, perhaps? *He asked me about doing the catering for his law firm's Links for Literacy event a few months ago. Sure, that's probably it.*

The phone shrilled again and Theodosia grabbed for it. *Must be Jory calling back,* she decided.

But it was Ann Marie, Timothy Neville's secretary, asking for Drayton.

"*That was Timothy* Neville," Drayton told them as he hung up the phone. He'd just had a ten-minute, mostly whispered conversation, and Theodosia and Haley had both tiptoed around him.

"What did *he* want?" asked Haley, rolling her eyes in a supreme expression of exasperation. She was not a fan of Timothy Neville, the octogenarian president of the Heritage Society. He was too old, too rich, too powerful for her taste. That and he scared her half to death.

"Timothy feels the murder of Roger Crispin has put a terrible stain on the reputation of the Heritage Society," said Drayton. "In what is already a disastrous year."

"Disastrous?" said Theodosia. "How so?"

Drayton looked grim. "As you well know, funding for our organization is still tight. Donations are way down and our much-talked-about expansion plans for a new Heritage Society library have been put on hold. Now Timothy is thinking about canceling the Spring Art Auction this Saturday."

"Oh no," said Theodosia. "That was slated to be a major fund-raiser."

Drayton nodded. "We were counting on the proceeds to cover operating expenses. Of course, when a strange and terrible tragedy like last night happens, it's difficult to ask the membership to dig deep and really run up the bidding. Makes them awfully nervous."

"Timothy didn't have anything to do with Roger Crispin's death," said Haley. "I mean . . . no one at the Heritage Society was really involved."

"We know that," said Drayton, "but Timothy's decided to hire a private investigator anyway."

"It feels like Timothy's jumping at shadows," said Theodosia. She knew Timothy fairly well and liked and admired him. He was a levelheaded fellow renowned for making careful, calculated moves. Hiring a private investigator seemed a trifle out of character for Timothy. Very alarmist.

"Maybe Timothy *is* being a touch reactive," said Drayton. "But Roger Crispin's auction house deals in antiquities and that's precisely what the Heritage Society is all about. People may think there's some sort of scandal brewing somewhere."

"Is there?" asked Haley.

"I fervently hope not," replied Drayton.

4

The Heritage Society had always been one of Theodosia's favorite edifices. An enormous gray stone building, it had the requisite lofty ceilings, cypress-paneled rooms, heavy leaded windows, and Oriental carpets that whispered underfoot. Dimly lit glass cases held displays of English silver tankards, rich oil paintings, antique maps, and French tea sets, all hinting at earlier, genteel times.

Palatial in scope, the place had always reminded Theodosia of a great hunting lodge in some dark, mythic forest. Perfect for bounding into with your pack of hounds after a chilly day spent meandering forests of golden leaves. A great place to snuggle up on gigantic leather sofas in front of a roaring, spitting fire.

With last night's shooting so fresh in her mind, however,

Theodosia wondered if the Heritage Society would ever exude its magical presence over her again. Now the twisting stone corridors, heavy furnishings, and dimly lit great hall seemed dark and secretive and more than a little ominous.

"*I invited Theodosia* here tonight," began Drayton, "because of the—what would you call it?—*adjunct role* she played last evening."

At Drayton's words, all eyes at the long conference table turned toward Theodosia, suddenly making her feel very much alone and in the spotlight. Of the dozen or so people seated here tonight, she was the only female in attendance.

Yielding the meeting to Timothy Neville, Drayton promptly sat down, then cleared his throat. Dressed in a tweed jacket and snappy red bow tie he projected the picture of confidence, yet his manner betrayed a slight nervousness.

"I, too, have introductions to make," began Timothy. Seated at the head of the table, he made a sweeping gesture toward the man on his right. "This is Harold duPont, the Heritage Society's attorney. Harold is senior partner at the law firm of Basset, Banners, and duPont. And, as you are all well aware, Harold is a former state legislator."

Harold duPont, a silver-haired executive in his late sixties, rose then nodded politely at the group, his face devoid of expression. Yet his hooded eyes continued to sweep the room even as he sat back down, and Theodosia had the distinct feeling the illustrious Mr. duPont, who would probably be no slouch in a courtroom, might be committing the faces of the various board members to memory.

Timothy gestured to the person on his left. "And we have one more guest who merits an introduction. I'd like to introduce Orrin Hudson from Starkey Investigations."

Orrin Hudson bounded to his feet and smiled a broad, barracuda smile. Though he was in his mid forties, the PI looked extremely fit and had the kind of short-cropped salt-and-pepper hair that gave him a lean, hungry German shepherd look.

"Starkey Investigations is a small, rather exclusive firm that specializes in corporate work," continued Timothy. "And Mr. Hudson was recently . . ."

"A detective with the Charleston Police Department," a dismayed Theodosia whispered to Drayton. "Remember him? He's a real horse's patoot."

Drayton peered speculatively at Orrin Hudson, then nodded. "Yes, I believe I do," he whispered back. "And for the record, your character assessment is dead on."

Theodosia had butted heads with Orrin Hudson when she'd been inadvertently pulled into the murder investigation of Harper Fisk, an antiques dealer who'd been a good friend of Drayton's. Hudson had tried to strong-arm her then, and Theodosia had no doubt he'd probably employ the same bulldozer tactics today.

Timothy was staring directly at Theodosia and Drayton now, giving them a look of admonishment. Basically, his dour headmaster look.

"Mr. Hudson has been retained to look out for the specific interests of the Heritage Society," continued Timothy in a clipped manner. "To make sure there are no ugly repercussions stemming from the incident of last night."

Theodosia raised a hand. "You mean like an investigation?" she asked.

Timothy frowned and cleared his throat. "Please, don't get me wrong. Certainly we'll cooperate with the police investigation in every way possible. It's just that we want the Heritage Society portrayed in the best possible light."

"We need to control the spin," piped up Orrin Hudson.

Now Drayton looked askance. "Spin?" he said with a jerk of his head. "I didn't realize Mr. Hudson's firm also dealt in public relations."

"They do not," snapped Timothy. He cast a sharp eye at Orrin Hudson, a rebuke for his "spin" comment. "But we certainly don't want to get blindsided by anything negative," explained Timothy. "The Heritage Society finds itself in an acutely vulnerable position right now, financially speaking. And, as you all know, we have our Spring Art Auction scheduled for this Saturday, although there have been suggestions from various board members that we cancel that event or at least postpone it indefinitely." Timothy paused, looking unhappy.

Sensing possible discord among the board members, Drayton leapt to his feet. "My suggestion is to stay the course," he told the group. "Oftentimes, the best way to put a terrible event behind you is to boldly soldier on. The sooner we get things back to normal, the sooner our donors will reestablish a comfort level with us."

"You don't think Mr. Crispin's murder Sunday evening was a terrible blight on us?" asked Cyril Haney, one of the board members.

"A most unfortunate incident," agreed Drayton. "But

completely beyond our control. The best thing we can do is carry on and put our trust in the police department to resolve this homicide and bring the perpetrator to justice."

Timothy cast an eye toward Orrin Hudson. "Mr. Hudson, I trust you still enjoy a productive and amicable relationship with the Homicide Division of the Charleston Police?"

Orrin Hudson gave a resolute nod. "Absolutely."

Theodosia bent her head and dropped her voice. "I think they kicked him out," she whispered to Drayton. His under-the-table answer to her was a firm but gentle kick to her shin.

"So you *will* be able to keep us in the loop during the ensuing investigation?" Timothy asked Orrin Hudson.

"Count on me, sir," said Orrin Hudson.

His eyes flicked down the length of the table and seemed to settle on Theodosia. Something passed across his face. *A flash of recognition?* she wondered.

"Drayton," said Timothy, raising his voice. "Since you are so adamant about keeping the Spring Art Auction on our docket, would you be willing to assume responsibility for it?"

"Absolutely," said Drayton. His answer rang out as supremely hearty, but a sudden look of panic fell across his face.

"Excellent," purred Timothy. "Of course, we'll have to let Simone, Mrs. Crispin, know that the Society has decided to proceed with the auction. It's certainly the courteous thing to do." Timothy continued to level his probing gaze at Drayton.

"I'd be happy to pay a visit to Mrs. Crispin," volunteered Theodosia. "In the company of Drayton, of course."

"Good, good," said Timothy, looking slightly skeptical. "Then it's all settled. The Heritage Society's Spring Art Auction shall proceed as scheduled this Saturday evening. And it shall be managed under the very capable direction of Mr. Drayton Conneley, our own parliamentarian." Timothy reached down, rummaged in his vintage leather attaché case for a moment, then pulled out a fat manila file folder. Slapping it down, he slid it across the broad table to Drayton. "Here is the list of objects that have been officially accepted, as well as our agreement with the caterer," said Timothy. "Who, I might add, was supposed to be in attendance here tonight. All I can say, Drayton, is good luck!"

"*I can't believe* I volunteered for this," said Drayton ten minutes later, once the boardroom had cleared out. He put his head in his hands and sighed deeply. His bare-faced enthusiasm about staying the course had just landed him a mountain of work.

"You'll be fine," said Theodosia, patting his shoulder. And Drayton, being a type A personality, *would* be fine. Organized and systematic in his thinking, he was a lot like Haley. And Theodosia.

"There'll be a million details!" moaned Drayton.

"Which you and I shall very capably deal with," said Theodosia. She flipped open the manila folder Timothy had given them, spread out a few sheets of paper.

"We've already committed to events at the tea shop," continued Drayton, allowing himself to wallow in his woe-is-me attitude. "Plus Haley wants us to pitch in and help at Gracie's shop!"

"Good point," said Theodosia as her eyes roved down the list of galleries whose works had been accepted. "Maybe we bit off more than we can chew."

Drayton looked up, slightly miffed. "Oh, do you think so?"

Theodosia shook her head. "Actually no. I think we'll be fine. Busy, certainly. A little nuts, maybe. But we'll make it happen."

"In addition, *vous* and *moi* have now been tapped to deliver the heartfelt sympathies of the Heritage Society to Simone Crispin," said Drayton. "I can't believe you actually *volunteered* for that little errand!"

"Chalk it up to my insatiable curiosity," shrugged Theodosia. "I've never met the woman and thought it might be interesting."

"Well, she's a very smart cookie for one thing," said Drayton. "And extremely tough-minded. She—" Halting midsentence and suddenly doing a double-take, Drayton cast a knowing glance at Theodosia. "You have an ulterior motive," he said in a slightly accusing tone.

Theodosia shrugged. "Not really." *Oops. Am I really that transparent?*

"Yes, you do," insisted Drayton, a slight look of triumph spreading across his face. "I can see you mentally toting up a list of suspects. Which means you're wondering if Simone Crispin might have somehow been involved in her own husband's murder!"

"Hey," said Theodosia. "Can I help it if I'm addicted to watching *Law and Order?* The first thing those detectives do in an investigation is take a good hard look at the spouse." *The first thing any police department probably does.*

"Might I remind you this is not dress rehearsal for a teleplay," rasped Drayton. "This is real life!"

"Which makes it all the more critical to get a face-to-face with her," said Theodosia. "Aren't you curious to see if she's upset? If she's gone into mourning? Or what if Simone Crispin is simply carrying on as usual? Personal reactions, with all the little nuances, can be very telling."

"You're incorrigible," accused Drayton. "And here I thought you were doing this in the spirit of volunteerism."

"There's some of that, too," admitted Theodosia. "But sure I'm curious about Simone." Theodosia slid the list of art donations over to Drayton. "Along with a few other folks. Here, take a look at this."

Pursing his lips, Drayton put his half-glasses on and stared down at the typed sheets. "What?" he asked, alternately blinking and frowning.

"Remember how upset Jester Moody was last night?" asked Theodosia. "About his Chinese sword not being accepted into the auction?"

"He was jumping out of his skin," replied Drayton. "I've never seen Jester so downright hostile."

"And all his hostility was directed squarely at Roger Crispin," said Theodosia. She slid a manicured finger down the list. "But take a look at this. There was no blackballing, no petty rebuffs. Jester Moody's piece is on the list after all."

Drayton stared at the list, digesting this new information. "You're right. All Jester's Sturm und Drang was for naught." Lifting his head, Drayton's eyes widened as he stared at Theodosia. "Oh no! You don't suppose . . . ?".

5

❧

Subtlety and subterfuge had never been Theodosia's strong
suit. Years ago, fresh out of college, she'd plunged head-
first into the grind-'em-up-spit-'em-out world of advertising and marketing and had immediately butted heads with
several male account executives. Tough guys, good old
boys, who didn't think women should be heading up business groups. But Theodosia had persisted. She'd worked
hard, toughened up, and turned a deaf ear. And after sur-
viving more than a few nasty bouts of infighting and back-
biting, she had emerged as an account executive in her own
right. Had even been handsomely rewarded with a com-
fortable corner office, personal assistant, and her own roster
of blue chip accounts.

Fact was, Theodosia had always lived her life with that

same brand of fortitude. She remained confident in her abilities, was determined to never give up ground, and was imbued with a burning penchant for fair play and justice.

So it was no surprise that, once Theodosia bid good night to Drayton, she spun on her heels and walked back down the dim, echoing main corridor of the Heritage Society and into the great hall. Where the lights burned low and black and yellow police tape now drooped like desultory spiderwebs.

She stared at the chairs, all shoved to one side of the hall. She noted the movie screen, still up but tilting precariously, and wondered to herself just who might have had it in for Roger Crispin, the steely head of the Crispin and Weller Auction House.

From what she knew of Roger Crispin, he was a fairly hard-nosed businessman. Then again, lots of people shared that trait. You almost had to be tougher than nails these days. Were sometimes *forced* to be.

But, as Drayton had cautioned her, auction houses were breeding grounds for contention. Sellers were often desperate, buyers sometimes greedy, and valuations, made on a whim, could be astronomical or meager. These elements could certainly come together in a lethal clash.

Theodosia could still feel the sense of panic that had pervaded the hall last evening. There was a residual energy left over and it resonated on a visceral level. She'd never been one to believe in ghosts or hauntings, even though many Charlestonians swore there were *hundreds* of ghostly inhabitants in their old, highly atmospheric city. But Theodosia could certainly feel this. An electrical energy that sprang from . . . what? Fear . . . panic . . . death?

Walking the length of the room, her footsteps echoing hollowly, Theodosia came to the spot where the tea table had sat last night. Right above was the lip of the balcony. The balcony that ran around three sides of the large room.

Obviously, someone could have sprinted upstairs from either of the front stairways. The lights had been out during Drayton's performance and the crowd's attention riveted on the storm as well as the projections on the giant screen behind him.

Theodosia supposed someone could have slipped past her and gone up the back stairway as well. She'd been hustling in and out of the small kitchen, so it was possible someone had tiptoed by unnoticed.

As if drawn by some unknown force, Theodosia moved toward the back stairway and began tentatively to make her way upstairs. Just as it had been last night, the stairwell seemed dark and narrow and dangerously steep. She moved slowly, testing each step to see if there was one that creaked. Testing her memory at the same time to see if she remembered hearing a telltale sound. She didn't.

No chalk outline shone from the bare floor of the balcony. Then Theodosia reminded herself that, even though Roger Crispin had been shot up here at point-blank range, he had landed downstairs.

On top of my cake. Why do I have absolutely no desire to ever bake a cake again?

Theodosia gazed about. Nothing looked moved or out of place. The desk with all the AV equipment was still shoved against the back wall, extra chairs were stacked here and here. The only thing different was that an overhead light was on now. Shrugging, Theodosia turned and was about to start back down the stairs. With the light behind her now, it was even more dark and shadowy in the stairwell, and Theodosia fumbled around, searching for a light switch.

Here it is.

Forty watts of dim light bounced off the inside of the stairwell. It wasn't much, but at least it would keep her from taking a misstep.

Halfway down, a flash of white fuzz stuck on the lip of a step caught her eye. Theodosia hesitated.

What's that? she wondered. *Dust?*

No, it's something else.

Bending down, Theodosia reached out and tentatively touched the little piece of fluff, wondering what it was, but telling herself at the same time that it was just something that had dropped off someone's shoe.

And then she saw it wasn't dust at all, but a feather.

A feather? How on earth did . . . ?

"Hello there!" A loud male voice rang out below her.

"Hello?" she answered in a somewhat tremorous tone.

Who else could be sneaking around here?

"Anyone there?" came the deep voice again.

Although she'd been properly startled, Theodosia decided this was not an altogether unfriendly voice that she was hearing. And when she arrived at the bottom of the staircase, she was surprised to see a young, thirtyish-looking man with bright blue eyes and a tousle of blond hair waiting for her.

"Are you with the Heritage Society?" the man promptly asked her. And then, without bothering to wait for her answer, launched into a rapid-fire apology. "Sorry, to be so late. We're breaking in a new sous chef and you have no idea what a can of worms *that* turned out to be. And then, when I finally glanced at my watch, I realized I was supremely late. For the meeting, I mean. Which means the Heritage Society will probably never hire us again and probably would prefer to fire our worthless butts except for the fact that it's too late to find another caterer." The man flashed her a winning smile as he thrust a sheet of paper into Theodosia's hands. "Anyway, here it is. Final menu with a carved-in-stone price." He stopped, took a breath. "I'm really sorry," he added for good measure.

Theodosia quickly scanned the sheet of paper. "Your restaurant's doing the catering for Saturday night?" she asked.

He gave a good-natured shrug. "As I so elegantly overexplained, yes. Yes, we are."

"And you are . . . ?" she asked him.

"Parker Scully."

Theodosia took in his well-tailored linen jacket worn casually over his T-shirt and khakis, his relaxed air, and his direct, no-nonsense pattern of speech. "You're not from around here, are you?" she asked, staring into cobalt-blue eyes that seemed to be blessed with amazingly long lashes.

"I kind of am," he told her. "I was born just a little bit north of here in Murrell's Inlet, but then my parents moved north when I was still a kid. The last four years I've been living in Manhattan, which was kind of a rat race and the reason I moved back home. At least I *hope* Charleston's going to be home."

"What did you do in New York?" Theodosia asked.

"Managed a trendy bistro on East 56th. Place called Tycoon." He flashed her a megawatt grin. "Ever heard of it?"

"Um, no," said Theodosia, slightly taken aback by his abundant enthusiasm. "But it sounds like fun."

"Trust me, it wasn't," laughed Parker Scully. "Try to imagine cranky, overworked advertising executives rubbing shoulders with society-ladies-who-lunch."

"Sounds like Darrin from *Bewitched* meets the women from *W* magazine," quipped Theodosia.

Parker Scully gave an appreciative chuckle. "Very good. What did you say your name was again?"

"I didn't."

"But you're with the Heritage Society," he said. "At least I hope you are since I just entrusted you with all the pertinent details for Saturday night's auction soiree."

"I'm Theodosia Browning," she said, offering Parker Scully her hand. "Nice to make your acquaintance."

A wide grin split his face as he shook hands with her. "I know who you are," he declared. "You're the tea lady, last night's unlucky caterer. Hope I've got better karma going than you did."

"So do I," said Theodosia.

"I wanted to meet you last night," said Parker Scully. "But, given the rather bizarre circumstances, never got the chance."

"You were here?" Theodosia asked, surprised.

Parker Scully nodded. "Little old me and I'd guess about two hundred of Charleston's blue bloods, all of whom are probably under suspicion for murder right about now. Not that I'd ever presume to count myself among them."

"The blue bloods or those suspected of murder?" asked

Theodosia as they walked through the great hall and out one of the double doors onto the patio.

"Hah, good one!" said Parker, dodging her question. "Did you know Roger Crispin very well?"

"Not really," said Theodosia. She thought for a moment. "Well, maybe a little bit. But only because of the Heritage Society. He's a member, I'm a member."

"And now so am I," said Parker Scully.

"A board member?" Theodosia didn't recall seeing Parker Scully's name on the list of board members, but that didn't mean a whole lot. The list was always shapeshifting as members who'd served two or three terms stepped aside and let new blood come in.

Parker Scully laughed. "Nah, I'm just a humble caterer and restaurateur. I'm one of the partners who own Solstice over on Market Street. Maybe you've heard of it?"

Theodosia searched her memory. She *had* heard something about the restaurant Solstice.

"We're kind of a French- and Mediterranean-influenced bistro, but we also have a *tapas* bar," Parker Scully explained.

"Delaine," said Theodosia.

"Pardon?" said Parker, giving her a quizzical look.

"A good friend of mine mentioned your place to me. It's fairly new, right?"

"Six months and counting," replied Parker. He reached an arm down and rapped on the edge of a wooden planter. "Knock on wood."

Theodosia thought for a moment as they walked. "My friend said . . . let me think now . . . oh yes, she said you have a wine list to *die* for."

"Well she's right," Parker Scully grinned. "Or at least we're in the process of developing a world-class wine list. I just got back from a buying trip through France and Germany, where I discovered some absolutely incredible wines. A Chateau Lagrange Bordeaux, some luscious Côtes du Rhône wines, even a Christoffel Urziger Riesling with almost Eiswein acidity. Now I'm making plans to expand our wine list to include something like four hundred different vintages."

"Are you serious?" asked Theodosia. "How can you keep them all straight?"

"How many teas do you stock at your tea shop?" Parker asked her.

Theodosia thought for a few moments. "Maybe a couple hundred?" she offered, thinking how skillfully he'd mousetrapped her. *Clever guy.*

Parker Scully just grinned.

"Yes," she said, somewhat intrigued by this brash but rather attractive restaurateur. "I see your point."

6

 ❧

"Miss Dimple," *called* Haley, "would you like a slice of fresh-baked cranberry orange bread?"

Sitting at a table near the little stone fireplace, early morning sun streaming through the Indigo Tea Shop's leaded windowpanes, Miss Dimple was busily scratching away in a pair of black ledgers, efficiently tallying the tea shop's previous week's receipts.

"And I can offer the perfect complement to Haley's cranberry orange bread," said Drayton as he sped over to Miss Dimple's table and poured out an aromatic stream of steaming gold liquid. "Take a sip of this tea and tell me it isn't the finest oolong you've ever tasted."

Miss Dimple obliged him. "Delightful," she declared as

she set her cup down and rolled her eyes as if to punctuate her words.

"This yellow-gold oolong is one of China's best kept secrets," declared Drayton. "Tea connoisseurs adore its fragrant, smooth liquor and subtle honey-nectar notes. This particular oolong was grown in Fujian Province up in the Anxi Mountains."

"If you ask me," called Haley from across the room, "that Chin Sun Oolong from Thailand is even better. You should brew Miss Dimple a pot of that!"

"Haley," said Drayton, hustling across the tea room. "Instead of jabbering away, trying to play tea one-upsmanship, will you kindly explain to me why these various twigs and branches are spread all over our front counter?"

"Those are mine," said Theodosia as she emerged through the green velvet curtains that separated the kitchen and her little office in back from the tearoom. "I'm the guilty party."

"What on earth are they for?" asked Drayton, looking askance. "More importantly, what are you going to do with them?"

Theodosia picked up a twist of dried vine and formed a circle. "I've been making grapevine wreaths and garlands. For decoration."

Drayton threw her a questioning glance. "You don't think our little tea shop exudes enough charm as it is?" he asked. "Look around, we're fairly *oozing* coziness. Between the teacup chandelier and the framed tea labels, the Indigo Tea Shop looks absolutely fabulous."

"But we're ab fab because Theodosia *keeps* fussing," argued Haley.

"Yes, but——" began Drayton.

"Why don't you pop a chill pill, Drayton," laughed Haley. "Theo and I are planning to decorate the wreaths and garlands with teacups. We've been saving all the chipped cups and saucers and are going to tie them into the grape vines with pink and green gossamer ribbons. We're just trying to add a festive touch for the big teacup exchange this Saturday."

"Oh," said Drayton, suddenly taken aback. "That's *this* Saturday. Oh my." He put a hand to his cheek, crossed an arm across his chest, Jack Benny–style.

Sensing Drayton's vulnerability, Haley rushed in for the kill. "Did someone *forget* about the teacup exchange?" she challenged. "Even though a certain master tea blender and events manager scheduled it a full three months ago?"

Drayton straightened up and tugged unhappily at his vest. "Ah, therein lies the problem," he began by way of explanation. "That particular event was scheduled so far in advance it completely slipped my mind." He raised a hand and zoomed it past his head. *"Pffft."*

"Drayton's been tapped to honcho the art auction this Saturday evening," Theodosia explained to Haley and Miss Dimple. "He has a very full plate right now, so you'll have to give him a little latitude."

"Isn't it a good thing the kitchen staff didn't forget," said Haley, a rising note of triumph in her voice and a wide Cheshire Cat grin across her face. "Good thing the menu's already been thought out and planned."

"Thank you, Miss Parker," said Drayton contritely.

But Haley wasn't finished. "I also happen to know that Theodosia ordered place cards and such. So all we really need to do is finish the garlands and wreaths. Which you seem to think are *extraneous* to our shop."

"Extraneous was not the word I used," said Drayton. "I was merely curious as to their exact usage."

"You three," spoke up Miss Dimple suddenly, "are an absolute riot. No wonder I adore coming here." She chuckled and her stocky five-foot-tall, pleasingly plump frame shook like a bowl of Jell-O. "I declare, I'd probably do the bookkeeping for free just because of the laughs I get."

Drayton peered at her, a look of speculation on his face. "Speaking of bookkeeping, are you busy later this morning?" Miss Dimple was the bookkeeper for several shops up and down Church Street, so she was forever dashing off to the Chowder House or Pinckney's Gift Shop or Antiquarian Booksellers.

"Not really," said Miss Dimple. "Why? Do you want me to stay and help?" she asked, anticipating Drayton's question. Miss Dimple always loved to stay and help.

"Yes!" all three of them answered in unison.

"Would you please?" begged Haley. "As you can clearly see, our poor Drayton is slightly addled today."

"Honey," said Miss Dimple, "I would think you're *all* a little upset considering what happened the other night with poor Mr. Crispin. Let me tell you, that story's been splashed all over the TV and newspapers!"

"You're right," said Theodosia. "We're still not over that one." *Not by a long shot,* she thought to herself, still wondering what to do about the strange feather she'd found stuck in the stairwell. *Keep quiet about it? Keep investigating? Tell Burt Tidwell?* Mulling over her options, Theodosia decided the latter two were probably her smartest move.

"You know," said Drayton, "I think I'm going to drag the outdoor tables around to the front. The temperature's supposed to be in the high seventies, so it's definitely nice enough for an outdoor seating."

"And good for revenue," said Miss Dimple.

"Lucky I happened to make *gallons* of she-crab soup," declared Haley.

"What else are we serving, Haley?" asked Theodosia.

"Chilled poached trout on a bed of field greens garnished with blue cheese and toasted almonds and *jambon et fromage*," said Haley. "Which you all know is a fancy French way of saying ham and cheese."

"Indeed it is," replied Theodosia, "but served on mini French baguettes with a dash of Dijon mustard your little sandwiches are really quite special."

"It's the poached trout that whets my appetite," declared Drayton. "With a menu this creative I'm definitely going to put our little French tables out."

Theodosia nodded. Their half-dozen little gueridon tables were authentic, marble-topped cafe tables that she and Drayton had purchased at an auction down in Savannah. A French restaurant by the name of Mon Petit had gone out of business and they'd picked up the little tables at a very good price. When clustered on the sidewalk outside the tea shop, the tables always looked very European, and customers were instantly drawn to them.

Glancing up as the door flew open, Theodosia noted that their usual morning customers were already beginning to trickle in. *Better get cracking,* she decided. *Deal with morning teatime, an always-busy lunch crowd, and then Drayton and I have to pay a visit to Simone Crispin this afternoon. Can we get it all done? That remains to be seen!*

Delaine Dish wiggled a little finger and flashed a broad pussycat smile at Drayton. She'd dropped in for lunch and brought along a friend. Dressed in a crisp suit of sea-foam green, Delaine gestured and waved like mad. Obviously, she was aching to introduce Drayton and Theodosia to her luncheon companion.

Theodosia was finally able to scuttle over to Delaine's table and slip into an empty chair beside her. "Drayton's awfully busy right now," she explained. "But I promise he'll stop by in a few moments."

Grabbing one of Theodosia's hands, Delaine beamed at Theodosia. "Honey," she said, "I just wanted you to meet Maribo Pratt."

"Hello," said Theodosia, smiling at an exotic-looking woman with long dark hair, high cheekbones, and luminous brown eyes that seemed to tilt slightly. She was in her late thirties, but except for a little crinkling under the eyes could have passed for a decade younger.

"Maribo is one of my newest and dearest friends," cooed Delaine. "She owns the Segrova Gallery over on Unity Alley."

The proverbial lightbulb suddenly popped on in Theodosia's head as she recalled exactly who Maribo Pratt was.

An up-and-coming gallery owner who'd garnered a fair amount of outstanding press.

"Of course!" exclaimed Theodosia. "Nice to meet you. I read about the Segrova Gallery in that terrific write-up you got in *Charleston Art Scene* last year. You spoke so passionately about Russian art it made me want to rush right out and start building a collection."

Maribo nodded eagerly and waved a manicured hand. "Russian art is still one of my passions. Especially the Russian Impressionists of the fifties and sixties, as well as the artists known as the Soviet Nonconformists. But right now, at this very moment, Baltic art has become the new, big thing."

"Can you believe it?" exclaimed Delaine, positively oozing enthusiasm. "*Baltic art* is what Russian art *used* to be. Hot, hot, hot. Isn't that absolutely *amazing*?"

Theodosia wasn't sure whether Delaine thought it was amazing art or amazing that Baltic art was suddenly so allfired popular. Didn't matter. Delaine found a lot of things amazing. For a while anyway.

"All right, ladies," said Drayton, materializing at their table with a pot of tea. "Try a cup of this oolong."

"Drayton!" exclaimed Delaine, who immediately launched into a gushing introduction of Maribo as well as a glowing description of the Segrova Gallery.

"Your gallery sounds marvelous," Drayton told Maribo as Delaine continued to prattle happily on. "I'd love to drop by some time. I took a connoiseurship course at the Gibbes Museum last winter and really got intrigued by Russian and Eastern European painters."

"There's absolutely no time like the present!" Delaine announced in a loud voice. "What about dropping by Segrova after lunch? I'm sure you two can steal away for a little while. Let the minions carry on with business."

"Therein lies the problem," chuckled Drayton. "We *are* the minions. No, I'm afraid Theodosia and I already have plans to duck out this afternoon." He turned his gaze on Maribo. "We're going to visit Simone Crispin. Formally convey the sympathies of the Heritage Society."

Maribo's lovely face crumpled. "Oh, my goodness," she said. "I've been following that story in the news! The poor man!"

"You knew Roger Crispin?" Theodosia asked her.

Maribo nodded sadly. "Roger and I served on the Charleston Art and Antique Council together. He was a wonderful fellow, so knowledgeable. And I know he's done so much for the community."

"Drayton, dear," interjected Delaine, "let's not spoil what's been a lovely luncheon so far by dredging up that sordid little episode."

"No, of course not," murmured Drayton. He smiled at Maribo. "Are you enjoying the poached trout?"

"Oh yes!" she exclaimed. "Only time I had better was when it was fresh caught in Montana."

"And I just *adore* this she-crab soup," said Delaine, not wanting to be left out.

"Where are my manners!" cried Maribo, suddenly digging into her straw handbag. She pulled out two embossed squares of vellum and handed one to Theodosia, another to Drayton. "Please, I'd love it if you both came to my gallery opening tomorrow evening. I'm premiering a new painter, Draco Vidak. This is the first time his paintings have ever been viewed by an American audience, so it's quite a coup."

"Thank you," said Drayton, squinting at his invitation and looking extremely pleased. "This sounds like a marvelous show. Draco Vidak. This artist is Russian?"

"Baltic," announced Delaine. She gave Theodosia a gentle nudge. "I'm bringing a date," she announced with a smile that bordered on smug. "Care to guess who it is?"

Somehow Theodosia just knew it had to be Jester Moody.

"It's Jester Moody," chortled Delaine, savoring her big announcement. She batted her eyelashes and grinned. "He's going to be my escort, isn't that fun?"

"I'm sure you'll have a lovely time," murmured Theodosia. *Amazing,* she thought to herself. *Delaine said she was going to date him and now she is. Score major points for the power of positive thinking. Or for Delaine's predatory skills.*

"This tea is absolutely luscious," said Maribo, a twinkle lighting her eyes. Obviously, Delaine had been crowing about Jester Moody to her, too.

"If you're a tea lover, you simply must come back here this Saturday," Drayton urged her. "We're having a teacup exchange and tea tasting. I'll be brewing some first flush Singbulli Estate and some Royal Golden Yunnan," he said, leaning in toward Maribo. "The Yunnan is like drinking velvet."

"I'd love to come," enthused Maribo. "I've even got some Russian teacups I could bring." She looked around the table. "You did say it was a teacup exchange, didn't you?"

"Quite right," said Drayton. "Sounds like they'd be perfect," he added, smiling at Maribo.

"You know, Drayton," said Delaine, sensing, or perhaps hoping for, a faint spark between them. "Maribo lived in Europe for a while. And she drives a Rolls Royce."

"Hold everything," laughed Maribo. "Before anyone gets too impressed, please realize my car's an '84 Corniche. I test drove the thing on a whim two years ago down in Savannah and fell utterly in love. Of course a Rolls is an absolute bear when it comes to repairs. Hard to find Rolls Royce–certified mechanics and always tricky to find parts."

"But a beautiful auto, just the same," responded Drayton. "And where did you live in Europe?"

"Paris," said Maribo.

"The City of Light," enthused Drayton.

"I had a lovely little walk-up just off the Rue de Rivoli," said Maribo. "Not that far from the Louvre."

"No wonder you were inspired to open your own gallery," said Drayton. "Living so close to all that fantastic art."

Theodosia was clearing dishes when Burt Tidwell walked in. She'd called his office an hour ago and left a voicemail. He hadn't been at his office and she guessed he was probably out for lunch somewhere. She knew for a fact that Burt Tidwell *always* made time for lunch.

Tossing her a heavy-lidded glance, Tidwell shuffled to a table and sat down heavily. Drayton was beside him thirty seconds later, armed with fresh linens, flatware, a hibiscus-design footed teacup and saucer by Ucago, and a small pot of tea. Noting the setup at Tidwell's table, Theodosia had to smile. She wasn't sure whether it was done on purpose or not, but Drayton inevitably seemed to give Tidwell the most delicate of teacups.

"Detective Tidwell," she said, hurrying over to his table. "Could I interest you in a light lunch?"

Tidwell shook his great head and his jowls sloshed slightly. "Thank you much, Miss Browning, but I've already eaten. A lovely bowl of okra gumbo at Poogan's Porch. With a side order of their rather peppery country sausage."

"Perhaps a dessert then," she said. "I happen to know Haley just pulled a pan of her special green tea–infused brownies from the oven."

The corners of Tidwell's mouth suddenly turned upward. "Green tea brownies sound like a delightful sweet treat," he told her.

"With a dollop of crème fraîche?" Theodosia asked, knowing full well he'd reply in the affirmative.

"Dollop away," Tidwell instructed her.

Tidwell was scraping up the final few crumbs when Theodosia pulled the little plastic baggy from her apron pocket and tossed it onto his table. She'd deliberated about withholding it, but decided she probably needed Tidwell's help after all. She also knew the consequences for withholding evidence could be severe. After all, her father had been an attorney.

"Pray tell, what is this?" Tidwell asked, his eyes darting between the final scraping of crumbs and a quick assessment of the baggy.

Tidwell's version of multitasking, Theodosia decided.

"Something I found at the Heritage Society last night," said Theodosia. "It was stuck on one of the steps in the back stairwell that leads to the loft."

"You've been investigating," Tidwell said in a reproachful tone. His beady eyes drilled into her. "Or, rather, removing potential evidence from a crime scene."

"I know that—" she began.

"And now it's potentially tainted," he went on.

"Hey," Theodosia said, her tone sharpening. "I was merely looking around. Can I help it if I happened to glance down and notice this little item? Which, I might add, your crime scene team *failed* to discover."

Tidwell poked at the baggy with one of his big fingers. "Offhand, I'd have to say it looks like some sort of feather."

"That's what I thought, too," said Theodosia, grimacing inwardly. She knew that feathers were one of the staple items Gracie Venable used in her millinery business. Which, of course, made her feel horribly disloyal. After all, Gracie had asked for help and she'd promised to give it. And Haley had pretty much begged her to look into things, too. Now here she was, turning over what could be a key piece of evidence to Burt Tidwell.

Theodosia sighed. But what choice did she have? She wasn't a forensic investigator, she didn't have access to a crime lab.

Since Drayton and Miss Dimple seemed to have everything in the tea shop under control, Theodosia sat down next to Tidwell.

Sensing her nervousness, he picked up the plastic bag,

stared at her with beady eyes. "I don't know how much you know about forensics," he murmured.

"Not much," she admitted.

"The French investigator Edmond Locard is often credited with being the father of forensics," Tidwell told her. "Locard theorized that for any two points of contact there is always a cross-transference of material from one to the other."

"So this could lead to something," she said to Tidwell. "If, in fact, there was this cross-transference. From murderer to victim. Or the *area* the victim was in," she stammered.

Tidwell continued to stare at her. "It's possible."

Theodosia drummed her fingers nervously on the table. If she was lucky, the feather would serve to *eliminate* Gracie as a suspect. The feather could be from a duck or a grouse for all she knew and might incriminate the real killer.

"Talk to me," said Theodosia, fully expecting some quid pro quo for handing over what might be a useful piece of evidence. "What can you tell me about the gun that was used?"

Tidwell reached for his teacup, took a delicate sip, set it down with a *clink*. For such a huge man he didn't seem to have any trouble handling the tiny china teacup. "It would appear the perpetrator used some type of silencer," he finally told her.

"Do you know the type and caliber of bullet?" Theodosia asked.

Tidwell fixed her with a baleful stare. "Yes, of course." They continued their impromptu standoff, but his eyes broke away first. "I don't have to tell you we're looking hard at Gracie Venable."

These were the exact words Theodosia didn't want to hear. "So now Gracie's been upgraded from witness to suspect," she said, her tone heavy with sarcasm. "If you can call that an upgrade." Theodosia decided Tidwell's pronouncement might also be a rush to judgment.

"Miss Browning," said Tidwell, "we are public servants performing our assigned tasks as best we can. And this, this homicide investigation, is a decidedly serious matter. One of Charleston's most prominent citizens was rather rudely dispatched with, in case you hadn't noticed."

"Oh, I noticed, Detective Tidwell," said Theodosia, scrambling to her feet. "How could I *not* notice when a dead body comes slamming down on top of my tea table!"

7

Crispin and Weller Auction House was located in a three-story Civil War–era red brick building on Beaufain Street, just a stone's throw from the King Street antiques district. In this most charming part of Charleston, visitors are always pleasantly surprised to discover the mother lode of English antiques. Much of the British-made furniture, silver, glassware, and paintings were brought over in the eighteenth century to furnish the homes of well-heeled, well-bred Charlestonians. More recently, the goods needed to stock these thriving antique stores have been acquired by savvy dealers who scour flea markets and auction houses all across the British Isles as well as up and down the Eastern Seaboard.

Theodosia and Drayton were greeted in the lobby by an acerbic-looking little man in his seventies who turned out to be Russell Weller, Roger Crispin's erstwhile partner. Weller wore wire-rimmed glasses that gave him a hard, glinty-eyed look, and he seemed to project a disapproving, somewhat sour air. His blue and white pinstripe suit was a distinct contrast to the rather staid and "tweedy" atmosphere of the auction house.

"So sorry about Roger," Drayton told him as the two solemnly shook hands. "He was such a tremendous asset to the Heritage Society. Roger never hesitated to give us both time and energy. As you can imagine, we're absolutely heartsick over the circumstances."

"Thank you," rasped Weller, who looked as though he'd just been interrupted and couldn't wait to get back to what he'd been working on. "I'll tell Simone you're here."

Russell Weller disappeared through a swinging door, leaving Theodosia and Drayton to wander the rather large and grandiose gallery. Sparkling chandeliers hung overhead, spilling their light on antique French buffets and writing desks. Gleaming oil paintings hung on the walls and glass cases filled with old porcelains seemed to be sandwiched everywhere. Scattered throughout the enormous room were dozens of enormous, colorful vases that could only be termed *jardins*.

"Weller's a little like Timothy Neville, isn't he?" whispered Theodosia, peering at a lovely collection of antique tartan ware enameled boxes. "But without the money and manners."

"Good lord," exclaimed Drayton. "Don't ever let Timothy hear you say a thing like that! Weller's always been a bit standoffish and antisocial. I understand that he and Roger barely exchanged more than fifty words a year." He paused. "Did you happen to notice that awful suit?"

"If I didn't know better," said Theodosia, "I'd say Russell Weller was trying out for a part in *Guys and Dolls*." Indeed, the navy pinstripe suit did have a certain racy, gangster patina to it.

"Sometimes you can be a very wicked woman," said Drayton, trying hard to keep the corners of his mouth from twitching upwards.

Peering into another of the lighted glass cases, Theodosia remarked, "They really do have some nice pieces here, don't they?"

"Crispin and Weller handles only the *crème de la crème*," responded Drayton, stepping up to a tall, antique case. "Come, look at this."

Theodosia ducked around a bronze statue of a garden nymph to stand next to Drayton.

The elegant old case displayed a half dozen very tasty objects. A Chinese Yi-Shing teapot in the shape of the Buddha's hand, a silver urn, two Greek marble heads in almost perfect condition, and a cloisonné vase. And on the top shelf, a gleaming fanciful marble egg, rimmed in gold and encrusted with rubies, pearls, and sapphires.

"Tell me that isn't a real Faberge egg," said Theodosia, awestruck.

"I assure you it's quite authentic," said Drayton. "Rather marvelous, wouldn't you say?"

Theodosia gazed at the Faberge egg. Until now, she'd only seen photos of the famous eggs that had been created for the Tsars of Russia by Carl Faberge and his skilled team of artisans, jewelers, and goldsmiths. But as her eyes drank in the splendor of this Faberge egg, she realized the photographs she'd seen didn't do them justice. Here was impeccable craftsmanship merged with elegance like she'd never seen before. A splendid little sculpture fit for a king. Indeed, fit for a Tsar!

"Most of the Faberge eggs that made it into this country were eventually incorporated into the Forbes collection," said Drayton. "But a year or so ago, that entire collection was purchased by a wealthy Russian industrialist and taken back to Moscow."

"I hope the collection was put on display in a museum," said Theodosia. "So everyone can enjoy it."

"We can only hope," said Drayton.

Twenty minutes later they were still waiting for Simone Crispin.

Drayton paced, glanced at his watch, snorted loudly, and stewed inwardly. "This is awful! Waiting for Simone is like *Waiting for Godot*," he said, referencing Samuel Beckett's existential play where the title character never does show up. "Where on earth could she be?" he huffed.

"Simone is such a pretty name," said Theodosia, trying to deflect Drayton's attention from what was fast becoming a tedious wait. "Do you know, is she French?"

"Not one whit," sniffed Drayton, "although she pretends to be."

Finally Simone Crispin swept into the gallery to greet them.

Tall, with a regal bearing, she looked almost like an older

version of Delaine. Mid-fifties, heart-shaped face, arched eyebrows, hair pulled into a swirl atop her head. But whereas Delaine had a softness and vibrancy about her, Simone Crispin seemed cool and brittle.

Theodosia peered closely at Simone. *Was her skin really that nice and tight or had she had some work done?* she wondered.

"My dear Mrs. Crispin," began Drayton, after he'd made polite introductions. "All of us at the Heritage Society are so *terribly* sorry about your tragic loss." Drayton was conducting himself as a proper gentleman again. A far cry from the fidgeting, stewing visitor he'd been a few moments earlier.

Simone Crispin gave an imperceptible nod. A sign for Drayton to continue.

"We are also heartsick that such a terrible tragedy would take place at the Heritage Society." Drayton's clasped hands spread open in a supreme gesture of appeal.

Simone nodded again. "We do not choose our place of death," she murmured, a sad smile lighting her face.

The words *drama queen* suddenly popped into Theodosia's head as she watched Simone closely. *Could she be enjoying this little bit of theatrics?* wondered Theodosia. *Just a teensy bit? Could it be that Simone isn't all that heartbroken?*

"You are so right," said Drayton. "The choice is never ours. Which is why the Heritage Society wishes to carry on with our auction this Saturday evening." He paused for several beats. "That is . . . provided you do not harbor any *serious* reservations." It was more a question than a statement.

"I have no problem whatsoever with the auction proceeding as planned," purred Simone. "In fact, I'm sure Roger would have wanted everyone to carry on."

"That was our thought, too," murmured Drayton. "But you are a kind and generous woman to give the Heritage Society your blessing on this event."

"Thank you for stopping by," said Simone, beginning to edge away.

"Do you know . . . ?" began Theodosia, deciding to take a quick shot in the dark. After all, she was here and this might be the only chance she had at talking with Simone. "Do you know if the police have any suspects in mind?"

Drayton telegraphed a warning glance to Theodosia, which Simone seemed not to notice.

"Yes, they do," said Simone, who didn't seem to object to Theodosia raising the subject. "At first they suspected his death was somehow related to a business deal gone awry, but . . ." Simone put a hand to her heart and her eyes drilled into Theodosia's. "My husband was also guilty of, shall we say, certain infidelities." Her voice sounded bitter, but she looked completely unruffled.

She's a cool character, thought Theodosia. *On the other hand, so is Russell Weller. That antisocial act can cover up a lot.*

At Simone's mention of infidelities, Drayton blanched. For him the conversation had clearly veered off in the wrong direction, way outside his comfort zone.

"I'm sure you've spoken to the police about Roger's . . . ah . . . relationships," said Theodosia, trying her best to look sympathetic. "Of course, that's usually the first thing the police ask about. Possible enemies, current or past, as well as personal *involvements*."

Simone nodded and a fierce light shone in her eyes. "You're quite correct. And you might be interested to know that I've advised them to take a very careful look at a young woman who recently became a tenant in one of Roger's commercial properties."

"Again," said Drayton, interrupting suddenly. "Thank you *very* much, and please know you have our absolute deepest sympathies." Nervously, he grasped for Simone's hand and pumped it heartily. "All of us at the Heritage Society are so very grateful for your understanding."

"You're very welcome," said Simone, favoring him with a dazzling smile. "Perhaps we'll speak again on Thursday. Roger's funeral, you know. St. Stephens."

"Of course," said Drayton, plucking at Theodosia's sleeve. "Sorry, but we really must be going!"

"Gracie!" exclaimed Theodosia once Drayton had managed to pull her outside. "Simone was talking about Gracie Venable! She's trying to steer the police toward Gracie when she has absolutely no reason to."

Drayton mopped his brow with a hanky. "Did you have to be so all-fired direct?" he asked sharply. "My goodness, the entire conversation took a horribly uncomfortable turn due to your probing questions!"

"Probing to you, maybe," said Theodosia. "I'd say Simone relished the whole thing. Made her feel important and painted her in a sympathetic light. You know, the poor wronged widow."

They climbed into Theodosia's Jeep and she started the engine.

"You don't suppose Simone really does have evidence of

some sort of"—Drayton searched for the right phrase—"hanky-panky, do you?" he asked. He'd settled for that rather tame descriptor rather than call it an out-and-out affair. He, too, had gotten to know Gracie Venable and had grown to admire her gumption and feisty spirit. He didn't want to think about the possibility that Gracie might have enjoyed a liaison with Roger Crispin.

Theodosia shook her head. "If you ask me, Simone's accusations sound like sour grapes." She turned the wheel sharply, pulled her vehicle into the street, and accelerated into traffic. "The possibility exists, you know, that Simone is trying to deflect attention off herself and onto Gracie."

"Good heavens, you can't believe the woman had a hand in doing away with her own husband!" said Drayton.

Theodosia stared straight ahead. She knew that spouses and family members were the first ones to come under police scrutiny these days. Probably because spouses and family members were also responsible for a high percentage of murders.

"Of course, I don't know that Roger and Simone had the happiest of marriages," commented Drayton.

"That was my impression, too," said Theodosia. "Otherwise she wouldn't have been quite so eager to bring up the *infidelities* part. So . . . Roger and Simone live . . . lived . . . where?" she asked.

Drayton thought for a moment. "Charming brick Georgian-style home over on Tradd Street. The one with the spectacular wrought-iron gate on the side. Although, I think Simone spends a fair amount of time in the country. They also own a farm, Hilloway I think it's called, somewhere off

Rutledge Road. You know, not too far from the Wildwood Horse and Hunt Club. Seems to me I heard she was into organic gardening or something like that. Doesn't believe in poisoning the earth with chemicals."

"Sounds like Simone doesn't live all that far from Aunt Libby's," said Theodosia. Her Aunt Libby Browning lived at Cane Ridge Plantation just off Rutledge Road, too. It was a former rice plantation where her father had also grown up. Now he was buried out there alongside her mother. In the small family plot surrounded by a crumbling stone fence and sheltered by an enormous live oak. A place shrouded in memories and tradition.

"Thanks goodness Simone gave us her blessing to proceed with the auction," sighed Drayton. "If she'd objected I don't know what I would have done. As it is I still need to follow up with a dozen or so galleries, contact Sheldon Tibbets about a quick story, make sure the great hall is set up again, and finalize the menu with the caterer."

"I met your caterer," said Theodosia, thinking back to her quick meeting with Parker Scully. "He seemed responsible enough. I don't think you'll have to worry."

"I always worry," said Drayton as they bumped along. His mind had obviously leapt ahead to finalizing the details for Saturday night, whereas Theodosia was still pondering their meeting with Simone Crispin and the murder of her husband Roger.

"Do we have time to make another stop?" Theodosia asked suddenly.

Drayton glanced at his watch, an ancient Patek-Phillipe that perpetually seemed to run a few minutes slow, and pursed his lips. "It's three," he said. Drayton got fidgety whenever he was away from the tea shop during business hours.

"Which means afternoon teatime is well under way," reasoned Theodosia. "So even if we head straight back they'll still be closing things up in a little while."

"I *suppose* Haley and Miss Dimple are covering things adequately," fretted Drayton. "What did you have in mind?"

"*Oh good heavens,*" exclaimed Drayton as they rocked to a stop in front of Passports, Jester Moody's elegant shop on King Street. "What's this about?"

"Chalk it up to curiosity," said Theodosia as she pushed the driver's side door open.

"That's exactly what you said about Simone," said Drayton, easing himself out of the Jeep, looking nonplussed. "And look what an unpleasant conversation *that* turned out to be."

"I seriously doubt this visit will be any friendlier," remarked Theodosia as they crossed the sidewalk and stepped into Jester Moody's rather intriguing little shop. "Come on Drayton, buck up!" she whispered.

Stepping inside Passports was like stepping inside Beijing's Forbidden City, Theodosia decided. Right into the imperial storeroom of the Last Emperor. Han figures, Tang horses and warriors, and exquisite oxblood and celadon vases sat majestically on Chinese rosewood tables and elegant lacquer shelves. An enormous terra-cotta statue that looked suspiciously like one of the ancient warriors excavated at Xian loomed against a back wall covered in gold brocade and highlighted by pinpoint spotlights. The faint scent of sandalwood incense hung in the air.

"Oh my," exclaimed Drayton. "Jester's certainly changed things around. Stepped up his caliber of merchandise, I'd say."

Jester Moody glanced up from where he sat at an ornately carved rosewood desk. An array of small jade figures were spread out before him and a customer, a gray-haired gentleman in a cream-colored suit, sat across from him, handling the various jade pieces.

"Hello there," called Drayton, taking the initiative, putting a friendly note in his voice.

Jester glanced quickly at the customer across from him. When he seemed satisfied that the man was busily engrossed in examining a small jade horse with a jeweler's loupe, he rose to greet Theodosia and Drayton.

Theodosia noted Jester's almost noiseless approach as he glided across an elegant expanse of Chinese rug. *Silk,* she decided. *That rug has to be loomed of pure hand-spun silk. Handmade and hand knotted. How much would something like that cost? Fifty? Sixty thousand dollars?*

"Drayton," said Jester, a scowl across his darkly handsome face, "I wasn't expecting you."

Drayton tried to keep it light and snappy. "Jester, this is Theodosia Browning . . . you remember Theodosia, don't you?" he asked and Jester nodded slowly. "We were just passing by and decided to pop in and take a gander at your shop. You know, Theo's absolutely passionate about Chinese art."

Jester raised an eyebrow and favored her with a remote look. "You're a collector?"

"Of sorts," said Theodosia. "I have a few Chen Lung celadon tea bowls and a lovely Chinese landscape painting that I think might have been done by Zhou Lung."

"You should bring it by sometime," said Jester, mildly interested now. "Let me authenticate it. Those monochromatic pieces are fetching big prices these days, especially from wealthy Taiwanese collectors."

"I'm delighted you've elected to donate one of your Chinese swords to the auction," said Drayton.

"It certainly took long enough to get my notice of acceptance," growled Jester.

"You were afraid your piece had been turned down?" asked Theodosia.

Jester narrowed his eyes and gazed at her in stony silence.

"Because, as I recall," she went on, "you were quiet upset the night of the Poet's Tea. Worried your piece hadn't made the cut."

Jester suddenly shrugged. "I'm a passionate man, what can I say? It's the nature of the beast." He pivoted a half-turn and focused his attention on Drayton. "Now *you're* the man in charge of the auction."

"That's right," said Drayton.

"Then your dropping by is rather serendipitous. I haven't had a chance to deliver my piece to the Heritage Society since my notification was so late in coming. Any chance you could take it with you now?"

"It would be our pleasure," responded Drayton.

"If you'll follow me," said Jester, starting toward the back room where his office and storeroom were located. "I have it all wrapped and ready to go."

"Wonderful!" said Drayton as he followed Jester into the back.

While Theodosia waited for Drayton, she wandered about Passports, admiring the collection of Chinese art objects. She noted that Jester seemed particularly fond of Chinese bronzes, elaborate ritual vessels that had been placed in ancestor graves some four thousand years ago. Most bronze vessels had been created to hold wine or grain and were decorated in archaic script and fanciful animal motifs. One in particular, a tripod-style vessel that sat high atop a cabinet of inlaid wood, caught Theodosia's eye. Embellished with rows of flanges and patinated a rich green, it was spectacular to behold. Wanting to read the particulars about it, Theodosia reached up to grab the descriptor card that had tipped over. As she did so, her hand brushed against something soft. Startled, she drew back, then found herself gazing at a dozen Chinese calligraphy brushes hanging on a teak brush rack. From large to small, they hung, brush side down, in a neat and orderly row.

Beautiful, she thought as she stared at the Chinese brushes. *And perfect for Drayton's calligraphy. I wonder how much they cost?*

Turning over the little tag, Theodosia flinched. Four hundred dollars! Yipes. Even though his birthday was coming up in a few months, that was still a pretty stiff price to pay.

Turning her attention back to the shop, Theodosia continued to poke about, looking at Chinese art objects. She'd come here to take an up close and personal look at Jester Moody, but now that she was here, she really didn't view him as a likely suspect. If Jester had intended to kill Roger, he certainly would have been more subtle about it. *Wouldn't he?*

She thought about that for a moment.

What would Jester's motive have been? Anger over some imagined slight concerning the auction? Or was there some other agenda? Had Crispin and Weller been tapped to handle some of Jester Moody's pieces and the deal had gone sour?

Hmm.

"*Jester's certainly a* prickly fellow," Theodosia said, once they slid the bubble-wrapped Chinese sword into the back of her Jeep and bolstered it in place with rolls of bubble wrap and a couple cardboard boxes. Their visit had pretty much confirmed Theodosia's suspicion that Jester Moody wasn't the sweetest pickle in the jar.

"Prickly," said Drayton, arranging a final bit of bubble wrap. "That's a funny description."

"But it's true. There's warm-fuzzy and then there's cold-prickly. Jester Moody's definitely in the latter category."

"I hear you," said Drayton.

"I also get a funny vibe off him."

"Funny strange or funny bad?" asked Drayton.

"Yes," said Theodosia.

Drayton's nose twitched ever so slightly. "Hmm," was all he said.

They both took a step back and Drayton grabbed the tailgate and slammed it shut as Theodosia glanced over her shoulder toward Passports. Reflection from the late afternoon sun bounced off the front windows in a dizzying pinwheel of light. But from where she stood, she could just make out the shadowy figure of Jester Moody peering out at them.

8

Hurry up, Theodosia, yelled Haley. "We've got to hustle over to Gracie's."

"Are you quite serious?" asked Drayton as he and Theodosia pushed their way through the back door of the tea shop. "Haven't you two put in a full day already?"

"We promised her," said Haley, rounding the corner and posing with hands on slim hips. "Remember?"

"I remember," said Theodosia, dropping her pocketbook on top of her cluttered desk and glancing at a King and Croswell tea catalog that had just arrived that morning. "I wish I didn't, but I do."

"And you," said Haley, tossing Drayton an accusing look. "You were so upbeat about rushing to Gracie's aid."

Drayton gazed at her placidly, like an old turtle. "Did you want me to come along and help?"

Haley considered his question for a few moments, then finally answered: "No, I think you'd just get in the way."

Drayton threw his hands up in mock exasperation. "The story of my life."

"You two are absolute lifesavers!" exclaimed Gracie Venable. Crouched on her knees, she pawed through a huge cardboard box spilling over with floppy silk flowers.

"We told you we'd be here to help," Haley reminded her. "And we meant it."

"Where do we start?" asked Theodosia. Although Gracie's shop seemed to be taking shape, her workroom was still a disaster. Half-opened cardboard boxes were stacked everywhere with hat blocks, felt fabric, rolls of sizing, and bolts of straw cloth spilling out.

"Just start unpacking," Gracie told her, "and I'll try to figure it out from there."

"Okay," said Haley, ripping into a cardboard box. "Oh, my gosh," she exclaimed. "Look at these strands of pearls. Gorgeous."

"They're faux pearls," said Gracie. "Don't get too wound up."

"But you've got like ten-millimeter pearls, tiny seeds pearls, and big Baroque pearls," said Haley. Grabbing a handful of strands, she held them up, like a pirate gloating over a treasure chest. "These pearls would look great entwined in our garlands," Haley enthused.

"Then take some with you," said Gracie. "As many strands as you need."

"Really?" asked Haley. "Don't you want us to pay for them or something?"

Gracie waved a hand. "Don't worry about it."

"What's this?" asked Haley. She was like a kid in a candy store, going from box to box. Now she had pulled out a hat block.

"That, my dear girl," said Gracie, "is the form I use for making buckram blocked hats."

"You're kidding," said Haley. "I didn't know you had to start from scratch. I thought maybe you bought the basic straw and felt hats and then shaped and decorated them."

"Some people do that," allowed Gracie, "but that's the difference between hat decorating and true millinery. For a custom hat one must always start from scratch."

"So you . . . what?" asked Haley, shifting the hat block around in her hands, looking slightly puzzled.

"Let's say you wanted a fancy hat to wear to a fancy tea party . . . or even the Kentucky Derby," said Gracie. "I'd take your measurements and then select the appropriately sized hat block. Then I'd take a piece of buckram"—she pulled out a roll of the stiff cloth—"and mold it over the block in the basic shape I wanted. Using a steamer to help steam it into shape. For discussion purposes, let's say you have your heart set on a Victorian-style hat. You know, wide brim, rounded top, lots of floral decor."

"Sounds yummy," said Haley, obviously fascinated.

Gracie pulled out a bolt of pink Shantung silk. "So then I'd cover the buckram form with this fabric, pinching and pleating just so, then sew in a matching lining. Then, just like decorating a cake, I'd trim it." Gracie stuck her arm into another cardboard box and came up with streamers of ribbon. Pink, pearl, peach, and lavender.

"My favorite colors," said Haley. "A French palette."

"I'd maybe add a ribbon hat band," continued Gracie, "then use this same ribbon to create a nosegay of tiny roses. Sew on a sprinkling of seed pearls for good measure."

"Hat making seems like a very involved process," said Haley.

"Oh, honey," laughed Gracie. "That's just the tip of the iceberg. We haven't even talked about felt blocking or braided straw hats or wire frame construction."

"You mean you can actually make a hat frame from wire?" asked Theodosia. She was as fascinated with the millinery process as Haley was.

"Wire lets you achieve the perfect weightless hat," explained Gracie. "It's the only way to go when working with deliciously sheer fabrics." Standing on tiptoes, Gracie reached up and grabbed an elegant mauve-colored Edwardian-style hat from where it had been hung on the wall, slightly above their heads. The hat looked sheer and breezy, like a whisper of wind might send it soaring. "Here." Gracie handed the hat to Haley, who accepted it reverently, studied it, then passed it on to Theodosia. "Try it on," urged Gracie.

Carefully, Theodosia set the elegant hat atop her head. "It *is* weightless!" she exclaimed.

Gracie held out a hand mirror. "Take a look."

Staring in the mirror, Theodosia was surprised, as always, by her comely visage. Fair complexion, sparkling blue eyes, broad, intelligent-looking face, full-formed mouth. And a swirl of naturally curly auburn hair that was barely contained by the lovely Edwardian hat.

"I love it," declared Theodosia. "Makes me feel like a proper Charleston lady." She could just imagine herself serving a pot of Moroccan mint tea at a garden party. Amidst sunbeams, blooming flowers, and flitting butterflies. *Gossamer butterfly wings and a gossamer hat,* thought Theodosia. *Whose heartstrings wouldn't be stirred by such lovely, lighthearted imagery?*

"Now watch this," Gracie told her. With the hat still sitting atop Theodosia's head, Gracie reached up with both hands and gently manipulated the brim, causing one side to dip down slightly, the other side to turn up. "You see?" said Gracie. "Wire framing means you're not dependent on crown and brim blocks to fashion the basic form. You're able to achieve subtle movements and create unusually shaped hats."

"Could I learn this?" blurted out Haley. "Could I be your apprentice?" Haley was fairly dancing on the balls of her feet. "This is all so fascinating. What are some of your other hat decorating tricks besides ribbon?"

Reaching for another box, Gracie pulled out a handful of bright-colored packets. "Feathers," she told them. "Ostrich, goose, pigeon, and turkey feathers are pretty much millinery staples. All dyed in a rainbow of colors."

Theodosia watched as Gracie popped open one of the clear plastic packets and allowed an arc of feathers to pouf out. And she was suddenly jerked back to the here and now, reminded of the feather she'd found stuck in the stairwell at the Heritage Society.

"Neat," said Haley. She picked up an errant feather, held it flat on her palm, and gave a gentle puff. The little bit of fluff sailed gracefully across the room.

"I've even got handbags trimmed in feathers," Gracie told them. "Of course they come from a vendor in Hong Kong. All ready-made." She pulled out a jade-green silk evening bag, trimmed in seed pearls and matching marabou, and held it up.

"Absolutely adorable," breathed Haley. "Want me to unpack them and create some sort of display?" she asked. "I think the feathery purses would look great next to the floral hair clips."

"Good idea," said Theodosia. "You tinker with displays on the sales floor, I'll work in here with Gracie."

"Okay," said Haley. "Great."

"Oh, honey, put these out, too, will you?" asked Gracie. She tossed an armful of feather boas across the top of the box filled with purses. "They just arrived this morning. Turkey feather boas. Pink, Paris yellow, turquoise, cinnamon, and, of course, red for the tea ladies." She smiled at Theodosia. "You know all about those gals, don't you?"

Theodosia nodded as she stood there mulling things over. She didn't want to just blurt out to Gracie that she'd discovered a feather at the Heritage Society and needed an explanation. She knew her little find was barely more than circumstantial evidence.

On the other hand, she did want to give Gracie some sort of heads up that Tidwell was probably going to follow up on the feather. And, Theodosia also felt it was important to tell Gracie that Simone Crispin was pointing an angry, accusing finger at her. Better to find out now than get blindsided by a wave of whispers and innuendoes.

So . . . what to do? How to handle this?

In the end, Theodosia decided to just tell Gracie about Simone. After all, the feather thing could turn out to be nothing and just go away on its own.

"Gracie," said Theodosia in a conversational tone. "I stopped by Crispin and Weller today."

Frown lines pinched together between Gracie's eyebrows. "Did you," she said.

"Simone Crispin—you know, Roger's wife—seemed to think there was, uh, something going on between you and Roger."

"You don't really pay attention to vicious gossip like that, do you?" asked Gracie. The tone of her voice seemed light, but her expression and body language telegraphed a high level of anxiety.

"Most gossip is just plain drivel," agreed Theodosia. "But I've got to be honest with you, Gracie. Simone Crispin seems intent on nudging this murder investigation in your direction. She seems to regard you as a viable suspect." There, she'd said it.

"The police have already talked to me," said Gracie. She unpacked a few more hat blocks and placed them on her worktable.

"No," said Theodosia. "The police just stopped by for a quick look-see. Believe me, they'll be back in full force. And when they do they'll be asking some fairly hard questions." Theodosia hesitated. "And they'll expect truthful answers. Think about it, Gracie. These are smart guys. If you have something to hide, these are not the guys to play cat and mouse with." Theodosia thought about Burt Tidwell, a major and immovable force in the Robbery Homicide Division. Now Tidwell was chief of homicide detectives. The man certainly *looked* like a buffoon, didn't *seem* like he possessed the stealth of a large cat. But in an earlier incarnation, Tidwell had cut his teeth as an SAIC, a special agent in charge, with the FBI. And after Tidwell had departed the bureau and moved to Raleigh, North Carolina, he was the one, the only one, who was able to crack the case of the Crow River Killer. All in all, Tidwell was not an investigator to be trifled with. He was too smart, too dogged, too maddening in his pursuit. You'd best bring your lunch if you intended to go a few rounds with Burt Tidwell. You'd best be awfully nimble.

Gracie straightened up and turned to face Theodosia. It was only then that Theodosia saw she was crying.

"Gracie!" exclaimed Theodosia. She certainly hadn't intended her words to have *that* kind of affect.

Tears coursed down Gracie's cheeks and her shoulders shook with sobs. "I *did* have an affair with Roger Crispin," she admitted. "I can't say I was in love with him but"—she sniffed and wiped at her nose—"I was in *like* with him. Roger was a good man. Smart, funny, extremely attentive. Women like that, you know."

"I know," said Theodosia, pulling a hanky from her jacket pocket and handing it to Gracie.

Accepting it, Gracie blew her nose and gazed mournfully at Theodosia, looking sad and miserable. She seemed ready to say something else, then just mumbled, "Thanks."

All the bravura that Gracie seemed to possess had suddenly crumbled. And Theodosia wondered how the police would react when they learned that Gracie had lied to them. If she'd lied to them.

"Gracie," said Theodosia. "Did the police ask about your relationship with Roger Crispin?"

Gracie blinked rapidly, causing a clump of mascara to puddle under her eyes. "They kind of danced around it."

"And you told them . . . ?"

"Nothing," said Gracie. "It's none of their business. It wasn't relevant."

Wasn't relevant, thought Theodosia. Well it certainly was now. Especially since Simone Crispin seemed intent on trying to railroad Gracie for her husband's murder.

"Gracie," said Theodosia, keeping her voice low. "You were rattled and nervous when the police paid you a visit yesterday morning, and rightly so. Then you came to my shop and asked for my help. And I want to give it, I really do. But my advice, and you're probably not going to like this, is to talk to Burt Tidwell first thing tomorrow morning. Tell him *everything*."

But Gracie seemed suddenly overwhelmed. "If any of this gets out," she wailed, "I'm out of business before I even open. Potential customers will see me as someone embroiled in a nasty *scandal* instead of the owner of an exciting new millinery shop. And the press . . . well, if this gets into the newspapers it'll just kill me."

"It's not going to get around," said Theodosia. "I'll have a little chat with Tidwell myself. See what he can do about putting a muzzle on Simone."

"That's who they should be looking at," said Gracie. Her anguish was suddenly replaced by cold fury. She stared at Theodosia, chest heaving, eyes blazing. "Ice water runs in that woman's veins. If anybody could have pulled the trigger and murdered poor Roger it was Simone!"

Theodosia's head was spinning as she drove home. She was a little upset that Gracie had asked for her help, but not revealed her prior relationship with Roger Crispin. Did that make her a liar? Or just a scared, innocent party?

Turning into her back alley, jouncing down old cobblestones, her Jeep headlights splashed across the rear brick wall of the Indigo Tea Shop. And revealed Jory Davis lounging on the wrought-iron bench that sat on the two-foot strip of lawn at her back door.

Slamming her Jeep into park, Theodosia hopped out and ran over to Jory, delivering a big hug and a quick kiss.

"Hey stranger, I thought you were going to call first!" She pushed a mass of auburn hair off her face and fixed him with a winning smile. "If I'd known you were just sitting here waiting for me, I would have been home sooner." Her heart, which had felt so heavy, suddenly lifted, and she took a deep, cleansing breath. It would be comforting, she decided, to talk to Jory. Especially after the go-round she'd just had with Gracie Venable. Jory was a smart lawyer who could offer an outsider's opinion on all of this. Or, he could even be enlisted to help if need be.

Trooping up the back stairs, Theodosia unlocked the

door and pushed her way into the kitchen. Earl Grey, all seventy-six shaggy pounds of him, came flying at them, eager to administer enthusiastic doggy kisses and amuse them with crazed spins and joyous tail wags.

"Want me to take the pup for a quick run around the block?" Jory asked Theodosia. Dressed in a windbreaker, jeans, and tennis shoes, he looked like he'd come over with exactly that in mind.

What a guy, she thought. "Do that and I'll brew us a nice pot of jasmine tea." The mild, slightly sweet tea imparted a lovely soothing aroma. Pulling her freezer door open, Theodosia asked Jory, "Can I tempt you with a coconut macaroon? Or maybe a raspberry chocolate chip muffin?"

"Yes to both," answered Jory, as he clipped the leash to Earl Grey's collar. "Fire up the microwave and us fellas will be back in a flash."

Twenty minutes later they were all ensconced in Theodosia's living room. Theodosia and Jory on the couch, with tea and desserts set up on the low table in front of them. Earl Grey sprawled out on the Chinese carpet next to them, his gentle, rhythmic breathing already an indicator that he was slipping into doggy sleep.

"This is so cozy," said Jory, smiling at Theodosia as she poured him a cup of tea.

"It's all working, isn't it?" she asked, glancing about. For more than a year now, Theodosia had been striving to create a personal space that would convey the genteel old-world charm of Charleston yet still remain soothing and envelope her like a cocoon. And she was just about there. What had once been a Country French, chintz-and-prints type of apartment had been utterly transformed into a rich, elegant living space. Now Aubusson carpets, Baroque mirrors, oil paintings crackled with age, Tiffany-style lamps, and chairs and sofas upholstered in pale mauve lent a classic feel. She'd even jumped off the cliff and painted her dining room a lovely, deep eggplant color. Which made the Hepplewhite table and chairs she'd inherited from her grandmother suddenly look perfectly at home. She'd even been inspired to purchase a small mahogany secretary and fill the lower shelves with leather-bound books while the top two shelves held prized antique teacups.

Yes, Theodosia decided as she passed a plate of macaroons to Jory, *it took a lot of hard work, but this place looks phenomenal.*

Jory accepted a macaroon, but made no attempt to nibble it. Just sat and stared at Theodosia with a slightly goofy look on his handsome face.

"What?" she asked him. "What?"

"I've got some absolutely spectacular news," Jory told her.

Since he was suddenly grinning ear to ear, Theodosia figured this had to a mega-announcement. The kind of news where you celebrate by going to dinner at the Library at the Vendue Inn and order an expensive bottle of champagne. Perhaps even Cristal or Moët-Chandon. Because maybe, hopefully, cross your fingers, Jory's recent legal maneuverings had been so absolutely stellar, had brought so much prestige and goodwill to the firm, that he's finally being made partner at Ligget, Hume, Hartwell!

"Tell me," said Theodosia, eager to share in his obvious joy.

"I've been asked to head up our New York office!" announced Jory.

Theodosia stared at him, stunned. "I didn't know Ligget, Hume, Hartwell had a New York office," she finally managed after a few seconds.

"We don't actually," said Jory, a sly look on his face. "Not yet, anyway. But we have two highly prestigious, revenue-producing clients up there . . . so the firm has decided to open one!"

"And you've been given the honor of heading up this office," she said, a trifle wary, putting what probably should have been boundless enthusiasm on the back burner for the moment.

"And I want you to come with me!" said Jory, a loopy grin still pasted across his face.

"To New York," said Theodosia, still getting used to the Jory-might-move-to-Manhattan concept.

"Absolutely to New York," said Jory with unbridled enthusiasm. "Hey, can you imagine the two of us in the Big Apple? Broadway, nightclubs, super restaurants, all those great museums!"

Theodosia thought about that for a few moments. Plays, nightclubs, and museums in New York were wonderful as an abstract concept. But she knew in her heart of hearts that there would be a trade-off, a price to pay. There was *always* a trade-off. *Hustle-bustle, razzle-dazzle for the genteel Southern way of life? Is that a good thing?* she wondered.

"What about the tea shop?" she asked, trying to ignore the hard lump that had suddenly formed in the pit of her stomach.

"Don't worry about the tea shop," enthused Jory. "Let Drayton and Haley run it. They're brilliant, just like you are! Relax and be an absentee owner for a while!" Overcome with enthusiasm, Jory grabbed Theodosia's shoulders and pulled her close to him. "Think of it. Madison Avenue." He looked at her with eager, shining eyes. "You could jump back into the game if you wanted. That's where all the big, hot ad agencies and PR shops are. New York."

Theodosia blinked. Was this really her Jory? All enthusiastic about moving away from Charleston? He'd grown up here. He had family here. And now, wonder of wonders, he was suggesting she jump back into the advertising business? The 24/7 rat race she'd spent a dozen plus years in and bid sayonara to a couple years ago? *No way,* she told herself. *No way am I ever gonna get caught up in that miserable drudge again. The Indigo Tea Shop is my oasis, it helps center me. And most important, it's my entrepreneurial dream come true.*

"Honey," said Jory, his voice filled with longing. "This is important to me." He beamed at her. "And I want us to get *married*!"

Theodosia gave it a long beat before she answered him. "Wow. You did a lot more than just drop by, you dropped a bombshell!"

"Yeah. Yeah, I guess I did," said Jory, looking more than a little stunned himself.

Theodosia smiled at him, trying to muster some excitement and enthusiasm. But the smile she offered felt like it was stretched too tight across her face. She was not unaware that Jory, in all his wild enthusiasm, had waxed poetically about his career move first and the possibility of their marriage second.

Maybe Jory's just caught up in the moment, she reasoned to herself. *Excited by the opportunity and honor that's been bestowed upon him. Sure, that's it. That must be it. Right?*

9

"A hair lower," instructed Haley. She was determined to get their new decorations dispatched with before they threw their doors open for business. She and Theodosia had finished the wreaths and garlands earlier that morning, adding dried hydrangeas and strings of pearls to the twists of grapevine, then tying in colorful teacups with gauzy silk bows. Now the decorations looked very elegant and fanciful. Like something right out of the Mad Hatter's tea party.

Drayton cocked his head as he slid the wreath a hair lower. "If I move this any lower it's going to incinerate when we light a fire," he snapped. "These twigs and sprigs are tinder-dry."

Haley heaved a deep and noisy sigh. "It's almost *summer,* Drayton. A fire isn't going to be an issue."

"You never know," said Drayton as he slid the wreath a notch higher, eyeballed the spot, then gently set the wreath onto a table. "We're getting into hurricane season. There could be a chilly evening or two." Drayton put a nail up to the spot he'd selected, held it in place, then gave three sharp whacks with a hammer. "There." With a self-satisfied look on his face, he slipped the teacup wreath onto the nail. "That's a job well done if I do say so myself."

"What about the garland?" asked Haley. "We have to deal with that, too. As soon as I weave in a few more strands of pearls."

"I know, I know," said Drayton. Picking up his cup of tea, he took a calming sip. "You don't have to henpeck me," he warned. "I'm a smart man. I get it."

Drayton and Haley had been going at it for the last ten minutes, hanging the wreaths, trying to figure out the best place for the matching garland. And, as Theodosia glanced at the wreaths from behind the counter, she had to admit they did look awfully neat.

"People are going to try to buy these things off the walls, you know," warned Drayton. "They always do. Remember that teacup Christmas tree we made two years ago? With all the bone china miniatures?"

"One woman offered three hundred dollars!" boasted Haley, as she dashed toward the kitchen.

Theodosia wasn't worried. Most of the items on display at the Indigo Tea Shop *were* for sale. And for a good reason. She loved nothing better than to wander through the low country, stopping at auctions and tag sales to pick up old paintings, framed bits of lace, teacups, and the odd piece of furniture.

She would display these items for a while, sell them to eager customers who fell in love with them, then have a marvelous excuse to go back out and do it all over again. It was fun to constantly refurbish her shop, offer something new that would catch her customers' eyes. In fact, once she was able to carve out a little more time, she planned to mount rare bone china saucers and antique silverware inside shadowboxes.

Theodosia wondered idly what kind of antiques she'd find in Manhattan. Probably exquisitely fine ones. Exquisitely expensive ones, too. But, of course, she wouldn't have the fun of hunting them down herself. Wouldn't have the delight of driving through the low country, over lazy, wandering streams and through swamp forests of cypress, longleaf pine, and live oak. When the sun was blazing and haze hung over the old, abandoned rice fields like spun gold.

"You're awfully quiet this morning," Drayton said to Theodosia as he reached into the overhead cupboard and brought out three Brown Betty teapots and two fancier ones. "Is everything okay?"

"Sure," she nodded. "No problem."

"Anything I can do?" he asked.

"Help me with the spoon tiebacks?" Theodosia asked.

Drayton gave an enthusiastic nod. "Of course."

Over the last couple weeks, Theodosia had definitely been in the throes of redecorating. Well, maybe not redecorating so much as enhancing. The wood-planked floors, exposed beams, and brick walls of her tea shop were really quite cozy and charming just the way they were. But now, besides adding eye-catching items to the walls, Theodosia had hung new dusty rose–colored velvet curtains at the front window and had curved and fashioned two antique silver spoons into perfect curtain tiebacks.

"Grab that left curtain right about midpoint and pull it back so I can get a sense of where we are," Theodosia instructed Drayton. As he did so, she slipped the curved teaspoon around the curtain, then stepped back a few feet to gauge the effect. "Perfect," she said, liking what she saw. She quickly slipped the spoon tieback around the opposing curtain, adjusted it briefly, then smiled.

"Now, for the pièce de résistance, let's drape the long garland over the top," Theodosia announced to Drayton.

"Ah, that's where it's going," said Drayton. "I was afraid Haley would want to try it a dozen different places. She's been dreadfully bossy this morning."

"I have not," called Haley, who'd been listening from her post in the kitchen. "I'm just a very proactive person!"

Theodosia whirled about to answer Haley and, in so doing, caught the ruffled sleeve of her blouse on the edge of a teapot Drayton had just set down. She felt a sharp jerk and then one of their Royal Winton chintz-patterned teapots went crashing to the floor!

"Whoa!" called Haley, sticking her head out. "Cleanup in aisle seven."

"Listen to her," said Drayton. "She doesn't know when to quit. All that youthful exuberance can be quite overwhelming, don't you think?" He peered closely at Theodosia. "Whereas you, my dear, look a tad jangled. If I didn't know better, I'd say you have a lot on your mind today," he added in a much softer tone of voice.

Theodosia nodded. Did she ever.

Haley came bustling over with a broom and dustpan. A neatnick of the first magnitude, she could always be counted on for cleaning, spiffing, and sprucing. Bending down, she dispatched with the shattered teapot in a matter of seconds, checking to make sure there weren't any jagged shards caught between the floorboards.

"Thanks, Haley," said Theodosia. "Sorry about the teapot, guys. I don't know what's wrong with me today. Just klutzy, I guess."

"No problem," said Drayton. "Now I have an excuse to order a couple pieces of Carolina Chintz by Charles Sadek. It's a gorgeous, almost watercolor-looking floral pattern and the price is extremely affordable for genuine porcelain."

Haley carried the broken shards out to the Dumpster, then reemerged a few minutes later bearing an enormous glass cake saver filled with baked goods. "We're going to serve a somewhat limited menu today," she told them. "'Cause we've got the China Society coming at three for their special tea service."

"What do you mean by 'limited'?" asked Drayton, lifting an eyebrow.

"Cinnamon apple scones and blueberry sour cream muffins," said Haley, raising the glass lid to show them. "And for lunch we'll be offering a cranberry-Waldorf salad accompanied by marmalade and cream cheese tea sandwiches."

"Haley, that's not limited," said Theodosia. "In fact, everything sounds positively heroic, considering you're preparing several courses for our afternoon guests as well."

"It's limited for me," said Haley, lurching back toward

the kitchen. "But I can't stand around jawing. I've got to get busy and prep."

Haley had been up at the crack of dawn to hit the downtown farmers' market. Marching the rows of fruit and produce stalls, she'd select fresh brown eggs, homegrown lettuce and herbs, and whatever else tickled her fancy. But always, always demanding of the grocers that their ingredients be just-picked fresh.

Drayton, who wasn't the least bit phobic about eating a two-day-old tomato, had dubbed her the *market martinet*.

"Drayton?" asked Theodosia, trying to shake the ominous feeling of a huge decision hanging over her head. "Have you thought about our tea offerings for this morning?" Usually, Drayton had a few special teas in mind to share with their customers. And sometimes he simply waited to see how Haley's menu shaped up, then made choices that complemented her lunches, desserts, and savories.

"Here's the thing of it," said Drayton. "I've decided to brew a Pussimbing Garden Darjeeling and a Keemun Hao Ya 'A' as our pouring teas. The Darjeeling is delightfully smooth with a big aroma and the Keemun is roasty with a bright aftertaste."

"Perfect," murmured Theodosia. Drayton was a wonder when it came to selecting the perfect teas. Then again, he was a certified master tea blender and had done considerable tasting at the big tea auctions in Amsterdam.

"Of course," Drayton went on, "if one of our customers has a yen for something different, I'm always happy to oblige. It's never any trouble to brew an extra pot of, say, a

Japanese Bancha, a lovely Assam, or maybe even a Sri Lankan breakfast tea. Plus I'm also going to whip up a somewhat unorthodox strawberry-banana green tea cooler for lunch. Just because we're serving a slightly lighter fare and we'll be seating guests at our outdoor tables again."

Theodosia smiled to herself. When the Indigo Tea Shop had first opened, it had taken a small amount of coaxing to get Drayton to break with tradition. But now he was the one pushing the envelope on tea coolers and infusions and had developed some very innovative recipes.

"I have a feeling this is going to be a hectic day," said Theodosia, squaring her shoulders.

Drayton nodded. "The exact same vibe has been rippling through me, as well. I'm still hip-deep in this auction thing for the Heritage Society and . . . say there," he said, watching Theodosia gather up her somewhat unwieldy grapevine garland. "Let me hang that for you."

"Give me a minute," said Theodosia. "I want to stick in a few more dried flowers."

"This thing is already bursting with flowers and teacups," laughed Drayton. "What are those lovely big blossoms anyway? Dried hydrangeas?"

Theodosia nodded. "Hattie Boatwright over at Floradora taught me this surefire drying technique. It pretty much works like a charm, provided you've got a nice dry spot to hang them."

"Well I'll be," said Drayton, looking rather pleased at Theodosia's creation.

* * *

"*Nice to see* you again, Miss Browning," announced a gruff voice at Theodosia's elbow. She finished pouring a cup of Darjeeling then turned to the table directly behind her to see who'd spoken. With the sun in her eyes, Theodosia didn't recognize her luncheon guest at first. Putting a hand up, she squinted, and was dismayed when he came into focus. Orrin Hudson, the rather boorish private investigator the Heritage Society had hired, was sprawled at one of her outdoor tables. Looking, she thought, a little too smug for his own good.

Oh great. Just what I need.

"Can I get you a spot of lunch, Mr. Hudson?" Theodosia asked. When in doubt, take the high road. Be polite but a trifle distant.

Orrin Hudson slid mirrored glasses up onto his forehead. "I'd settle for a quick conversation," he told her.

"I'm awfully busy right now," Theodosia replied, all business. "Maybe you could give me a jingle later. I'd be happy to chat then." *Sure. Right.*

"I know all about your friend," Orrin Hudson murmured in a low, condescending tone. "Your friend is harboring a nasty little secret, and I know what it is."

"I have no idea what you're talking about," Theodosia replied briskly. She glanced about, hoping nobody else was tuning in to this rather one-sided conversation, trying to catch bits and pieces.

"I'm talking about your friend Gracie," continued Hudson in his same maddening tone. "Gracie Venable was, shall we say, romantically *involved* with Roger Crispin." He tucked his chin down and lifted his brows, as if waiting for her to confirm or deny.

She would do neither. "How would you know anything about that?" Theodosia asked, knowing full well Simone Crispin must have told him. Had, on the pretext of confiding in him, probably revealed her little marital secret and then probably steered Orrin Hudson hard in Gracie's direction, hoping the police would follow.

Remember, Theodosia reminded herself, *the best defense is a strong offense. Simone may well have something to hide.*

"You know," said Hudson, "I make it my business to know things." Now he looked downright smug.

"That's all very interesting," said Theodosia. "But once in a while I make it my business to know things, too. And I have a feeling I'm a *lot more* plugged in to what's going on than you could ever hope to be."

Although she hadn't meant to elicit a harsh reaction, her words seemed to infuriate him. "You stay out of this!" snarled Orrin Hudson, pushing his chair back and struggling to his feet.

Kapow! thought Theodosia. *I just hit a tender spot.*

"Because when everything hits the fan," shouted Hudson, "you're going to be very sorry!"

Hudson twisted his mouth into a grimace, slid his mirrored sunglasses over his eyes, and fixed her with a hard stare. Theodosia noted that his sunglasses were exactly like the ones state troopers sometimes wore, and they seemed to impart on Hudson a false sense of security. Or maybe she was just being overly paranoid.

* * *

"*Theo*," *asked Drayton*, looking worried. "Have you seen our large silver tray? I mean the really huge one with the scalloped edges?"

"No, I haven't," she told him as she dumped a load of cups and saucers into the large plastic bin they used for dirty dishes. "I was hunting around for it yesterday and never did locate it." She frowned, tried to clear her head. Orrin Hudson's visit had left her feeling rattled and disjointed. She wanted to remain loyal to Gracie, but could the woman be hiding something? Could Gracie have been spurned by Roger Crispin and then, in a fit of anger, shot him?

"Drat," said Drayton. "I bet that tray is still sitting over at the Heritage Society. Between the storm and the bizarre shooting of Roger Crispin, we never did get all our catering supplies packed up."

Now why didn't I notice that tray when I was snooping around there two nights ago? thought Theodosia. *Because I ran into Parker Scully that's why.*

"Tell you what," said Theodosia. "I'll scoot over and take a look. I have a feeling the last place I saw that tray was in their little kitchen." In her mind's eye Theodosia could see the giant serving tray leaning against the backsplash. Just where they'd left it.

"I do believe you're right," fretted Drayton, glancing at his watch. "Better shake a leg, though."

10

※

In theory it was just going to be a snatch and grab. Sprint the few blocks to the Heritage Society, dash into the kitchen for the tray, then take off again. What Theodosia hadn't counted on was running into Timothy Neville, the octogenarian president of the Heritage Society.

"Theodosia," said Timothy, cocking his small, compact head to one side. "We haven't conversed much since I returned from England." Theodosia and Earl Grey had stayed at Timothy's enormous Italianate mansion over on Archdale Street while he was away. Housesitting, watching over his priceless antiques, doling out Fancy Feast to his old cat Dreadnaught. The two of them had only had time to exchange a few words the day Timothy arrived home, supervising the arrival of his luggage and countless crates of antiques just as Theodosia was exiting his home carrying armloads of clothing.

"Drayton told me your genealogy research went very well," said Theodosia. She tucked the tray she'd just retrieved under her arm and slowed her pace to stay even with Timothy as they wandered down the long hallway together. Brooding paintings of prominent South Carolinians stared down at them from the walls, the Oriental carpet whispered underfoot. "Most of your research was centered in Bath?" she asked.

"Bath, Winchester, Salisbury . . . I traveled about quite a bit." Timothy seemed to have something on his mind but was obviously going to take his own sweet time getting to it. "Lots of lovely tea shops over there," he added.

"I've visited a few," Theodosia told him. *A few?* she thought. *More like dozens. Maybe even a hundred.* When you lived and breathed tea, a trip through the English countryside, with its plethora of charming little cottage tearooms, was a dream come true.

Arriving at the door to his office, Timothy beckoned her in. Theodosia followed obediently.

"Take a look at this oil painting," he said to her. Stepping over to his desk, Timothy eased himself down in a large chair. Theodosia had always suspected that chair had been set higher to make Timothy a head taller, subsequently creating a more commanding presence. She walked to the opposite side of his desk and sat down in one of the rather uncomfortable high-back black leather armchairs that always made her feel a trifle enclosed. Like being in a confessional.

Timothy snapped on a high-intensity tensor lamp and a small puddle of light spilled across the dark oil painting that rested on his desk. Theodosia immediately saw that it was a portrait, a three-quarters view of a man's head and shoulders. And from the portrait style it looked like it might have some age on it. As though it had probably been painted in the latter half of the eighteenth century.

Theodosia studied the subject, a young man dressed in a thick, buttoned coat and a high, white, knotted collar. The face was youthful, his demeanor robust and proud, as though he'd just accomplished some amazing feat for his country. Although the background was dark and the glaze crackled, Theodosia could make out the faint outline of a Greek temple. *Very much the Neoclassical style,* she told herself.

"It's lovely," she told Timothy. Even though it was unframed, just canvas on stretchers, the painting was really quite stunning. Glancing at the lower right-hand corner of the painting, Theodosia noted the scrawled signature—Rt. Peale. "How much do you know about this artist?" she asked. She was pretty sure she knew the artist's pedigree, but wanted to hear it from Timothy's lips.

Timothy's face took on a beatific glow. "I've had this painting authenticated by two different sources," he told her. "And both are quite positive the artist was Rembrandt Peale."

"That's fantastic!" cried Theodosia. Rembrandt Peale was an Early American painter. A prodigy who, at the tender age of seventeen, distinguished himself by persuading George Washington to sit for a portrait. Peale went on to immortalize other prominent live subjects, including Thomas Jefferson and Andrew Jackson.

"Stunning piece, isn't it?" asked Timothy, who was just this side of gloating.

"Where did you get it?" asked Theodosia.

"It was bequeathed to the Heritage Society as part of an estate," Timothy told her. "An elderly woman who lived in the guest house of what used to be an old plantation down by Blufftop. A Mrs. Estelle LaPointe-Parsons. She passed away last month. Almost ninety with no direct heirs." Timothy was almost gleeful.

Gazing at the painting, Theodosia silently wondered how Mrs. LaPointe-Parsons had come to own such a glorious piece of artwork. Had she possessed a keen eye and purchased it at auction years ago? Had it been handed down to her? Or had Mrs. LaPointe-Parsons stumbled upon this painting in the attic of the guest house she'd moved into? It wasn't uncommon in the South to discover treasures that former owners had long relegated to attics, coal bins, or storage sheds. One generation decrees a painting or piece of sculpture outmoded or passé, then, decades later, a new generation suddenly finds it back in vogue, highly collectible, and, if they're really lucky, skyrocketing in value.

"I decided last night," said Timothy, "that this Rembrandt Peale will be the key piece in the Heritage Society's auction Saturday night."

"Really," said a surprised Theodosia. *It was funny,* she mused. *Two nights ago Timothy was nervous about going ahead with the auction. Now he's all set to put a Rembrandt Peale up for bid.*

"You certainly did an about-face," Theodosia told him.

"At the board meeting you weren't even sure you should hold the auction."

"Mmn," said Timothy, obviously not relishing a reference to his mercurial nature.

"An even more pertinent question might be," continued Theodosia, "why sell the Peale at all? Why not hang on to it? Add it to the Heritage Society's permanent collection."

"Money," was Timothy's terse answer. He lifted his head, squared his jaw, and stared at her with hooded eyes. "You have no idea what kind of deficit the Heritage Society is running these days."

"You're right," stammered Theodosia. "I don't know." This was surprising news to her. For as long as she'd been associated with the Heritage Society they'd been a fiscally stable organization. Operating in the black with an ever-constant revenue stream. "Drayton said times were tough, but I didn't know circumstances were getting desperate."

Timothy gave a shrug. "Drayton's not on the finance committee, so he doesn't know every dire detail. Plus, I've instructed all board members to remain closedmouthed. If this should get out . . . well . . . let's say it would make for rather nasty gossip."

And you might lose your job, thought Theodosia.

Even though Timothy Neville had been a veritable powerhouse, tirelessly raising money for the Heritage Society year after year, pulling proverbial rabbits out of hats, the fact of the matter was Timothy was slowing down. And so, too, were the Heritage Society's sources of revenue. Theodosia was well aware that almost all museums and nonprofit agencies were struggling mightily to elicit member contributions these days. The economy was still a little shaky, money was in short supply.

Still, it would be a shame for Timothy Neville's tenure to come to an abrupt end just because he was a victim of circumstances, of difficult financial times.

Of course, she had to hand it to Timothy. Putting the Rembrandt Peale up for bid was a brilliant maneuver. This tasty little painting by Peale would easily capture the hearts and minds of an upper-crust Charleston audience. Probably enticing rabid art lovers to part with hundreds of thousands of dollars. Once again, like a phoenix rising from the ashes, Timothy Neville would be a hero.

"Do you have an estimate as to what this painting's worth?" Theodosia asked.

Timothy managed to contain his smile. "Anywhere from two hundred to three hundred fifty thousand dollars. Almost half the Heritage Society's annual operating budget." He stood up abruptly, thrust his hands into the pockets of his perfectly pleated dove-gray trousers, and jingled his loose change. "Do you know what that means?" Timothy asked. "We could salt away half a year's budget in one evening alone!"

"Did you ever think about putting this painting up for auction in New York?" Theodosia asked. "Contract with a firm like Sotheby's so you could get an international audience bidding on it?"

Timothy nodded. "The idea occurred to me. But I prefer to give our local art collectors and connoisseurs the opportunity to own it."

He's also hoping that whoever buys the Peale will ultimately donate it back to the Heritage Society, thought Theodosia. *He'd really love to keep the painting, but can't justify doing so. But whoever is high bidder on this piece, you can bet he or she will be lobbied endlessly by the Heritage Society.*

Theodosia decided Timothy's plan was ingenious. He'd raise a ton of money, garner major press, and please Charleston's art collectors to no end. Best of all, the Rembrandt Peale would probably remain in Charleston. Under Timothy's watchful eye.

Across the desk, Timothy was humming to himself, a faint smile on his lined face, holding a magnifying glass to the painting. Timothy was old, Theodosia decided. And he was decidedly hidebound and cantankerous. But he was also incredibly brilliant. Exactly what the Heritage Society needed.

She was in the throes of mentally singing Timothy's praises when another thought struck her.

"Did you ever consider asking Crispin and Weller to handle the sale?" Theodosia asked abruptly.

"Of course," said Timothy. "Roger was on our board, after all."

"Did Roger ever look at this painting?"

"He did," said Timothy.

"What was his opinion?" asked Theodosia.

Timothy's eyes filled with sadness. "I'm afraid we'll never know. Roger died before we were ever able to discuss it."

The phone on Timothy's desk buzzed abruptly. "Yes?" he said, snatching the receiver up and holding it to his ear. He listened for a few seconds, then said to Theodosia, "Give me a minute will you?"

Propelling herself out of her chair, Theodosia grabbed her tray and headed for the door. She knew she should hurry back to the tea shop. She'd only planned to be gone a quick ten minutes and now nearly half an hour had elapsed. But a few steps from the doorway Theodosia stopped short.

In the back of her mind she'd always known Timothy possessed a prized collection of antique weapons. But she'd never put two and two together until just this minute.

She waited patiently until Timothy was off the phone and then said, "Timothy. Everything's in place here, right? I mean . . ."

He picked up her thought-wave immediately. "You're asking if one of my pistols is missing? If someone might have crept in here during the Poet's Tea and lifted one? Breathe easy, Miss Browning. Because the answer is no. Nary a piece is missing. And the police have already examined my pistols and determined it couldn't possibly have been one of them that inflicted the fatal wounds on Roger Crispin."

Theodosia thought for a moment. "Whoever shot Roger probably used a silencer, right?"

"That is what the police seem to be implying," said Timothy.

"Which points to a more modern gun," said Theodosia. "Would you know what kind of guns take silencers?" If Timothy was a weapons expert, she figured he just might know.

"Good heavens, no!" Timothy exclaimed. "My knowledge of firearms is confined solely to antique weapons. I'm intrigued by early manufacturers, maker's marks, silversmithing, that sort of thing. You'd have to ask a real firearms dealer about an apparatus like a silencer."

"Who's your dealer?" asked Theodosia. Maybe she would do a little checking, after all.

Timothy frowned and shook his head. "I don't have a dealer per se. I've purchased pistols from a number of local antique dealers and auction houses."

"Crispin and Weller?" she asked.

"Yes," said Timothy slowly. "I believe I obtained my Blunt and Syms single shot through Roger. But before you go leaping to conclusions, know, too, that I have also purchased pistols from March Forth and Bayside Antiques. And . . . oh, let's see, who else? Well, the British Calvert came from Jester Moody."

"Jester Moody sells antique guns?" asked a stunned Theodosia. "I know he handles swords, but I thought he was primarily an Asian art dealer!"

Timothy stared at her with hooded eyes. "Actually, he used to have a second shop down in Savannah where he sold quite a few antique weapons. Had an elegant pair of Belgian dueling pistols a few years back. Although I think those went to a collector over in Monck's Corner. A rather dour old chap by the name of Chester Drury."

"Does Tidwell know all this?" Theodosia asked. "I mean about these antique dealers also handling weapons?"

Timothy blinked. "I would imagine so."

Theodosia didn't believe in coincidences. Wasn't a fan of numerology, astrology, or studying the bumps on a person's head. She firmly believed that coincidences were more often human engineered. So when she spotted Detective Burt

Tidwell posturing on the outdoor patio, looking all the world like some sort of bizarre mythological statue surrounded by boxwood, climbing roses, and jasmine, she was pretty sure he was here for a reason. Which pretty much dashed any hope of a speedy and clean getaway.

"What are you doing here?" Theodosia asked, even though she quickly decided she'd try to turn his appearance into a serendipitous opportunity for gleaning new information. In other words, she'd ply *him* with questions concerning firearms.

"Why am I here?" asked Tidwell. "One might ask you the same thing."

Theodosia lifted her tray. "Running errands. See?"

"And, true to my nature, I am merely poking about," Tidwell replied.

"Is that a circuitous phrase for investigating?" she asked him.

Tidwell made a bellow of displeasure, something akin to the noise a walrus or bull elephant might make. "Not a favorable attitude to take regarding a humble civil servant."

"But you came here looking for me," she said. They'd wandered over to a pond filled with bright orange koi. The caretaker had turned on the fountain and a spill of water splashed forth from a stone urn held by a stone cherub, then swirled and burbled merrily into the pool, hopefully delighting the koi. With a halo of sun shining and the flowers in bloom, butterflies flitted about the garden, too. Lovely monarchs and mourning cloaks that reminded her vaguely of Gracie's airy hats.

Why couldn't the weather have cooperated like this the other night? Theodosia wondered. *Maybe the evening wouldn't have unfolded as badly as it did.*

"Listen," said Theodosia, shifting her tray from her right hip to her left. "Did your ballistics people take a hard look at Timothy's antique pistols?"

Tidwell raised a furry eyebrow. "Tell me you're not accusing poor Timothy Neville of murdering Roger Crispin. If so, it probably won't be long before *my* name appears on your personal witch-hunt list."

"Please," said Theodosia. "Of course I know Timothy's completely innocent. I'm just trying to rule out his antique pistols as the weapons du jour. Since they were"—she fished for the right word—"convenient."

"Miss Browning, I feel quite confident in telling you that the police are not searching for a convenient antique weapon."

"You're quite sure?" asked Theodosia. "Because there seems to be a plethora of them around. Crispin and Weller is a source, Jester Moody—"

"You are searching for answers that fit suppositions," Tidwell told her. "A completely nonproductive methodology."

"It's a lot better than badgering the wrong suspect," Theodosia shot back.

"Ah," said Tidwell, a self-satisfied expression spreading across his broad face. "Now that you've opened that little can of worms, why don't you kindly elucidate for me the true nature of the relationship between Miss Venable and Roger Crispin."

"Don't you think you should be posing that question to Gracie Venable?" asked Theodosia, steeling herself so as not to reveal anything via facial expression or body language. What Gracie had told her was in complete confidence, and she was determined it would remain that way.

"I already did," replied Tidwell, looking rather speculative. "But the woman was not terribly forthcoming. In fact, you might say she was a bit dodgy."

"Dodgy," repeated Theodosia. "I wasn't aware that was an actual word."

"We must play scrabble some time," said Tidwell, a faint smile playing about his mouth.

"So the Robbery Homicide Division continues to investigate Gracie Venable as Orrin Hudson gleefully urges you on?" she asked.

Tidwell let loose a disdainful snort. "Hudson is an idiot, a loose cannon at best."

"And aren't we lucky to have him on retainer, looking out for the welfare of the Heritage Society," said Theodosia. "If that's what you call it."

"Sarcasm is never becoming to a woman," replied Tidwell.

"Neither is anger," said Theodosia. "But until you pull your men off Gracie's back, I'm going to continue looking for the *real* killer."

11

Last night, when Jory told Theodosia that Drayton and Haley were brilliant, she had acknowledged his remark on an intellectual level. Yes, of course they were, she'd told herself. They were also personable, creative, and amazingly hardworking.

But now, seeing the tea tables set in anticipation of the China Society's visit, there was no question in Theodosia's mind that her two associates were utter geniuses possessed of magical powers.

Chinese brocade fabric draped luxuriously across each table. Gigantic peonies in black lacquer vases stood as magnificent centerpieces. Red linen napkins, pleated like Chinese fans, were tucked next to a dazzling array of blue and white Chinese teacups and saucers, famille rose plates, and gold bowls decorated with bamboo motifs.

"It looks like we're expecting the emperor and his imperial court," exclaimed Theodosia. "I had no idea we had all this Chinese accoutrement in our possession."

"We don't," said Drayton, pleased by Theodosia's favorable reaction. "Some of it's borrowed, some of it's bartered."

"Don't you love it?" asked Haley as she came bounding out of the kitchen to greet Theodosia. "Doesn't the tea shop look gorgeous?"

"I think we'll have to add a formal Chinese tea to our event repertoire," said Theodosia. The Indigo Tea Shop had long relied on mystery teas, chamber music teas, mother-daughter teas, Victorian teas, and even chocolate teas to entice customers. And customers, in turn, seemed to adore these special event teas. Probably because they offered a grand excuse to get dressed to the nines and enjoy tea and savories with friends.

"Wait till you get a load of Haley's menu!" announced Drayton. He was poised behind the counter, setting out a dozen different Chinese-motif teapots. Theodosia was pleased to see he was using some of their Spode and Wedgewood teapots as well as several smaller Yi-Hsing teapots.

"Tell me," she said, caught up in their excitement.

"First course," said Haley, "are my special Chinese ginger scones. Then we'll serve tiny Peking duck spring rolls garnished with hoisin sauce and shredded lettuce, then a pair of crabmeat wontons and a cream cheese puff. For dessert we'll have two courses. Miniature moon cakes and caramelized Asian pears with almond cookies."

"Not to be outdone by young Miss Parker here," said Drayton, "I am prepared to brew some lovely smoky Lapsang

Souchong, a tippy Yunnan, and a grand Keeumun."

Theodosia stared at the two of them, her heart near bursting. They were so enthusiastic, so delighted that *she* was delighted. How could she possibly leave them? How could she ever move north with Jory? Surely, it would break their collective heart.

Instead Theodosia said, "You don't need me anymore," in a breezy, teasing manner. "I'm superfluous to the cause."

"Oh come now," laughed Drayton. "I hardly think so."

"No, I mean it," said Theodosia. "For a tea shop to be successful there are really only a couple critical components. Wonderful, fresh-brewed tea and spectacular food to start with. And, of course, a cozy, relaxed atmosphere. But nowhere is it written that the CEO-slash–marketing maven is in any way essential to the operation."

"Yeah right," laughed Haley as she moved from table to table, lighting tea warmers. "That's a good one."

"You're in a strange mood," said Drayton as he measured out spoonfuls of Lapsang Souchong. "What kept you dawdling at the Heritage Society for so long? That fellow Tidwell came sniffing around the tea shop and I finally sent him over there. Was Timothy bending your ear? Regaling you with his depressing financial news?"

"Do you know much about that?" asked Theodosia.

Drayton nodded as the bell over the front door jingled and a crush of women began to push their way in. "We board members are always talking amongst ourselves," he said in a low voice. "Nothing's really a secret, you know."

*   *   *

The China Society wasn't really an academic group, it was more like a ladies' tea group from North Charleston. Their leader, Miss Velba Moore, was apologetic when all but two tables showed up.

Ultimately the spare tables turned out to be a *good* thing for Theodosia and Drayton. Because once the ladies of the China Society were seated and happily sipping tea, two other small parties showed up. A pair of newlyweds who'd been ensconced in the bridal suite at the Featherbed House B and B a few blocks away, and fellow shopkeepers Delaine Dish and Brooke Carter Crocket. Brooke's shop, Heart's Desire, was one of Charleston's premier estate jewelry shops on Church Street.

Since Haley always prepared more food than was actually needed, Theodosia and Drayton surprised the newlyweds, as well as Delaine and Brooke, with the same delightful scones, spring rolls, and wontons that the ladies of the China Society were enjoying.

"Are y'all sure this is low fat?" drawled Delaine once they were into their second course. She seemed especially paralyzed by the little spring roll in front of her. "If I gain weight and have to squeeze into double digits I'll just *die!*"

"Listen to the queen bee here," cracked Brooke, who was fifty-something and more than sensible. "She thinks wearing a size ten is the end of the world. Hah!"

"It is when you're in the fashion industry," snapped Delaine. Her shop, Cotton Duck, was one of the *tres* popular boutiques in Charleston. Never understated, always shooting for over-the-top, Cotton Duck offered a dazzling array of evening pajamas, linen shifts, hand-painted silk blouses, beaded bags, and fluttery scarves. If you had tickets to the opera, the symphony, or any of Charleston's endless social soirees, you'd best grab your charge cards and pay a visit to Cotton Duck first!

"People expect me to be a role model," Delaine told them as she picked delicately at her food. For some reason the duck garnished with lettuce was verboten, the ginger scone was not.

Selective calorie counting, decided Theodosia. It was something she'd certainly been guilty of on more than one occasion.

"And then, of course, there are the sample sizes," explained Delaine, pushing a shard of delectable duck breast aside with her fork. "I have to really fight to squeeze into those teensy sizes."

"My fighting days are over," declared Brook as she helped herself to a dollop of Devonshire cream. "My philosophy is to just stay active and enjoy life. There are enough hurdles and travails in the world without worrying about an extra pound here or there."

"Then let's have Drayton bring on the wontons," said Theodosia, who had slipped into the extra chair at their table.

"Oh, Theo, there's something I want to show you," said Brooke. She reached down and plucked a distinctive-looking blue box from her straw handbag. "That cute little lady who's opening the new hat shop brought it in to my shop."

"Gracie Venable?" said Theodosia. *What was this about?*

"Her custom hats are to *die* for!" exclaimed Delaine. "I've already got one and am going to have her make me a second one. The Summer Classic Horse Show's coming up, you know."

"Take a look at this," said Brooke, flipping open the lid on a small blue box. "She just consigned this piece to my store."

Theodosia and Delaine stared at the gold and ruby-encrusted pearl pendant that was nestled on a pouf of blue velvet.

"Oh, my goodness!" exclaimed Delaine. "Is that what I *think* it is?"

Brooke nodded. "It's a genuine Faberge piece, all right. But not rare like the eighteenth-century ones created by Carl Faberge for the Russian Tsars. Those are almost impossible to find and cost gazillions. This little egg is a fairly new commercial piece. Designed, no doubt, by one of the Faberge descendants."

"Still," said Delaine, her eyes lighting up as she appraised the little pendant, "it's gorgeous. In fact, I've got a raspberry pink linen dress with a keyhole neckline that would showcase that piece beautifully. Size eight." She smiled and batted her heavily mascaraed eyelashes.

Still staring at the blue box, Theodosia reached out a hand. "May I see it?" she asked. Brooke passed her the box and Theodosia immediately noted the embossed *CandW* on the jewelry box's lid. "From Crispin and Weller," Theodosia murmured.

"Most recently, anyway," said Brooke. "Wasn't that a terrible tragedy about the senior partner? And very strange circumstances, too, from what I understand."

"Tell us about it!" cried Delaine. "Theodosia and I were *there*. We practically *witnessed* the murder."

"How awful," said Brooke. "Have the police come up with anything? It seems that with a room full of people they must have zeroed in on one or two prime suspects."

"They have," said Delaine, glancing sideways. She pointed a manicured index finger at the box Theodosia was holding. "And *she's* one," Delaine told them in a loud whisper. "Gracie Venable, the hat lady!"

Theodosia's brows instantly knit together. "Why would you say that, Delaine?"

Delaine was suddenly all wide-eyed innocence. "Honey, I'm just repeating what I *heard*. Far be it from me to spread rumors, but there is chitchat going around that Roger Crispin and Gracie Venable had a *thing* going. You know, a liaison."

"Really?" said Brooke. Her normally placid face was lost in thought. "I kind of wondered if she got the Faberge pendant from him. I knew that Roger picked up a few smaller Faberge pieces at an auction in Vienna last year."

Theodosia remained silent. She just stared at the Faberge egg pendant. Twinkling and flashing as it caught the afternoon light, it hinted at the mystery and past grandeur of the Romanoffs, the intrigue of life at court with the last Tsar, Tsar Nicholas. The dazzling little jewel hinted, too, at the secret relationship between Gracie and Roger Crispin. And, perhaps, another tragic death?

What were Delaine's exact words? Theodosia asked herself. *Oh yes . . . Her custom hats are to die for!*

As Theodosia rose in her chair, eager to abandon this rather uncomfortable thread of conversation, Delaine's hand clamped tightly about her wrist.

"Don't look now," said Delaine in her stage whisper, "but that lady in the too-bright green suit has just removed a picture from your wall! And I do believe she's going to stash it in her purse!"

"I think she plans to buy it," responded Brooke in a droll voice. "In fact, there goes the wreath, too."

"That's par for the course around here," said Haley as she hustled over to refill Delaine and Brooke's teacups. "We sell a ton of stuff to customers. T-Bath products, wreaths, antiques. Good thing Theodosia's always finding new stuff."

"Doesn't that put you under tremendous pressure, dear?" asked Delaine. "Always searching for new and appropriate decor?"

"Not really," said Theodosia, who was still lost in thought, pondering the relationship between Gracie Venable and Roger Crispin. "In fact," she murmured, "it's usually lots of fun."

"Atta girl," said Brooke.

"*I was afraid* our guests would buy the decorations right off our hallowed walls," said Drayton. "And they did. *Now* what are we supposed to do?" He sounded annoyed but looked pleased. "Along with your T-Bath products, those beaded bags and toile-patterned tea towels sailed right out the door. As did the two Victorian language of flowers prints. And I *was* hoping the teacup wreaths and garland would manage to stay put for at least a week or so." sighed Drayton. "Especially since we've got the teacup exchange Saturday."

"Maybe I could whip together a couple more wreaths?" proposed Theodosia.

"You'd have to be awfully quick about it," muttered Drayton as he slid his glasses on and began totaling up the day's receipts.

Theodosia glanced at her watch. If she jumped in her Jeep right now, this very minute, she could make a mad dash out to Aunt Libby's place, where dozens more grapevine wreaths and garlands were drying in one of the barns. She could cart them back here and stash them in back. Then she and Haley could decorate them with their signature teacups and ribbon in between doing everything else they had planned!

Yeah, right.

On the other hand, a quick spin out to Aunt Libby's would be a dandy way to clear her head. Of course, she'd have to push like crazy. The opening at the Segrova Gallery was tonight, and Jory was supposed to pick her up promptly at seven.

"Theo!" yelled Haley from behind the counter, where she was ringing up a final purchase of T-Bath products. "Telephone. It's Jory returning your call."

Theodosia dove into her office and snatched up the phone on her desk. "Hi there," she said. She suddenly felt jittery and nervous and hated herself for feeling that way. They'd always been good together. Had always served to *calm* each other.

His voice boomed into her ear. "You left me a voicemail earlier."

"Right," said Theodosia. "I was just checking to see if we were still on for tonight."

"Tonight?" came his distracted reply.

Uh-oh. "Remember?" prompted Theodosia. "The Segrova Gallery is having that big opening?" She'd asked him last night if he wanted to go with her and he'd promised to carve out some time for the event. Now it didn't sound good.

"Gosh," said Jory, and Theodosia could hear papers rattling in the background. "Things are really crazy here." A pause. "I don't think I can make it, Theo. Not tonight. But you go. Have fun."

Have fun, she thought. *Gulp. Is it my mistake or have things suddenly cooled big time?*

"Listen," she said, trying to sound upbeat but suddenly feeling awful. "While I've got you on the phone . . . you know the auction house, Crispin and Weller?"

"Yes," said Jory slowly. "Our firm does their legal work."

"Right," said Theodosia. "You mentioned that." She stared at the wall across from her desk. Her memorabilia wall, a lovely collection of framed photos, favorite tea labels, and opera programs. Hanging there was a picture of Jory and her, too. Taken last summer on his sailboat, *Rubicon.* When they'd raced in the Compass Key sailboat race and come in a respectable third in their division.

"Well," Theodosia continued, "I was wondering what you could tell me about Simone Crispin. I mean, she's been trying to stir up a veritable hornet's nest. Pointing fingers at a friend of ours, Gracie Venable—"

"Who was reputedly having an affair with her husband," finished Jory.

"I can't . . ." replied Theodosia, her voice trailing off. She didn't really want to tell Jory what Gracie had confided in her. It was awfully personal, and Gracie was probably embarrassed enough as it was.

A long, awkward silence spun out, and then Jory said in a quiet voice, "I'm afraid anything I could tell you about Simone would be privileged information."

"I'm just trying to steer police *away* from Gracie," said Theodosia. *Come on, Jory, please don't be like this. Just because I'm not ready to pack my suitcase and run off to New York with you at the drop of a hat. Give me some time. Give me some breathing space so I can think everything through.*

Jory hesitated for a moment. "Be careful, Theo. Simone is very well connected. And from the rumors I've heard . . . well, I'm not so sure you *should* steer the police away from Gracie."

"What rumors?" Theodosia asked, her heart sinking.

"Theodosia," he said. "We need to talk. Just not right now."

"*Theo,*" *said a* visibly worried Drayton five minutes later, "you look like you're running on autopilot. Please tell me what's going on. You haven't been quite yourself today. And after that phone call from Jory . . . well, I want to know what's wrong. I want to *help.*"

Wiping her hands on a tea towel, Theodosia gazed deeply into Drayton's kindly old eyes, deciding she wouldn't tell him everything. Maybe half. A small sin of omission.

"If you must know," she began, "Jory asked me to marry him."

"That's *wonderful* news!" exclaimed Drayton. "Cause for celebration, in fact." He peered at her with speculation, the smile suddenly slipping from his face. "Yes . . . hmm . . . I'm sure that explains why you're so glum. Marriage. Such an awful prospect for the future!" he snorted.

"Drayton, you don't know the half of it," responded Theodosia. "Jory also wants me to move to New York with him. To Manhattan. He's been offered a post to head up his firm's new satellite office."

Drayton's eyebrows arched in sudden surprise and he fingered his bow tie nervously. "I see. That *isn't* such good news." He peered at her, filled with nervous energy now. "You're not going to, are you?" he stammered. "Move, I mean? Leave us? Leave this?" Drayton was visibly shaken.

Theodosia shook her head. "I don't know. At least, I don't *think* so."

"But Jory's absolutely leaving?" asked Drayton. "With or without you? He's going to relocate?"

"That's the impression I get, yes. He's absolutely thrilled by his firm's offer."

"Oh dear," said Drayton, letting the news sink in. "Well, it certainly *is* an honor of sorts," he allowed. "But move to New York?" He shook his grizzled head. "It's a world-class city, to be sure. But New York simply doesn't hold a candle to Charleston!"

12

❧

A *kaleidoscope of* bright green foliage, sluggish streams, swamps, and overgrown rice plantations flashed by as Theodosia buzzed along Rutledge Road. Haley had opted to come along with her, and now both of them were enjoying this impromptu foray into the countryside. Whitetail deer, gray foxes, river otters, and even alligators were still to be found in theses piney forests and swamplands that stretched between Charleston and Savannah. And though much of the land was sparsely inhabited and seemingly untamed, it was also hauntingly beautiful.

"There's Aunt Libby!" exclaimed Haley as Theodosia pumped her brakes, spun into a right turn, then exploded through the stone gates that marked the entrance to Cane Ridge Plantation.

Libby Revelle, Theodosia's aunt and only living relative, was the chief resident at Cane Ridge, although Margaret Rose Reese, her companion and housekeeper, had pretty much settled into full-time residency as well.

Libby lifted a hand and waved as they bumped across a patch of gravel and rocked to a stop.

"Gosh, this is beautiful," marveled Haley, gazing around.

"One of my all-time favorite places," declared Theodosia.

Built in 1835 on Horlbeck Creek, Cane Ridge had once been a thriving rice plantation. Now it was the loveliest of quiet country homes, encompassing a Gothic Revival cottage replete with peaked and gabled roof and a dozen or so outbuildings in various tumbledown stages.

But when the sky dimmed to purple and the frogs picked up their insistent chorus in the nearby swamp, there was nothing finer than reclining in a giant wicker chair on the cottage's enormous piazza to watch a command performance of the evening stars and be assured that all was right with the world.

"Aunt Libby's house always reminds me of a Hansel and Gretle cottage," said Haley as they walked over to meet her.

Libby Revelle held out a silver pail filled to the brim with cracklins. "Better mark a trail for yourself then, Haley. So you can find your way back."

"I'm not about to go wandering off in your woods," said Haley, giving Aunt Libby a quick hug and taking the pail from her. "Theo once told me there were alligators out there. And quicksand."

Silver-haired and tiny, Libby gazed out over her property. Set on a gentle rise as they were, the view was calming but spectacular. A nearby quiet pond segued into marshland, then low fields stretched to meet piney forests. "Once in a while you hear an alligator bark," said Libby, her eyes twinkling. "As for the quicksand, it can be found pretty much all over the low country. Mostly in really swampy areas." She gazed out where the western sun was setting. "But over near the ruins of the old mill, a mile or so as the crow flies, there's a nasty boggy patch. And I've always suspected there's probably quicksand there, too."

Haley shuddered. She was a city girl through and through. And while she loved the beauty and serenity of the low country—what native of South Carolina didn't?—she felt a little lost once the sidewalk ran out.

"You always feed the birds this time of day?" Haley asked.

"She feeds the birds *all* day," laughed Theodosia. "The warblers, marsh wrens, cedar waxwings, and even herons and ibises show up in shifts. Libby lays out a veritable buffet. That's why all sorts of four-legged critters drop by for a handout, too."

"Small creatures need to eat, too," Libby reminded them.

"And these critters eat cracklins?" Haley asked, peering into the pail she held.

"Absolutely," said Libby. "Lately we've had a veritable population explosion of possums, raccoons, river otters, woodchucks, and weasels."

"I can't imagine why," commented Theodosia in a droll voice.

"But I didn't think you had to actually *feed* animals like that," said Haley. "I thought they all kind of preyed on each other."

"You're thinking of people, dear," said Aunt Libby with a subtle grin. She turned her gaze toward Theodosia. "You came for more grapevines?"

Theodosia nodded. She'd gathered what seemed like miles of grapevine last autumn, twisted it all into wreaths and garlands and hung it up to dry in one of the outbuildings.

"I hope you can stay for supper," said Libby as they watched Haley lug the silver pail down to a fallen oak whose hollow trunk now served as a kind of feeding trough. "Margaret Rose is making her famous Shrimp Kedgeree tonight."

"I wish," said Theodosia, who adored the curried shrimp and rice dish. "But we have to get back right away."

"Next week then," said Aunt Libby, putting an arm around her. "And bring Haley along, too. She's such a love. And dear Drayton. I always enjoy talking stamp collections with Drayton."

"*You know that* song?" asked Haley. "The one that goes, *Oh, they ran through the briars and they ran through the brambles?*"

"*The Battle of New Orleans,*" said Theodosia. "The one Johnny Horton sang."

"Exactly!" said Haley. "Well, that's what the back of your Jeep reminds me of. Briars and brambles. Or else it looks like we jammed a duck blind in there. Or those lumpy things that beaver's build."

"Beaver dams," said Theodosia.

"That's it," chuckled Haley. "Beaver dams."

"Funny concept," said Theodosia as they headed back toward Charleston. She was keenly aware that she hadn't as yet mentioned Jory's marriage proposal to her Aunt Libby or even to Haley. Or the fact that Jory's proposal seemed to hinge on both of them pulling up stakes and moving to New York.

She'd tell them in her own good time, she decided. After she'd had a chance to sort things out herself. After she figured out what to do.

"This isn't the way we came," Haley suddenly announced.

Theodosia knew that. She frowned and pushed her foot down on the accelerator. Bumping down that dirt road, hoping it intersected with Highway 17, she'd gambled on taking a shortcut in hopes of saving time. But from the looks of things—because none of these landmarks were even remotely familiar—Theodosia suspected she'd made a wrong turn. *Rats.*

"Is there a map in the glove box?" asked Haley. Popping open the little compartment, she ransacked through the usual jumble of sunglasses, insurance cards, and paper clutter, then pulled out a map. With a great deal of fanfare, Haley unfolded it, stared at it briefly, then turned it a half-turn to read it.

As Haley was tracing a line with her forefinger, Theodosia suddenly hit the brakes. Sluicing across the gravel road, Theodosia cranked the steering wheel left then right, fighting to control her fishtail skid, tires spitting up rocks as they scrabbled for purchase.

"What the . . . !" cried Haley as they slid sideways, heading for a stand of cypress. Bracing herself, she said, "This isn't gonna be a soft landing!"

But, wonder of wonders, Theodosia managed to gain control and hang on to the road. "Sorry," said Theodosia as they jolted to a stop. "Are you okay?"

"Uh . . . yeah," said Haley, still bracing herself, wondering just what had happened.

"Sorry that was such a messy stop. But that sign we just passed? The one that said Hilloway? That's Simone Crispin's farm!"

Haley fixed her with a blank stare. "Yeah? So why is that a reason for us to go spinning across the road like a crazed top?"

Oh, rats, thought Theodosia. *She doesn't know. Of course she doesn't know.*

"Haley," said Theodosia, turning in her seat to face her young assistant. "I need to bring you up to date on a few things . . ."

"I guess so," said Haley, struggling to fold the map.

"It's about Roger Crispin's murder . . ."

"Oh, oh."

Haley listened with rapt attention as Theodosia told her about Gracie confiding in her about her relationship with Roger Crispin. And also about the egg pendant that had probably been a gift from Roger and that Gracie was trying to sell on consignment in Brooke's shop. Theodosia also told Haley about Simone Crispin's behind-the-scenes machinations to steer blame, and the police investigation, squarely in Gracie's direction.

The information was obviously a lot for Haley to digest, for when Theodosia had finished, Haley just stared straight ahead and chewed her lip.

"I can understand that Gracie might have been involved with Roger," said Haley finally. "It's her business, after all." She held up an index finger to footnote her sentence. "Not that I approve, mind you, but it *is* her business. But . . . about this Simone Crispin person trying to point the police toward Gracie. That's utter nonsense! Gracie Venable doesn't have a murderous bone in her body. For gosh sakes, her main focus for the past few months has been trying to launch Bow Geste! Believe me, I know. I helped contribute to the business plan—my whole class did. I've seen how single-minded Gracie's determination has been!"

Theodosia chose not to point out that Gracie had, indeed, made time to enjoy another small diversion—that being the company of Roger Crispin. To bring that up again, however, would probably be in poor taste. And even though Haley wasn't prudish, she did seem genuinely disappointed by Gracie's actions.

"So that's the reason, or *reasons,* I should say," explained Theodosia, "why I suddenly got so hot and bothered when I spied the sign for Simone Crispin's farm."

Haley stared out the front window for a few moments and Theodosia could sense the gears humming inside her head. "Since we're still in one piece," Haley said finally. "I think we should go take a look."

Theodosia gave an encouraging smile. "I was hoping you'd say that. But, we'll have to be fairly discreet. Jory would have a cat if he knew what we were doing."

"We're be the hallmark of discretion," Haley assured her.

But snooping, even discreet snooping, wasn't going to be an easy task. Because once Theodosia had put her Jeep back in gear and they'd crawled a quarter of a mile down Simone's driveway, a high stone wall rose to their left while a swampy area stretched off in the other direction. Pressing forward, easing their way around a curve, they found their way blocked by a formidable-looking gate.

Climbing out of the Jeep, the two women tentatively approached the gate. There didn't seem to be any sort of security camera or device, so their movements probably hadn't been detected. And since they couldn't see the main house, they assumed no one there had gotten a visual sighting of them, either.

Haley put a tentative hand on the black wrought-iron gate and gave it a rattle. "Locked," she pronounced, then pressed her face between the bars.

"Can you see anything?" asked Theodosia.

"Nope. This driveway seems to curve off to the left. And all I can see straight ahead is that scrappy little stand of pines." Haley looked annoyed. "Now what?"

Theodosia shrugged. "Search me." It looked like the end of the road. Both literally and figuratively.

Haley cocked her head for a few seconds, then waved a hand, motioning for Theodosia to be quiet. "Listen," she said. "You hear that?"

Theodosia stood stock still and concentrated. She *did* hear something. She just wasn't sure what it was.

"This is gonna sound strange," said Haley. "But it kind of sounds like there's a cocktail party going on."

Slightly amused, Theodosia listened again. Haley was right. She, too, was picking up a high-pitched hum of conversation that sounded, for all the world, like chatter emanating from a busy cocktail party.

Is Simone having some sort of garden party? wondered Theodosia. *Some sort of celebration with friends?* She decided there was only one way to find out.

"We've got to check this out," Theodosia told Haley.

"Great," replied Haley. "What's the plan?"

They both stared at the eight-foot-high stone wall. It seemed to offer considerably more footholds and possibilities for climbing than the wrought-iron gate with its top row of spikes did.

"I suggest a technical alpine assent," said Theodosia, sticking her toe into a narrow crack and testing the hold. Once, years ago, she'd dated a semiprofessional rock climber who'd dragged her into the rolling hills and rocky ridges of the Piedmont on a climbing trip. Terrified and befuddled, she'd clung to the rope he'd dangled down to her, hoisting herself up instead of actually *climbing* the rock face. Now Theodosia racked her brain, trying to remember the few pointers he'd shouted at her. Leverage your weight, always look for toeholds, never crank your arms too far above your head. Of course, he'd been coaching her on climbing *real* rocks. But this had to be pretty much the same principle.

Theodosia found a second toehold, reached up, pushed her body against the wall, and searched for her next hold. There it was. Right at waist level. A really good-sized hold this time. She brought her leg up, stuck her toe in, and began her ascent, remembering to jam her hands into the crevices to support her upper body rather than use a pinch grip. Her form was awfully ragged, to be sure, but she was definitely making progress.

Thank goodness I've been doing my Pilates exercises faithfully, she told herself. *Well, fairly faithfully.*

"Careful, careful," cautioned Haley, as she followed Theodosia up.

The rocks were dry and crumbly and parts of the wall seemed like they might have been patched with tabby, a mixture of sand, lime, and oyster shells. Dubbed the "cement of the low country," tabby was certainly not the most durable of building materials. But the rock wall offered a wealth of knobs and holes and rocky projections. So, in a matter of minutes, Theodosia and Haley were able to hoist themselves onto the narrow top of the wall and peer across to the other side.

"We made it!" exclaimed Haley, looking around. "But no party." She hesitated. "No nothing." She suddenly sounded disappointed.

A white Federal-style home sat on a broad expanse of lawn. Two-storied with slender columns, the home had a double flight of stairs leading to the graceful porch, disguising the high foundation that was a practical necessity out here.

Though the home had undoubtedly been the scene of many parties and galas, today it sat quiet and still. One could almost hear the clocks ticking inside the empty house.

Nobody home, thought Theodosia.

Set further back from the home was a small, newer-looking building surrounded by a high wire fence. Inside were small blurs of birds.

"There's your cocktail party," said Theodosia. "Not a flock of babbling guests, but a flock of chickens!"

"Huh," said Haley. "Fancy chickens at that." Then peering

more carefully she added, "Looks like Silver Sebrights, and maybe Cochines."

"How on earth do you know what *breed* they are?" asked Theodosia, impressed as well as amused by Haley's quick response.

"Are you kidding?" exclaimed Haley. "Fancy, pedigreed chickens are all the rage these days. Don't you remember? Martha Stewart had *tons* of fancy chickens."

"So Simone is into chickens," said Theodosia. "Interesting."

"Not really," commented Haley, ready to leave. "Time to call it quits?"

"Not so fast," said Theodosia as she stared at the milling flock of chickens. "As Lucy used to tell Ricky, I've got some more *'splaining* to do."

Quickly, Theodosia filled Haley in about the feather she'd found clinging to the stairwell at the Heritage Society. And how she'd agonized about turning it over to Tidwell. And how she'd been more than a little nervous when she'd seen all the feathers lying about Gracie Venable's shop.

But rather than worry over Gracie's possible involvement, Haley was suddenly infused with enthusiasm. "Wow," she exclaimed, excited by Theodosia's revelation. "This changes everything! I mean, what if these chicken feathers *matched up* with the one you found? Then Simone Crispin would be incriminated big time! I mean, maybe she found out about Gracie and Roger and was crazed enough to murder her own husband!"

"Maybe," said Theodosia. "A matching feather wouldn't be proof positive of her guilt, but it might help put Simone at the scene. Get the police to take a harder look at her."

"That would be good," said Haley. "Instead of just seeing Simone as the poor, bereaved widow, they'd see her for what she really is. Cold and calculating, trying to cast aspersions on Gracie. Which brings us to our next logical step."

"Which is?" said Theodosia.

"We've got to go grab some of those feathers!"

Somehow, Theodosia knew that was exactly what Haley was going to suggest.

"If we grab a feather and it matches," Haley said excitedly, "then Gracie's off the hook!"

"Maybe not entirely off the hook," said Theodosia. She didn't want Haley to get her hopes up too much. There were still an awful lot of people who were suspicious of Gracie Venable. She herself was starting to get a little nervous.

"Halfway off the hook, then," said Haley, a hopeful note in her voice.

Theodosia thought about Haley's idea for about a half-second. "You're right," she said. "Let's climb down and go pluck a few of those feathers."

"Do chickens bite?" asked Haley as they clambered down from the wall and crept across the wide lawn toward the chicken enclosure.

"No, but they peck," Theodosia cautioned her. "Chickens can be high-strung and a little nasty." Her last encounter with chickens had been more than a few years ago, but she doubted that improvements in breeding had led to improvements in temperament. In fact, maybe just the opposite.

* * *

Inside the wire pen, the Silver Sebright bantams with their elegant black markings and the creamy buff Cochines with their trademark bouffant "do" gave them no trouble. But as they scrambled to pick up feathers, Theodosia heard the first faint sounds of barking.

Haley heard it, too. "Dogs?" she asked, a sudden look of panic flitting across her face.

"Let's go," was Theodosia's terse answer. Scrambling out of the pen, they slammed the wire door behind them as faint sounds turned to fierce, serious-sounding barks.

"Those sound like bona fide guard dogs!" cried Haley.

Or like hounds after a fox, thought Theodosia.

From around the side of the house, two black balls of fur, Rottweilers, suddenly appeared, streaking purposefully toward them!

No, hounds after us!

"Run!" yelled Haley.

"Hold it! Hold it!" cried Theodosia. "Stand your ground!" Everything she'd been taught about being confronted by unfriendly dogs involved standing your ground. Looking fierce, waving your arms like crazy, showing no fear.

"Are you nuts!" cried Haley, grabbing Theodosia's arm and giving her a hard jerk as the two chunky black dogs came closer into view. "Look at those hellhounds! They've got one thing on their brain . . . ripping us to shreds!"

"Good point!" cried Theodosia as they dashed across the lawn in an all-out sprint. She was a regular jogger, but she hadn't logged a mad heat like this since high school track.

"Oh my gosh! I think they're catching up!" shrieked Haley, managing a quick peek over her shoulder as they streaked for the stone wall. "They're almost on our heels!"

"We're gonna make it!" cried Theodosia. The dogs were rapidly closing ground, but the stone wall loomed just ahead. "Ten more paces, then climb as fast as you can! Fling yourself up that wall and keep kicking. Kick for dear life!"

They hit the stone wall at record speed. Whomping into it with enough force to inflict serious scrapes and scratches. But they were agile, determined, and definitely scared. Clambering, scrambling, they clawed their way up the wall, fighting for every inch, sensing warm dog breath on their ankles, nervous that at any moment those sharp fangs would rip into soft flesh.

"We made it!" screamed Haley once they'd gained the top of the wall. She threw her arms up in the air victoriously, looking all the world like a soccer player about to rip her jersey off.

Below them, the two giant black dogs let out disappointed snarls as they circled and whined, unwilling to concede the chase.

"Forget it, dogs," yelled Haley from her rocky parapet. "You're outta luck!"

Pacing nervously, growling, and rolling their eyes, the Rottweilers looked as though they realized their status as fierce guard dogs had been seriously blown.

Haley puffed and wheezed, trying to catch her breath. "You got the feathers?" she asked, once she was able to calm her breathing.

Fighting to calm her breathing, too, Theodosia fumbled in her jacket pocket.

She *did* stick them in there, right? She did still *have* them?

There was a panicky moment when Theodosia figured the feathers must have been lost in the heat of the chase. Just fluttered off somewhere. Then her fingertips touched downy softness and she triumphantly pulled out a bit of white fluff to show Haley.

"Got 'em!"

13

Colorful canvases hung from the white walls of the Segrova Gallery. A Russian symphony, String Quartet #8 by Shostakovich, wafted through the air, lending to the cultured yet slightly frenetic atmosphere. Champagne glasses clinked, giant dollops of gleaming black caviar were plopped upon rounds of golden toast to be gobbled voraciously. And everywhere, throngs of eager gallery patrons smiled, chatted, drawled exuberant *hellos,* and engaged in that elaborate greeting ritual known as the air kiss.

"Very impressive," said Drayton as he deftly snatched two tall flutes of champagne from the tray of a passing waiter. Pleased with scoring the glasses of bubbly, he quickly passed one over to Theodosia. When she'd called him at the last minute to see if he still wanted to attend the art opening with her, he'd been more than enthusiastic. Drayton was an art lover and had occasionally dabbled with oil and tempera paints himself, although he professed to be a rank amateur and never showed anyone the many canvases he produced. Secretly, his friends all assumed that Drayton was probably quite talented. Anyone who was a master tea blender, bonsai artist, and whiz at calligraphy could probably paint a fairly passable picture as well.

"These pieces are really quite stunning," said Drayton as they gazed at the collection of large expressionist paintings that hung on the walls. "Highly evocative, lovely compositions, and the colors . . . well, I must confess, I've always preferred moody paintings to a brighter palette. Probably a by-product of my misspent youth and somewhat dark nature." Drayton wiggled his eyebrows Groucho Marx–style at Theodosia as if to quietly dispel his I'm-so-dark soliloquy.

Theodosia, who had a pair of moody seascapes hanging above her own fireplace, had to agree with him. Still lifes were pretty to gaze at, portraits always compelling, and contemporary works were often provocative and tongue-in-cheek. But there was nothing like a dark, moody painting to evoke the primitive, poetic self that dwelled deep within her breast. In Theodosia's college days, she'd been an English literature major and had spent the occasional day roaming the highly atmospheric grounds of Magnolia Cemetery with its crumbling Civil War–era graves and gnarled live oaks dripping Spanish moss. Clad in a flowing purple velvet cape, determined to compose her own romantic, lyrical words, she would recite stirring passages from works by Jane Austen and Charlotte Brontë for inspiration. A little melodramatic, to be sure, but still quite soothing to her bohemian soul and so very appealing to the romantic within.

"These paintings are quite poetic," said Theodosia. They'd arrived at the Segrova Gallery a half hour ago and, with the wall-to-wall crush of guests, had only been able to inspect half of Draco Vidak's paintings so far. But they were definitely impressed by the ones they'd seen.

"Richly introspective," said Drayton. "Like the music of Erik Satie or the writings of Proust. These paintings, especially the ones with the saints and religious icons, put me in the mood to curl up in front of a cracking fire and sink into a contemplative reverie."

"I know exactly what you mean," said Theodosia, who enjoyed nothing more than collapsing on her antique fainting couch to have a good think herself.

"I'm sorry Jory couldn't make it tonight," Drayton said abruptly. "I'm sure you would have enjoyed the pleasure of his company far more than my own."

"Don't you dare say that!" cried Theodosia. "I'm having a great time playing art critic with you!" Much to her delight, Theodosia *was* enjoying herself immensely. Though still shaken by her mad dash from Simone's guard dogs, Theodosia was thoroughly caught up in the excitement of Maribo Pratt's gallery opening and the opportunity to hobnob with people she hadn't seen for a while. She'd already run into Angie and Mark Congdon who owned the Featherbed House B and B over near the Battery, and Marianne Petigru, one of the partners in Popple Hill Design Studio.

"I would imagine you and Jory have *volumes* to discuss," said Drayton. He was still worried by the news that not only did Jory want to move to New York, but that he'd asked Theodosia to relocate there as well. For Drayton, who'd been with Theodosia since the very inception of the Indigo Tea Shop, this was something that threatened his very being.

Theodosia patted her hair, suddenly nervous at having Jory's name brought up. With the intense overhead lights and crush of bodies, her mass of auburn hair, always full to begin with, seemed to be expanding at a rapid rate. She thought her tresses unruly when, in fact, they were simply bountiful. And dressed as she was tonight, in a simple pale green silk sheath dress accented with antique cameo earrings, Theodosia looked like a lovely, almost ethereal character straight out of a pre-Raphaelite painting.

"Maybe Jory and I don't have a lot to discuss after all," Theodosia murmured to Drayton a trifle wistfully. "Perhaps it's all been said."

Drayton peered at her. "Is there something you're not telling me?"

"Um . . ." began Theodosia. "Concerning Jory, no. You actually know about as much as I do. Which is pretty much next to nothing. But as far as other issues go, there *is* something I need to talk to you about."

"What?" asked Drayton, suddenly anxious. "What?"

Pulling Drayton aside, Theodosia quickly filled him in. She related her tale of finding the feather at the Heritage Society and turning it over to Tidwell. Then she segued into Haley's and her misadventure that afternoon. Theodosia told Drayton about their seeing the sign for Simone's country house, venturing onto the property and grabbing the feather, and then, of course, being chased by snarling dogs.

"Good heavens," said Drayton, his eyes going wide. "You two are a dreadful influence on each other! I hope you realize that, as a result of your blatant trespassing, you could have been ripped to shreds by those vicious animals. And the ensuing melee would have been *your* doing!" Drayton's voice continued to rise with excitement. "Don't you know not all canines are as even-tempered as your fellow, Earl Grey?"

"Shh . . . I know, I know," said Theodosia, thoroughly chastised but trying to calm Drayton, trying to get him to speak in a lower tone of voice. "But getting back to the issue of the feathers . . ."

"I hope you intend to hand this recently pilfered batch over to Detective Tidwell as well," said Drayton. He managed to look outraged, but Theodosia knew his curiosity was piqued.

"Of course I will," said Theodosia. *Aha, he is intrigued. Now he's got a small stake in this, too.*

"About Simone Crispin," continued Theodosia. "Do you know . . . was she in attendance Sunday night?"

"At the Poet's Tea?" Drayton shrugged. "I have no earthly idea. As you may recall, I was a trifle preoccupied that evening."

Theodosia thought for a moment. "Is there a guest list I could look at?"

"Afraid not," said Drayton, shaking his head. "The Poet's Tea was set up as a drop-by event. Just a fun thing to coincide with Spoleto. There was minimal PR, a few invitations to key Heritage Society members, that sort of thing. Very informal."

"Hmm," said Theodosia. "Too bad."

"Do you really think Simone Crispin would murder her

own husband?" asked Drayton. "She and Roger might not have had the best marriage in the world, but they always seemed cordial."

"That cordiality could have been an act," said Theodosia.

Drayton laid a gentle hand on Theodosia's shoulder and fought to lower his voice. "Theo," he said, "I know you don't want to face this, but there's a very real possibility Gracie Venable is guilty. She was at the Heritage Society that evening. And the fact exists that she might have had motive. The woman was involved with Roger Crispin, for goodness sake! Or at least I *think* she was."

"She was," said Theodosia, a sense of dread suddenly filling her. "She admitted as much to me." Theodosia knew that Drayton was voicing the same thoughts she'd been trying to push back.

"Haley is . . . a rather innocent sort," continued Drayton. "She's almost childlike in the fact that she always focuses on the good in people. It's a wonderful quality, to be sure. But Haley believes, with all her heart, that Gracie Venable is completely innocent. A victim only of malicious gossip and strange circumstances." Drayton paused, his grizzled face rearranging itself to give Theodosia a deeper, more meaningful look. "But you and I, we're a little more experienced in the ways of the world. I don't want to use the term *jaded,* but we both understand that people aren't always as they appear. And they're rarely as one *wishes* them to appear."

"I hear you," said Theodosia.

"You say that," said Drayton, "and I want to believe you. But you have this ferocious spirit that burns inside you. A spirit that compels you to rush to people's defense." Theodosia started to sputter, but Drayton held up a finger. "You also try to assume the weight of the world on your rather small but capable shoulders." He paused. "Please. You don't have to. You're not a lone crusader out there. You know that, don't you?"

Theodosia gazed at Drayton with a mixture of gratitude and amusement. "Thank you," she murmured. "I'll try to remember that."

"Now," said Drayton, looking purposeful, "I suppose you plan to attend Roger's funeral tomorrow?"

Theodosia winced. He had her there. Of course she was going to the funeral. That's where you always went to figure out who the bad guy was, right? He'd be the one lurking in the background, gloating over his crime.

"Do not think you are going alone," said Drayton, trying to sound stern. "I shall be right alongside you the entire time. Count on it."

"Thank you, Drayton," said Theodosia. There was something comforting in the fact that Drayton, a man who abhorred violence, never hunted, never hooked a fish, always transported tiny insects outside when he caught them in his house, was taking it upon himself to watch over her. Then again, that's what friendship was all about, she decided.

"Now," said Drayton, holding up his glass. "That said, shall we indulge in another glass of champagne?"

"Excellent suggestion," said Theodosia. Drayton's emotional and heartfelt words of support and warning were still echoing in her head. He was right. She had to be careful. And she wasn't alone. No matter how bereft she might feel about Jory moving away.

But as Drayton turned to search for another waiter bearing flutes of champagne, his face suddenly lit up. "Ah," he exclaimed. "If it isn't the lady of the evening!"

Maribo Pratt, dressed in a figure-skimming, glittery black pantsuit, was closing in on them fast.

"Isn't this delightful?" she cried, gazing around at the flurry of excitement. "Didn't I get a marvelous turnout?"

"A splendid evening," said Drayton, leaning forward to give Maribo a chaste peck on the cheek.

"Oh Theo! Drayton!" cried another shrill voice. Delaine Dish, who'd been five steps behind Maribo, suddenly pushed her way into their small circle, pulling an aloof-looking Jester Moody along with her.

Excited by the event, proud to have made such a good catch, Delaine preened in her frothy pink dress and pressed herself up against Jester Moody. "Isn't this fun?" she squealed. "Isn't this artsy crowd a gas?"

Maribo could barely contain her widening smile. "We got a spectacular turnout!" she exclaimed again.

Delaine looked proud. "I've been hammering on each and every one of my customers for a week, telling them they absolutely *had* to be in attendance tonight," she said. "After all, this opening is one of the most important social events of the season!"

At Delaine's rather pompous pronouncement, the corners of Drayton's mouth twitched. "I'm sure the Gibbes Museum and the Charleston Symphony will be heartbroken to hear they've been one-upped," he murmured.

Delaine's high laugh tinkled like glass. "Don't be silly, Drayton. You're talking about old-line stodgy institutions.

This is"—she glanced about, totally enthralled—"a completely different kind of vibe!"

"Kindly tell us about this rather impressive artist you're showcasing tonight," Drayton urged Maribo, anxious to deflect Delaine's hysteria and get back to the subject at hand. "I've had a look at several of the man's paintings and, I must say, I'm extremely impressed."

Maribo looked delighted. "Draco Vidak is one of the most important painters to emerge from Eastern Europe," she told them. "Vidak studied at the rather prestigious Art Lyceum in Belgrade, where he received the Pavle Simic Award. He then went on to produce an incredible body of work that I think rivals even artists like Kosta Milicic and Nadezda Petrovic. Sadly, Draco Vidak died in the Podgorica Penitentiary four years ago."

"What?" exclaimed a shocked Delaine. "You mean the artist is *dead*?"

Jester Moody finally spoke up. "All artists have to die in order to become famous," he said in a droll voice. "At least that seems to be the historical precedent."

"I'm absolutely heartbroken!" exclaimed Delaine. Her chin quivered, her mouth drooped, she looked like she was about to burst into tears.

"Then aren't you going to run out of Vidak's pieces fairly soon?" asked Theodosia. *Why,* she wondered as she spoke the words, *am I always the practical one?*

"Yes and no," Maribo told her slowly. "Fortunately for all of us, Draco Vidak was an extremely prolific painter. The man even continued to paint from his prison cell! And through some rather extensive wrangling and negotiations with his estate and certain government officials, I've been able to secure his remaining body of work."

Delaine glanced about the gallery, still looking utterly heartbroken. "What do the red dots on all the paintings mean?" she asked.

"Those, my dear," said Jester Moody, draping an arm around Delaine's shoulders, "are the pieces that are already spoken for."

"You mean they're *sold*?" wailed Delaine. "Already? That isn't *fair*! I was just beginning to warm up to Mr. Vidak's work. I was considering *purchasing* a piece as an investment."

"Not to worry," said Maribo, rushing to smooth Delaine's ruffled feathers. "I have another shipment of paintings that just arrived. They're over at the North Charleston Port Terminal tucked safely inside a bonded warehouse."

"When will those paintings be available?" asked Delaine, still sniffling and looking hurt.

"Those paintings go on sale to the public beginning this Sunday," said Maribo. Delaine was about to launch another vigorous protest when Maribo added: "Of course, I'd certainly give *you* a first look before they're put up for sale."

"Oh," said Delaine, suddenly pacified. "You'd do that for *me*?"

"Absolutely," Maribo assured her. "Special allowances are always made for special customers."

"Well, that would be very nice," said Delaine, sounding pleased. "I'd like that very much."

"Good," said Maribo. "I'm going to select one painting for the Heritage Society's Spring Auction, then the rest are yours to contemplate. Just drop by early Sunday afternoon."

"It's very generous of you to donate a piece of Vidak's work to the Heritage Society," said Drayton.

Maribo waved a hand. "It's a worthwhile cause."

"And an excellent way to garner notoriety as well as publicity," volunteered Jester.

"Nothing wrong with that," agreed Maribo.

Theodosia gazed at Jester Moody and wondered about his nasty remarks about Roger Crispin and the fact that, in an earlier incarnation, Jester had been an antique weapons dealer. She wondered, too, about the somewhat reclusive Simone Crispin with her fancy feathered chickens and slavering guard dogs. And the Faberge egg pendant that had been part of a collection purchased by Crispin and Weller then surreptitiously given to Gracie Venable. Lots of interesting goings on, she decided. But not exactly a wealth of clear-cut information.

"Draco Vidak's paintings *are* awfully compelling," Drayton whispered to Theodosia once Delaine was out of earshot. "And may, in fact, be a good investment. But Maribo is really stringing Delaine along with her *important customer* routine."

"And our dear Delaine is thriving on it," agreed Theodosia. "Which means she'll probably end up buying a painting."

"That wouldn't be the worst thing," said Drayton, peering at a depiction of Russian peasants working in a field. "They really are quite marvelous." He fumbled in his linen jacket for his glasses, slid them onto his nose and studied the information card that was tacked next to the painting. "This was painted when? Ah . . . nineteen ninety-eight, Podgorica Prison," he murmured. "Such a shame. Why is it poor artists are always picked on and persecuted in socialist regimes?"

"It isn't always artists who are persecuted," Theodosia

reminded him. "Certain religions or nationalities are often singled out, too."

"You're quite right," said Drayton, still caught up in the painting. "And isn't that a sad commentary on what's supposed to be a civilized world."

"*What are you* doing here?" asked a familiar voice.

Theodosia whirled about to see a darkly handsome face bobbing in front of her. Well, *almost* in front of her since Parker Scully was a good head taller than she was.

"I was invited," said Theodosia. "But a better question might be what are you doing here? Aren't you supposed to be popping wine corks and trying to enlighten Southerners on the merits of *tapas* versus grits?"

Parker Scully grinned at her, the roguish grin of a riverboat gambler. "I helped arrange a shipment of Beluga caviar for Maribo and she sent me an invitation." He looked around at the crush of guests and gave a short laugh. "Along with eight hundred of her closest friends. And here I thought I was someone special. Pretty pathetic, huh?"

"I thought you'd be working tonight," said Theodosia, although she was secretly pleased to see him.

He shrugged. "Hey, what can I say. Solstice wasn't all that busy tonight, and even a restaurateur deserves an evening out once in a while." He looked pointedly at Theodosia's empty champagne flute. "Say, can I get you another drink? A real drink? Maybe a good Montrachet or a Cabernet? Something that wasn't brought down from New Jersey in a tanker truck."

"I don't think they're serving *that* kind of wine," said Theodosia as they edged over toward the bar. She was not unaware of how tall Parker Scully was and how familiarly close he stood to her.

Theodosia, who was fairly intuitive to begin with, could fairly sense Parker Scully's interest in her. And, heaven help her, she knew he could sense her curiosity about him.

How is it, she wondered, *that I've spoken to this man a total of three times and yet I feel like I know him?*

It was a frightening, disquieting feeling. She'd always thought, always *assumed,* that she would end up with Jory Davis in a happily-ever-after scenario. They'd get married, pool their resources, maybe buy an enormous old home in the historic district. After that, the vision had always been a little murky. Like a fog bank drifting in from the Atlantic. Maybe her future *wasn't* all that predetermined after all. Maybe fate had a twist in store for her.

And the fact that Parker Scully had recently moved here from New York, and Jory was hot to relocate to New York, was beyond strange. Like some weird force field that had reversed itself.

"Here she is!" exclaimed Maribo, dragging a flustered-looking Drayton behind her. "Hiding over here with Charleston's most adorable restaurateur."

"I was on my way to the bar," explained Drayton, "when Maribo waylaid me."

"Ambushed is more like it," laughed Maribo. "And then Drayton introduced me to Sheldon Tibbets. You know, the lovely man who writes the arts column for the *Post and Courier.* He's so impressed with the show that he promised to mention the Segrova Gallery in his next column and maybe even do a sidebar on me!" Maribo's eyes sparkled. "Oh honey," she said, clutching at Theodosia's arm, "this is the most fun I've ever had, bar none. Thank *goodness* I was brave enough to take that trip to Saint Petersburg two years ago. I was so worried about being an outsider, but the people over there were so warm and friendly. They invited me right into their homes and apartments. That's how I started dealing in Russian collectibles and antiques, too. Fun things like dolls and teacups. Those poor people were *desperate* to sell whatever they had just to earn a few dollars."

Maribo waggled a finger, and the three of them followed her to the back of the gallery. Behind two gleaming white desks was a wall of built-in cupboards. Maribo reached up and pulled open one of the doors. "Look at this," she said as she removed a glass and silver object and handed it to Drayton. "Tea glass holders like they used in that movie *The Hunt for Red October*. Only these are the real thing, not just reproductions."

"Ah yes," said Drayton, his eyes lighting up as he balanced the silver holder in his hand. "Sean Connery as Captain Ramius."

"You saw the movie!" exclaimed Maribo, giving his arm a gentle, conspiratorial touch.

"No," said Drayton, "I read the book."

14

❧

Navy blue seemed to be the color du jour. Everywhere Theodosia looked in St. Philip's church, everyone was clad in navy blue. Navy blue dresses, navy blue hats, navy blue suits. Not as funereal as your basic black, but still properly somber, navy blue was obviously regarded as a serious, down-to-business color.

Sitting two rows back from Theodosia and Drayton, right next to Maribo Pratt, was Delaine Dish, Charleston's own fashion maven. Delaine had paired her tailored navy dress with a pair of blue and white spectator pumps, so her outfit managed to convey, *Yes it's a funeral and we're all in mourning, but for goodness sakes, it's summer in Charleston!*

The turnout for Roger Crispin's funeral was sizable. Across the aisle sat Timothy Neville and a large contingent of employees and board members from the Heritage Society. And scattered everywhere were antique dealers and gallery owners. Some from the shops on Church Street, many from Charleston's so-called antiques district, that area along King Street between Beaufain and Queen Streets that was populated with fine shops brimming with French, English, and Early-American antiques.

Theodosia recognized Summer Sullivan from the Legacy Gallery, Lawrence March from March Forth, and Tom Wigley from the Adolphus Gallery.

Drayton caught her gazing around and flashed an unhappy half-smile at her. Normally the pillar of decorum, Drayton was beginning to fidget. The temperature was warm heading toward hot inside St. Philip's Church, and people continued to file in even though the service had been scheduled to begin some ten minutes ago. But Drayton wasn't the only member of the congregation who was checking his watch and wondering when the service would get under way. All around them heads turned, fingers tapped, and a low buzz of conversation filled the air like a swarm of unwelcome mosquitoes.

Yet, through it all, Simone Crispin sat ramrod still in the front row off to their left, eyes straight ahead, looking cool and aloof. An ice queen staring at the veritable hedge of floral bouquets that had been sent for this final tribute, a testament to the fact that Roger Crispin had been so very well-liked.

Finally the service got under way. Organ music swelled and Roger Crispin's dark mahogany casket was borne in by eight young men, probably younger relatives, who looked as though they were struggling mightily despite their combined manpower. And then Reverend Charles Toussaint took his place at the podium.

Halfway through the Reverend Toussaint's measured but welcoming words, Theodosia turned her head to ease a kink in her neck and caught a flash of movement out of the corner of her eye. She did what she hoped was a surreptitious turn of her head and saw . . . *Gracie*.

Gracie Venable had tiptoed in late, exceedingly late, to take a seat in the far recess of the great church.

Theodosia twisted her head again and this time caught Gracie bent forward with her shoulders decidedly slumped, daubing a hanky to her eyes.

Poor Gracie. She said they weren't in love. Still . . .

"For goodness sake, will you look at this," Drayton muttered in Theodosia's ear.

She turned her head back to focus on the activity in the front of the church.

"Russell Weller," she breathed.

Russell Weller, Roger's business partner, was taking his place at the podium. Unrolling a crumpled piece of paper, he flattened it with both hands then stared straight out at the congregation, his face devoid of expression, light glinting off his steel-rimmed glasses.

Could Russell Weller have wanted to get rid of his partner for good? Theodosia wondered. *Possibly. But being somewhat antisocial, Russell Weller probably hadn't attended the Poet's Tea. Which means he would have to be in collusion with Simone. Which sounded way too much like a wacky conspiracy theory.*

"Can you believe that old fellow's been tapped to deliver

the eulogy?" whispered Drayton. "Even though he and Roger rarely spoke."

"Thank god he's not wearing that awful suit," Theodosia whispered back.

Forty minutes later the memorial service was concluded. Vespers had been uttered, hymns sung, and eulogies delivered just as floral sprays and bouquets began to visibly droop.

Theodosia and Drayton pushed their way outside to mingle on the front steps and catch a welcome breath of fresh air.

"My, the church was warm today," Delaine announced loudly, fanning herself with her hand and slipping off her jacket. "Or maybe it's all that champagne I drank last night," she joked.

"We went through a few dozen cases," said Maribo. Her dark hair swept upward, makeup impeccable, she looked like she was still reveling in last night's success. "But it was well worth it. A turnout like that is absolutely thrilling."

"You deserve every success," Drayton assured her.

"Say now," said Delaine, "you two are heading right back to the tea shop, right?"

"Of course," said Drayton. "There's work to be done, luncheons to be served."

"Well I think Maribo and I are going to drop by for lunch then," said Delaine. She turned toward Maribo. "That okay with you?"

"Great," said Maribo, smiling at Drayton. "I love your tea shop. And truth be told, I'm ravenously hungry. I was so swamped with loose ends this morning I didn't have time for breakfast."

"Ta-ta," called Delaine as she moved off. "See you two in a little bit."

"Later," said Drayton. "Goodness," he murmured. "Where on earth does Delaine get her energy from? Is she solar powered? Hydrogen powered? The woman just never *quits.*"

"Delaine's still in low gear," warned Theodosia. "Wait till she gets a little lunch in her. She'll probably crank into overdrive and regale us with details of her date with Jester Moody."

"I sincerely hope not," said Drayton, looking aghast. "Say, there's Timothy Neville over there. I need to have a word with him. Do you mind?"

"Not at all," said Theodosia as they watched Timothy gravely shake hands with Simone Crispin. "He looks worried," she added. "I hope the Rembrandt Peale fetches as much as he hopes it will Saturday night."

"How do you know about that?" Drayton asked sharply.

"Timothy showed it to me," said Theodosia. "Yesterday, when I went over to pick up the tray."

"Ah," said Drayton. "Either Timothy's not as good at keeping secrets as he used to be or he's *really* worried about money."

"*You realize Church* Street derived its named because of this very edifice," rumbled a low voice at Theodosia's elbow.

She turned to find Burt Tidwell's beady eyes gazing at her.

"You realize," she said, "this is the second incarnation of St. Philip's. The first one being destroyed by fire in the early eighteen hundreds."

"But the graveyard is the same," said Tidwell. Indeed, the graveyard flanking the Old World–style church contained the remains of signers of the Declaration of Independence and U.S. Constitution as well as a former vice president.

"I figured you'd show up here," said Theodosia. She hadn't spotted Tidwell inside during the service when she was gawking around, but figured he'd somehow make his presence known.

"Of course you did," replied Tidwell. "I've been channeling the Swamp Fox," he said, making reference to Francis Marion, South Carolina's Revolutionary War hero and guerrilla fighter. "Like an ethereal spirit from the forests and swamps, you never know when I'll spring from the mists."

Theodosia gazed at Tidwell. *An ethereal spirit with an expanding waistline,* she thought, but was too polite to say. Still, she had to allow that Tidwell did have a certain *Now you see me, now you don't* quality about him. Probably the hallmark of a savvy investigator.

"I have something for you," said Theodosia, edging out of the mainstream of people who were still milling about.

"Goody," said Tidwell, edging with her.

Reaching into her handbag, Theodosia pulled out a plastic baggy stuffed full of the feathers she and Haley had retrieved from Simone's country house yesterday. "Here," she said, handing it over.

Tidwell frowned. "More feathers. The lady has just presented me with additional feathers."

"Just take them, will you?" hissed Theodosia. She really didn't want people to see her slipping what could be incriminating evidence to Detective Tidwell. Especially if the evidence served to incriminate Simone Crispin!

"I'm going to need more," he told her, giving the little baggy a tentative shake.

Puzzled, Theodosia just stared at him. "What? You mean to run tests on?"

"No, to complete my featherbed sometime during this decade."

"Please don't be impossible," she told him. "I'll have you know I risked life and limb to get those."

Tidwell turned and stared into the crowd. "It wasn't a feather," he muttered out of the side of his mouth.

Blinking, not quite believing what she'd just heard, Theodosia said, "What? What wasn't a feather?" Now she was almost sputtering. "What are you talking about?"

"I'm referring to the first packet you gave me."

"You're kidding," said Theodosia. "Not a feather? Well, it certainly *looked* like a feather." She suddenly felt deflated, like the air and all her energy had suddenly run right out of her.

"The first rule of smart investigating is not to rely solely on your eyes," Tidwell told her in a maddening, lecturing tone. "One must also employ evidentiary testing practices."

"So you're telling me the evidence I collected at the Heritage Society was . . . what?"

Tidwell grimaced. "Organic material. Something that's been bleached and probably processed."

"Organic material?" said Theodosia. "What are we talking about here?"

"Best guess would be fur or hair," said Tidwell. "We're

not one hundred percent sure yet. Our crackerjack lab rats are still working on it. Running their tests."

Theodosia thought about all the fuzz, flosses, and fibers that were strewn about in Gracie Venable's workshop and her heart sank. This wasn't good. This wasn't good at all, she decided.

"You look utterly bereft," said Tidwell, a slightly puzzled look on his broad face. "And here I thought you'd be pleased. You who are so imbued with investigative curiosity."

Taking a deep breath, feeling regretful at what she was about to disclose, Theodosia said, "There's something else."

Tidwell's eyes narrowed. "What?" he asked in a wheedling tone. "Tell me."

"Gracie's trying to sell a pendant that Roger Crispin gave her," said Theodosia, feeling intensely disloyal. "As a gift. It's a pretty little egg pendant, a newer Faberge piece that she took to Heart's Desire for consignment."

Tidwell's big head seemed to nod of its own accord. "Yes, it's quite obvious they were much more than friends, Roger Crispin and this Gracie Venable. People do so love to talk, you know."

Theodosia squirmed. "I know."

"Yet you are still convinced of this woman's innocence?"

"I . . . don't believe Gracie harbored any . . . uh . . . destructive thoughts toward Roger," said Theodosia.

"Not a very clear-cut answer," said Tidwell, peering at her with hooded eyes.

"It's not a clear-cut matter," replied Theodosia.

15

❧

"*Funerals are so* upsetting," complained Delaine. "I'm feeling downright discombobulated." She lifted her shoulders to her ears then stretched her arms overhead in a languid gesture.

Lounging at the little table next to the stone fireplace, Delaine and Maribo looked positively relaxed while Theodosia and Drayton scurried about like madmen, ferrying steaming pots of tea and serving lunch to what had turned out to be a full house. Roger Crispin's funeral had lasted until after eleven, so things were more than a little backed up at the Indigo Tea Shop. Haley had held down the fort this morning with the very capable assistance of Miss Dimple, but lunch was a trickier matter.

"Oh, Drayton, dear," Delaine called in a loud voice, "could we get a little service please?"

Miss Dimple was front and center at Delaine's table in a heartbeat. "What can I get you, honey?" she asked, ready to present the little luncheon menus that Haley had run off on the computer this morning. "Want to start with a nice cup of tea? Maybe a Formosan Pouchong or a nice Dragonwell?"

But Delaine waved her off. "We prefer to have Drayton take care of us personally," she said, her manner just this side of haughty. "We're *special* customers."

"Suit yourself," said Miss Dimple as she scurried off to attend to the other tables.

Satisfied that all their customers had luncheon plates in front of them as well as refills on tea, Drayton finally popped over to Delaine and Maribo's table. "Would you care for some Dragonwell tea?" he asked, holding up a teapot. "It's a classic Chinese green tea. Very light and refreshing with a slightly sweet aftertaste."

"It's your own blend?" asked Delaine.

"Ah," said Drayton, "if it's *custom* blending you desire I have a vanilla cream fruit tea. A black tea carefully blended with hibiscus flowers, apple bits, and rose hips flavored with a bit of vanilla. Slightly nontraditional, but delightful just the same. I call it our White Point Blend, after our lovely White Point Gardens down on the Battery."

"Sounds awfully yummy," said Delaine. "I think I'd like to try it."

"Me, too," smiled Maribo. Though far less demanding, she hadn't gone out of her way to try to settle Delaine down.

"And we have two different lunch offerings today," Drayton continued. "Smoked turkey pâté on pumpernickel with a mixed green salad or cheese and mushroom quiche. Plus we've still got pumpkin scones left from this morning and I believe Haley has miniature cheesecakes for dessert."

After a few moments of consultation and indecision, Delaine and Maribo both opted for the cheese and mushroom quiche. But only if Delaine could have a tiny side salad topped with some of Haley's famous buttermilk dressing.

"We're running around like banshees," Drayton complained to Theodosia when he was back at the counter, "and Delaine is sitting there holding court like a grand duchess!"

"Of course," said Theodosia. "She's always that way, it's her personality. We're type A's, she's type M—maddening!"

Theodosia knew that the things that drove you nuts about Delaine were also the same traits that drove Delaine to excel. She was a whirlwind when it came to selling tickets for the Lamplighter Tour, surpassing everyone in sight. And Delaine could wheedle donations with the best of them. If the Hospital Aid Association was short on funds and wanted to solicit a curmudgeony millionaire, they sent Delaine in to work her magic. She'd flirt, cajole, and bully until she got her way. And she always got her way.

But, thought Theodosia, *you paid a price for Delaine. She could drive you a little crazy.*

"I hope you're saving room for Haley's miniature cheesecakes," said Theodosia, stopping by Delaine and Maribo's table a few minutes later.

"Are you insane?" shrilled Delaine. "Those things are like a *gazillion* calories."

"Oh no," said Theodosia, tipping her tray down for Delaine to see. Two Chinese blue and white plates each held a miniature cheesecake creation. Artfully drizzled with strawberry sauce, of course. "I can't imagine these desserts would even count, they're so tiny."

Delaine's arched eyebrows shot up. "You really think so?"

Theodosia was doing a masterful job at keeping a straight face. *A little sugar and a few calories aren't going to hurt her,* she told herself. *And after all, Delaine is dying for me to give her permission to eat this. Right?*

"I guess I *would* like a dessert after all," declared Delaine. "What about you, Maribo?"

"Count me in, they look wonderful." Maribo tilted her head and gave a wistful smile. "Gee, this is a great little tea shop. So cozy and quaint. I feel absolutely special when I step in here. My pulse stops racing and I even breathe a little slower. What a kick to leave the hurly-burly world behind for a while and step back into a gracious, more genteel time."

"Like Alice tumbling down the rabbit hole?" asked Theodosia. "But without all the crazy running around."

"And without the mad queen," added Delaine.

"Exactly!" said Maribo, gazing around. "A tea shop is a whole 'nother world. A place where you can decompress."

"Delaine," said Theodosia, suddenly turning serious as she cleared away their luncheon plates and placed their desserts in front of them. "Do you remember seeing Simone at the Poet's Tea last Sunday night?"

Delaine shook her head slowly. "Mm . . . I don't think so."

"You're still puzzling over Roger Crispin's murder, aren't you?" said Maribo. "You're such a good soul. Drayton was telling me last night that the police were leaning hard toward your friend Gracie Venable, but that you're trying to clear her name."

Theodosia shrugged. "Or shake something loose," she said.

Maribo reached out and put a hand on Theodosia's arm. "Bless your sweet, pure spirit," she said. "If there were only more people like you, the world would be a far better place."

"Say now," said Delaine, "I have a sensational idea. Speaking of Gracie Venable, why don't we drop by her new hat shop."

"What a good idea," enthused Maribo. "It'd be a kind of nonverbal way of showing our support. But are you sure she's even open?"

"Her official grand opening with all the hoopla is scheduled for tomorrow," said Theodosia. "But I'm pretty sure Bow Geste is open for business today. A quiet opening, as they say in retail."

"Wonderful," said Maribo. "Because I feel like celebrating last night's big success with a quick shop."

Delaine's eyes lit up like twin beacons. "Then we should definitely swing by Cotton Duck as well," she purred. "After all, a hat may be a lovely little accessory, but a woman's personal style is truly defined by her wardrobe!"

Theodosia was still pondering Tidwell's words from that morning as she waited for Drayton to prepare a pot of Ceylon black tea from the Dimbula district. This was a special request from a group of four ladies who had heard raves about Ceylonese teas and wanted to taste one for themselves.

Organic matter, she thought as her eyes traveled idly over the dozens of tea tins stacked behind the counter. *Tidwell said what I found was organic matter, like fur or hair. Hmm.*

"I'm thinking of creating a new blend using Ceylon tea," said Drayton as he efficiently ladled spoonfuls of the dark, rich tea into a chintz teapot, then carefully poured in hot water. "Maybe combine it with an Indian black tea so you have that classic Ceylonese fruitiness layered with something really full-bodied." Drayton reached over and tapped a small tin that held one of his special blends they'd dubbed Drayton's Jade Cloud. It was a delightful blend of Malaysian and Chinese black teas. "This has been a very big seller," he told Theodosia.

Theodosia stared at the tin of Jade Cloud. It was one of about twenty house blends that Drayton had created. Not only were they extremely popular with Indigo Tea Shop customers, but they all sold well via their Web site, too.

Of course, Theodosia had drawn on her background and put real effort into the marketing part. Schmoozing editors and getting feature articles about their house blends into local publications, appearing on Channel 8 in a few tea segments, and creating their distinctive packaging.

Staring at the labels with their elegant brush strokes, something clicked in Theodosia's brain.

Huh? she thought. *What was it that suddenly made my neurons start firing?*

She gazed at the brush marks on the tea labels again and thought how Drayton's skillful calligraphy had come into play. He'd done a masterful job creating Chinese and Japanese dry brush characters for the labels. Customers were always commenting on them. One woman had even tapped Drayton to create a Chinese character she could use as a logo for her Feng Shui business. Drayton had really labored over that little assignment. She remembered that he'd used an antique Chinese ink stone and ground the ink paste himself to get a nice thick ink. Then he'd made countless practice characters with his various brushes.

The thought that had eluded her suddenly came cartwheeling into her brain. *Brushes,* Theodosia thought. *What are brushes usually made from?*

"Drayton," she said, barely able to contain her excitement. "What are calligraphy brushes made from? What materials?"

He carefully placed the teapot on a tray and slid it over to her. "Oh, various things. Camel hair, horse hair, that sort of thing."

"I talked with Tidwell this morning," she said, "while you were chatting with Timothy . . ."

"Yes?" he said, staring at her with a quizzical look.

"He said the fluff I found in the stairwell at the Heritage Society wasn't a feather at all."

"Then what—" Drayton began.

"Tidwell said it was something organic. Like fur or hair."

"Okay," Drayton stared at her, nonplussed.

"Fur or hair could come from a calligraphy brush," said Theodosia.

"I'm sure I'm supposed to make some dramatic leap in logic here," said Drayton. "But for the life of me I just can't seem to find one."

"Jester Moody is into calligraphy," prompted Theodosia. "Jester Moody has a set of calligraphy brushes in his shop!"

"Oh," said Drayton, letting out a deep breath. "*Now* I see where you're headed."

"Which means you've got to go over there and get those

brushes," said Theodosia in a rush. "So we can have them tested."

Drayton reared back in surprise. "I can't just go *borrow* them. I'm sure they retail for hundreds of dollars."

"Four hundred," said Theodosia. "I looked at the price tag."

"That settles it," fretted Drayton. "There's no way we can squander four hundred dollars on a crazy hunch." He hesitated. "Can we?"

Theodosia thought for a moment. "No, but I've got another idea. What if you asked Jester if you could take the brushes on approval. Tell him you just want to hold them or think about them or something like that."

"On approval," Drayton repeated.

"Remember?" said Theodosia, suddenly liking the idea. "Like the old Mystic Stamp Company? When I was a kid they'd send me stamps on approval. Then, if I saw a few I liked, I'd keep the stamps and send them the money."

"I wonder if Mystic Stamp still does that?" said Drayton, a faraway look on his face.

"Never mind whether they still do it," said Theodosia. "The question is, will *you* do it?"

"Yes, yes I will. Since Roger's funeral this morning I've been more upset than ever about his murder. Besides, it . . . it feels like we're too close to quit now."

"Atta boy," said Theodosia. "I'll drive you over to Passports as soon as we close up."

"What are you two whispering about?" asked Delaine as she approached the counter to pay her bill. "You sound so conspiratorial."

"Just making plans for the teacup exchange," said Drayton quickly, knowing how good Delaine's radar was. "You're still coming, aren't you?"

"For a little while," said Delaine. "But I'm a working girl, remember?"

"Indeed, I do," replied Drayton, as he handed her change.

By three-thirty Haley had escaped out the back door, hoofing it down the street to Bow Geste where she was going to help Gracie put the finishing touches on her shop. Haley planned to return to the Indigo Tea Shop around seven or so that evening, so she could bake a few batches of Russian tea cakes and lemon bars for tomorrow. Theodosia had told Haley to just use whatever ingredients they had, but Gracie had insisted on buying her own.

At four o'clock, with everything cleaned up and the tables properly set for tomorrow morning, Theodosia and Drayton were ready to step outside and turn the key in the lock. So of course the phone began to shrill.

"Rats," said Theodosia, slinging her handbag over her shoulder. "Maybe we should just ignore it."

Drayton telegraphed his disapproval with a frown. "Perhaps it's a request for a reservation?"

Theodosia ran back and grabbed for the phone. "Hello? Indigo Tea Shop."

"Exactly who I wanted to talk to," said an upbeat male voice. "I was wondering if you'd like to come over for dinner tomorrow night."

"Uh . . ." began Theodosia.

"This is Parker Scully. I thought I better tell you that just in case you've received a few dozen of these brazen requests already today."

"Yes, I recognized your voice," said Theodosia, even as her brain was telling her to think fast. *Think fast? I feel like I'm almost paralyzed around this guy.*

"So what about it?" asked Parker. "Want to drop by Solstice and watch us be fey and trendy?"

"Actually," said Theodosia, trying to remain cool, "I was planning to stay in tomorrow night."

"Ah," said Parker Scully. "Let me guess. You're about to give me the old 'stay in and wash your hair' line. A wonderful ploy in screwball comedies from the forties but—dare I say it?—a little hackneyed in our zero decade."

"I was actually going to wash my hair *tonight*," laughed Theodosia.

"So was I," said Parker. "So why don't you drop by Solstice tomorrow evening and we'll greatly admire each other's shining tresses."

"You know what I mean," said Theodosia. *Sweet invitation, but . . .*

"Listen," said Parker Scully, suddenly turning serious. "Are you engaged or something? Is there another guy in the picture?"

Theodosia thought about that. She had no ring, just a sort of invitation to marriage. *Was that being engaged? Or was it just more of the loosey-goosey arrangement she and Jory had always had?*

"I'm not sure," she said, managing a half-laugh.

Instead of laughing with her, Parker Scully turned serious.

"I'd love to get to know you," he told her. "But I really don't want to step on some other guy's toes. Or make you feel uncomfortable in any way. That's just not my style."

I like your style, Theodosia thought to herself.

"Can I let you know?" she asked. "You caught me at kind of a bad time."

"Anytime," he told her. "I'll be here."

16

❧

"*He liked you,*" Theodosia told Earl Grey as she fastened his bright blue service dog cape around him. "Tidwell doesn't like many things, but he certainly liked you."

Earl Grey, slightly jazzed because he knew he was about to visit the O'Doud Senior Home tonight, thumped his tail loudly against the side of Theodosia's Jeep and gazed at her with serious brown eyes.

Drayton had picked up the calligraphy brushes from Jester Moody's shop as planned. And then, after placing a call to Tidwell, Theodosia had swung by his home on her way to the senior home.

Theodosia wasn't sure what had amused Tidwell more: her notion that the Chinese brushes might hold a clue or his meeting Earl Grey.

Tidwell had immediately started chiding her about her paranoia, but when she'd actually *shown* him the Chinese brushes, he'd fallen silent. She could see the wheels turning inside his head. He'd managed an indignant *hmph,* but he'd still promised to deliver the brushes to the police lab first thing in the morning. She figured Tidwell had spoken with too many witnesses who'd seen Jester Moody storming about last Sunday night to discount the credibility of the brushes.

Then she'd introduced Tidwell to Earl Grey. What a shocker. The large man had actually gotten down on his knees to talk eye-to-eye with Earl Grey. Had scratched behind Earl Grey's ears, chucked the dog under his furry chin, told him what a good boy he was.

And Earl Grey had responded with the same polite enthusiasm he showed everyone. The polite enthusiasm that said, *I am a trained service dog, and I'm here to brighten your day!*

Trust Earl Grey to know how to handle Tidwell, thought Theodosia. When nobody else could.

"*How do, Earl* Grey," called a friendly voice. Suzette Ellison, one of the night nurses at the O'Doud Senior Home, waved her hand in a friendly greeting. "Good to see you, too, Theodosia," she added.

Theodosia grinned. It was always this way. Then again, it was *supposed* to be this way. Earl Grey was the star tonight. It was his show, his "meet and greet" with the residents.

"You might want to pay a visit to Anna Pinchont," said Suzette. "She's in her room."

"Is her eyesight any better since her corneal transplant?" asked Theodosia.

Suzette shook her head, looking concerned. "Not really. And she says she doesn't think she can endure the stress of going through another one."

"I can't say I blame her," said Theodosia, who was already headed toward Anna's room.

"Knock knock," said Theodosia at the door. "Anybody home?"

"Come in," called a small, papery voice.

Theodosia and Earl Grey pushed through the door. A tiny, birdlike woman with a shock of white hair sat in a rocking chair holding a pastel pink MP-3 player in her lap. Pulling the plugs from her ears she asked, "Who's there?"

"It's Theodosia Browning, Mrs. Pinchont. I've brought Earl Grey for a visit. That is, if you're not too busy."

"Come on in," exclaimed Anna. "I was just listening to a little Smokey Robinson that my grandson downloaded for me. You like Smokey Robinson? The Motown sound?"

"Love it," said Theodosia, leading Earl Grey up to Anna's rocker. Allowing the leash to go limp, she let Earl Grey edge his own way up to Anna.

"My eyes aren't so good, but my ears are perfectly fine. Come closer, doggy. I can hear your toenails clicking against the floor."

"He probably needs a trim," laughed Theodosia. "A *peti*-cure."

Anna spread her arms as Earl Grey laid his head in her lap, just as he was trained to do. She closed her arms slowly about him, then lowered her head to rest her chin atop his head. A smile spread across her lined face. "He feels like suede," she said. "A wonderful suede puppy."

Earl Grey stretched out his neck, easing himself even closer.

"Oh, you like that!" said Anna. "Well so do I." She cupped a hand under his chin and talked to him in a low whisper. "You remind me of a dog I had when I was a little girl. I lived on a farm up by Orangeburg and I had the most wonderful Labrador named Asia. Asia was supposed to be my daddy's hunting dog, but he wasn't much interested in traipsing through swamps and such, so Asia became *my* best friend. And you know what we used to do, me and Asia? We used to have tea parties. Do you know what those are?"

"I think he does," said Theodosia. "In fact, Earl Grey's probably gained a good seven or eight pounds since he's become our official tea shop dog."

"Oh my," said Anna, running her hands along Earl Grey's sides. "Those ribs have to be in here *somewhere*."

Driving home that night, Theodosia felt exhausted but happy. They'd made the rounds that night and, of the dozen or so residents Earl Grey interacted with, he'd brought smiles to all their faces. And of that she was genuinely proud.

It was one thing to be a business owner and resident of a community, enjoying all the benefits there were to be had. It was another thing to give back to that community. To volunteer your time and try to make a difference in people's lives. *A most important thing,* she decided. *Always difficult to find time for, but it felt so good when you finally did.*

When her cell phone shrilled inside her purse, Theodosia almost didn't answer it. Then she remembered it could be Tidwell calling. So she fumbled around, driving one-handed, as she fished the phone out of her bag and popped it open.

"Hello," she said.

"Theodosia?"

It was Jory.

"Hi stranger," she said. She kept her voice light, but she was fairly sure he was able to detect the cautious note that was there, too.

"What's going on?" he asked.

What's going on? I'm on pins and needles waiting to talk to you. Trying to make a decision. Trying to get my mind straight!

Instead she said, "I'm just on my way home with Earl Grey. We were visiting folks at the O'Doud Senior Home tonight."

"Terrific," said Jory, although he didn't sound like he really meant it. There was a long pause and then he said, "Theo, we have to talk."

This doesn't sound good, Theodosia decided.

"About . . . ?" she said.

"About us," said Jory. "Look, are you coming with me or not?"

"When you put it that way," said Theodosia. "How could I resist?"

"I didn't *mean* it that way," said Jory. "Really. It's just that . . ."

"What?" said Theodosia. "What? There's something else going on, isn't there. . . ."

"Yeah," said Jory. "This fellow I work directly under, Harold Pritcher—the one who offered me the deal in New York—he's extremely put out with all your snooping."

"What?" she said, stunned. "What are you talking about?"

"Simone Crispin is raising holy hell around here," said Jory. "She says you're trying to implicate her in her own husband's death."

"And because of some statement I may or may not have made concerning Simone, this Harold Pritcher is taking his frustration out on you?" asked Theodosia. "Look Jory, this doesn't have anything to do with you. When I asked about Crispin and Weller and you told me anything having to do with them was privileged information, that was the end of it."

"But it *wasn't* the end of it," said Jory. "You were seen at the funeral this morning talking to Tidwell. Simone Crispin called here and pretty much burned up the phone lines."

"Oh please," said Theodosia. "I can't control Simone Crispin. I'm certainly not responsible for her actions or her out-of-control paranoia."

"But you're *involved*," said Jory. "Probably a little too involved. And Simone Crispin seems convinced you're out to get her."

"That just isn't true," protested Theodosia. *I'm out to find whoever was responsible for Roger Crispin's death. And to try to get Gracie off the hook.*

"Theodosia," said Jory, "try to see it from my point of view."

"*Your* point of view?" said Theodosia. "What about Gracie Venable's point of view. If Simone stopped pointing fingers herself and started cooperating we'd *all* be a lot better off!"

"Whoa!" said Jory. "You really are taking Gracie Venable's side in all this, aren't you?"

"I'm not taking anyone's side, Jory. I'm just doing what I do."

There was a pregnant pause and then, in a voice dripping with anger, Jory said, "Then maybe you should stick to doing what you do best, Theodosia. Serving tea instead of dishing up wild theories!" There was another pause and then he yelled, "Good-bye!"

"Oh my goodness," Theodosia said out loud, stunned by Jory's harsh words. He'd never yelled at her before. Never even come close.

Oh, my lord.

As if in a trance, Theodosia steered her Jeep toward the curb, eased to a stop, and slid the gear lever into neutral. She sat there for a moment, feeling hot tears well up, then leaned forward and rested her head on the steering wheel.

From his perch in the backseat, Earl Grey listened to his best friend's sobs. Laying his ears against his head, he eased himself forward until he was able to slide his long, furry muzzle into the crook of her arm. Then he sat there, half in the front seat, half in the back, trying his best to lend his silent strength and communicate his unconditional love to Theodosia as she cried her heart out.

17

❧

Dawn always shepherds in a new day. A fresh start. And even though Theodosia's sleep was fitful, her dreams haunted by vague notions of what might have been, a new day also meant a new perspective.

Half of the tea shop was filled with customers this Friday morning, the other half taken over by wreaths, garland, curls of ribbon, and extra cups and saucers. While Drayton stalked the tearoom, pouring steaming cups of English breakfast tea and Yunnan black tea, Theodosia and Haley hurriedly put together additional teacup-laden wreaths and garlands for tomorrow's big teacup exchange.

"We're going to need something for door prizes, too," Drayton told them as he paced nervously. He was still final-izing details for the Heritage Society's big auction tomorrow evening and feeling bogged down. "Have you thought about that yet?" he asked.

"No," said Theodosia. Suffering from lack of sleep, she was feeling more than a little overwhelmed. *Jory hung up on me? Let me go just like that? Woof.*

"What if I put together a few tea baskets?" offered Haley. "You know, a tin of tea, a jar of DuBose Bees Honey, a little silver tea strainer, and maybe a tea candle?"

"Good idea," said Drayton. "Theo, that okay with you?"

Theodosia gave an affirmative nod. "I think we could even do a basket filled with T-Bath products," she said. "We've got plenty of green tea lotion, and I'm pretty sure there's a full case of lavender bath oil tucked away in my office. Toss in a loofah and a bar of that hand-milled soap and you're good to go."

"Great," said Haley. "I have to check on my raisin scones anyway, so I'll run back and grab some of our T-Bath stuff."

"Are you okay?" Drayton asked once Haley was gone.

Theodosia shrugged. "So-so. It seems Jory and I are no more."

Drayton's face sagged. "Oh no. That's terrible."

"It seems I've become a bit inconvenient for him," said Theodosia.

"What on earth are you talking about?" asked Drayton, frowning.

"Simone Crispin—or rather Crispin and Weller—are major clients of Jory's law firm. Long story short, Simone's throwing her weight around like crazy and Jory's afraid my investigating is going to destroy his big career move."

"You mean his move to New York?" asked Drayton. "Which, if you ask me, is a hideous mistake."

Theodosia nodded.

"Somehow I just can't imagine Jory's scenario," said Drayton. "To say that a mere one-hundred-twenty-pound woman has superhuman career-destroying powers sounds very far-fetched to me."

"Try to convince Jory of that," said Theodosia unhappily. She picked up a chipped Sevres porcelain teacup, ran a snippet of ribbon through the handle, and tied it to her wreath, positioning it so the chip didn't show. "And you know what?" she continued. "Even though Haley is still begging me to help clear Gracie's name, I can't for the life of me figure out who could have murdered poor Roger Crispin."

Drayton favored Theodosia with a mournful look. "Maybe Gracie Venable really is guilty."

"That thought has been buzzing around in my brain, too."

"But deep down, in your heart of hearts," said Drayton, "I know you don't really believe that."

Theodosia hesitated. Deep down in her heart of hearts she'd once believed a lot of things. That Jory Davis might be the one for her. That she would someday live happily ever after. That nations would eventually coexist in harmony.

So. Did she believe Gracie was guilty or innocent? Theodosia decided she wasn't going to leap to any conclusions until she heard from Burt Tidwell concerning those brushes. Thus far, her wanton leaping had taken her nowhere.

Five minutes later Tidwell's call came in.

"We have no match," Tidwell told her without preamble.

"The lab ran a few preliminary tests, but they're convinced the two materials are not in any way related."

"Oh no." Theodosia held her hand over the receiver and beckoned to Drayton. "No go on the brushes," she told him.

"You mean no match?" he asked.

Theodosia gave a rueful look and shook her head. Then she turned her attention back to Tidwell.

"There's another problem," Tidwell continued. "Apparently Simone Crispin is extremely friendly with Chief Robert Lords, our illustrious chief of police. They sit on a board of directors together, something to do with art in the parks. Anyway, it seems Simone has been pouring her little heart out to Chief Lords and pushing hard for some sort of action against your friend Gracie Venable."

"I don't much care what Simone is telling people," said Theodosia. "The thing that worries me is, will the chief respond?"

"Unfortunately, he probably will," said Tidwell.

"Which means . . . what?" Theodosia asked him.

"Can't say," said Tidwell cautiously. "But I have a feeling this is all going to come to a head fairly soon."

"Another suspect bites the dust," said Drayton, once Theodosia had hung up.

"Could Jester Moody still have been the one up in the balcony?" asked Theodosia. "The one who shot Roger Crispin?"

Drayton plucked at his bow tie, looking thoughtful. "*Someone* was up there that night, that's for sure. The problem is, maybe that little bit of evidence you discovered is meaningless. Here we are, chasing around like lunatics, making suppositions and building theories, and it could all boil down to nothing at all. Maybe what you found was a little bit of schmutz that the cleaning people missed."

"It could be," said Theodosia. "The thing is, you watch all these crime scene dramas and forensic TV shows and you become convinced that forensic evidence is the big, hot thing. They discover a strand of hair or a shred of cloth and that always leads directly to solving the crime."

"Look what I've got, boys and girls," announced Haley as she came flying out of the kitchen, bearing a large tray. "Nice, hot, English raisin scones ready to serve to all our customers. Plus I whipped up a batch of my special honey butter."

"Excellent," said Drayton. "And not a minute too soon."

There was a five-minute flurry in which the scones and honey butter were delivered to eager customers and the teacups refilled. Then Theodosia and Haley set about clearing away the leftover wreath-and-garland decorations. After all, their luncheon crowd would begin arriving in less than an hour.

"You're coming to the grand opening this afternoon, aren't you?" Haley asked Theodosia as they worked.

"When do the festivities kick off?" she asked. She didn't feel much like dropping by Gracie's shop but knew Haley would be deeply disappointed if she didn't.

"Two o'clock," Haley told her, holding up two fingers to emphasize the time. "But I told Gracie I'd be there nearer to one. To help get everything set up. Hope you don't mind. I've got tomato bisque and spinach puffs all ready for lunch with chocolate eclairs for dessert. Oh, Drayton," she said as Drayton came trooping up to the counter. "I was telling

Theodosia that all you guys have to do is serve the bisque and spinach puffs and top the eclairs with a couple poufs of Devonshire cream. And then maybe clear the tables. I'll be back later in the afternoon to take care of the rest."

"In other words, you've idiot-proofed it," said Drayton.

"Your words, not mine," said Haley, happily.

Theodosia had never seen so many women trying on hats. It was wall-to-wall pandemonium as she edged her way into Bow Geste. Everywhere she looked women in fluttery summer dresses were exclaiming over elegant hats and accessories. It would appear, she decided, that Bow Geste was a smash hit!

Gracie Venable was buzzing about, too, looking delighted, snatching hats from display racks and delivering them to outstretched arms. "We've got to make sure your hat *frames* your face," she told one woman. And to another, "Oh, honey, that brim is awfully wide for your small stature. Let's try this one instead."

Delaine Dish was there, too. Probably, Theodosia figured, Delaine's curiosity had gotten the best of her. Delaine wanted to know exactly how many customers had been drawn to Gracie's grand opening. In fact, it wouldn't be out of character for Delaine to jot down names and send postcards to the ones who'd shown up today!

"Isn't this exciting!" enthused Haley when she spotted Theodosia. She was standing at a table toward the back of the shop, dispensing cups of rose-flavored Darjeeling. Anyone who had a spare hand was also offered a tiny plate on which

Haley had placed two triangle-shaped tea sandwiches filled with cucumber and chicken spread as well as two Russian tea cakes and a sliver of lemon bar. "It looks like Gracie's grand opening is an absolute smash!" Haley told Theodosia.

"And her hats are selling like crazy," added Delaine as she sidled up to the table. Delaine's eyes darted about, taking in the gaggle of delighted customers, the lovely hats that seemed to float from woman to woman, the showy displays of beads and boas, and the constantly ringing cash register. Being the prima donna that she was, it was quite apparent that Delaine wasn't exactly overjoyed that the women of Charleston were going gaga over Gracie's merchandise mix.

"I see you've found another pretty hat," commented Theodosia.

Delaine touched the brim of the delicate straw hat she was wearing, a *different* hat than the custom number she'd worn to the Poet's Tea. "I've heard that sunlight filtered through the very thinnest of straw brims is extremely flattering to the face," Delaine explained. "And there seem to be *dozens* of garden parties popping up on my social calendar."

"Mine too," said Haley, swooshing her long hair behind her ears. "Of course, I'm probably going to be *working* at them."

"Haley's such an *amusing* girl," said Delaine in her most bored tone of voice. "She must keep ya'll in *stitches*."

"Haley's the best pastry chef I've ever had the pleasure to work with," said Theodosia. "And while she certainly keeps us in stitches, she also pretty much keeps us in business."

"Touché," said Delaine with arched eyebrows as she slid off into the crowd.

"Oh my goodness, this has got to be the most exciting day of my *life*," gushed Gracie as she rushed up to greet Theodosia. "I can't believe anything could top the utter joy I'm feeling right now."

"I'm so happy for you," said Theodosia, returning Gracie's enthusiastic hug.

"You are so sweet to lend Haley to me," Gracie chattered as she pushed open the door to her workroom. "And to bring along such wonderful refreshments."

"That was all Haley's doing," said Theodosia as she followed Gracie into her workroom. "Of course, we were all delighted to help, but Haley was the one who worked overtime to whip up the tea sandwiches and cookies."

"And people are loving them," exclaimed Gracie as she pulled a box from underneath one of her worktables. "Now let's see, I thought I had more summer gloves stashed back here somewhere." She stopped suddenly and drew a deep breath. "I declare, I'm going to have a heart attack if I don't calm down."

"Take a breath," urged Theodosia who had experienced the same kind of panic attack when customers poured into the Indigo Tea Shop when they were already bursting at the seams. "Everyone's having a marvelous time trying on hats and nosing about your shop. They're not going to just desert you."

"You're right," said Gracie. "I'm just . . . oh, you know . . . worried."

"About the shop?" asked Theodosia. "About making your monthly nut?" Theodosia knew that finances was the common concern that bound many small-business owners together. That omnipresent worry over making enough money to pay rent, utilities, payroll, and taxes. And then have some left over for yourself.

Gracie wrinkled her nose. "Simone Crispin is calling the shots now as my landlord. And I get the sinking feeling she probably has her attorneys working day and night to find a loophole so she can boot me out of here."

"Simone does seem to play hardball," said Theodosia. *Is that what Jory's working on right now?* she wondered. *Gosh, I hope not.*

Gracie's face softened as she gazed at Theodosia. "I can't thank you enough for all you've done. Haley told me you've really been looking into things. Investigating."

"I'm afraid I keep coming up empty," said Theodosia, giving an apologetic shrug. "Sorry."

"Oh, don't apologize," said Gracie. "It's enough to know you're on my side. The world can be a very cold place when you don't have . . . well, when you don't have someone who cares about you."

"You miss Roger very much don't you?" said Theodosia. *Of course, she does. She has to.*

Gracie nodded furiously even as she wiped at her eyes. "More than you know. If only . . . if only I'd been able to say a proper good-bye to him."

"Honey," said Theodosia, "you had no idea that Roger was going to be shot!"

"That's not what I mean," said Gracie. She stood there with a wistful look on her face, a delicate pair of white lace gloves clutched in her hands. "Roger and I had decided to stop seeing each other," she explained. "We knew our relationship was wrong. We'd been trying to convince ourselves to call it quits for almost a week. I was going to say my final good-byes to him that night . . . at the Poet's Tea. But then Roger was all worked up about something."

"About what?" asked Theodosia. *That's right, Gracie did mention this once before.*

Gracie suddenly looked defeated. "I don't know. Something about the auction, I think."

"The auction?" said Theodosia. *No kidding.*

"I think so. But, like I said, I really don't know for sure. Roger didn't go into it. He just told me he'd returned from a day trip to Savannah and had learned something very important, something rather earth-shattering, to use his words. And then the program began, so he had to dash upstairs to do the slides and things for Drayton's reading." Tears welled in Gracie's eyes. "That was the last time I ever saw Roger alive."

Theodosia put an arm around Gracie's shoulders. "You have to remember the *good* things," she told her even as she wondered what it was Roger had discovered down in Savannah. *What could be earth-shattering?* she asked herself. *And what did it have to do with the Heritage Society's auction?*

A loud *knock knock knock* interrupted Theodosia's thoughts.

"Theodosia?" called Haley. "Gracie? We've got trouble out here." Haley's voice was loud and insistent, carrying a hint of panic.

"What's wrong?" asked Theodosia, flinging the door open.

But instead of running smack-dab into Haley, Detective Neal Beaderman's broad face loomed in the doorway.

"I've got a search warrant, ma'am," said Beaderman. "We need to clear these premises immediately."

"What?" said a stunned Gracie. "You mean tell everyone to *leave*?"

Beaderman was suddenly flanked by two officers in blue uniforms. And out on the sales floor, hats were being laid down nervously and women were watching the strange proceedings with stunned expressions.

"Hold everything," said Theodosia. "You're executing a search warrant *now*?" She shook her head, trying to remain calm, yet telegraphing to the police the notion that this was highly unorthodox. "Come on," she said, trying to put a bantering note in her voice. "You can see there's nothing *illegal* going on here at the moment. Hat stores aren't exactly hotbeds of criminal activity. Why don't you guys back off for a few hours." She lifted a hand to indicate Gracie. "Let this poor woman have her grand opening."

But Beaderman was shaking his head even before she'd finished. "I'm afraid I can't do that," he said.

"Please!" begged Gracie. "This is just gonna *kill* my business!"

Neal Beaderman looked grim but insistent. "Sorry, ma'am, I'm not the one issuing orders."

"You can't . . ." began a sputtering Gracie. But as she looked over the shoulders of the officers, she could see that her gala afternoon had come to a screeching halt. Her shop was clearing out, customers were beginning to scatter.

And then like an avenging angel, Haley appeared. Angry, gruff, infuriated. "Forget it, pal," she told Beaderman. "You're not gonna get away with this."

"Haley," said Theodosia. "Don't. You're not helping matters."

"Theo," Haley pleaded. "You've got to figure something out! They're acting like the gestapo!"

But with that official piece of paper being waved in everyone's face, there was absolutely nothing Theodosia could do.

18

~~~~

Late afternoon sun spilled into the Indigo Tea Shop like spun gold. The pegged wooden floors gleamed, the bricks reflected the mellow light, floor-to-ceiling shelves that held jars and tins of Darjeeling, Chinese black tea, African Redbush, and other wondrous offerings from faraway tea plantations seemed etched in neon.

But for Theodosia, who moved about the tea shop slowly, cleaning and picking up, there was no joy, no basking in the usual afterglow that came from putting in a hard day's work.

Gracie's grand opening at Bow Geste had been utterly ruined. Customers had skulked off, greatly embarrassed for her. Sales had been lost as the police dug and rooted though all her frivolous finery.

And what had they found? Theodosia asked herself. *Nothing. Nada.*

It had all been a big sham. A harassment designed to discredit Gracie. And Simone Crispin had probably been pulling the puppet strings.

As Theodosia brewed herself a cup of Japanese sencha, a faint knock sounded at the door. "I'm sorry, we're closed," she called. Then, when she saw a large, wavering image through the leaded glass, she knew who was standing out there.

"*I'm to blame,*" were Tidwell's first words. "I made mention of the egg pendant. It's circumstantial at best, but it seemed to add fuel to the fire. Then, when Simone Crispin applied pressure to Chief Lords, he presumably thought *he* was doing the right thing." Tidwell sat down heavily in a captain's chair and sighed. "I don't know," he said. "Maybe he was."

"And maybe he wasn't," said Theodosia, pouring Tidwell a cup of tea. "Whatever the case, please don't beat yourself up over it. Everything just got way out of hand. And to be perfectly honest, Simone isn't jumping to conclusions any more than I am. In fact I'm still suspicious that Jester Moody was involved." She paused, glanced at Tidwell who seemed to be deep in thought. "Did the lab ever test those brushes?"

Tidwell nodded. "Oh yes. That's one of the reasons I'm here."

"Well?" Theodosia asked, eyeing him cautiously.

Tidwell shook his huge head and his jowls sloshed sideways. Then he stared at her. "We got a hit back from the Fish and Game Department. It's elk."

"What's elk?" asked Theodosia, thinking this was some kind of non sequitur Tidwell had engineered just to rattle her.

"The feather you retrieved wasn't a feather at all. It's a bit of elk hair." He picked up his teacup, polishing off half of his beverage in one gigantic gulp.

As Tidwell's words sank in, Theodosia felt both stunned and puzzled. "Good heavens," she exclaimed. "Who raises elk around here?"

"No doubt the South Carolina Elk Ranchers Association," replied Tidwell.

"I didn't know there was one," said Theodosia. This was news to her.

"There isn't," said Tidwell. "I was just trying to be droll."

"Please don't," said Theodosia. "Things are bad enough already." She thought for a moment. "So the brushes we appropriated from Jester Moody's shop were . . . ?"

"Camel hair. *Old* camel hair, probably the same poor wretched beasts that once trekked the silk road. But camel hair just the same."

"Rats," said Theodosia.

"No," said Tidwell, as Theodosia picked up the little ceramic teapot that sat between them and topped off his cup. "We found none of that."

"Then we're back to square one," she said, ignoring his strange attempt at humor.

Tidwell's eyes carried a low gleam. "The possibility does exist, you know, that your friend is guilty."

"I still don't believe Gracie resorted to murder," said Theodosia. "If you could have heard the way she talked about Roger today . . ."

"Greed . . . anger," murmured Tidwell. "Those are primary motivators that drive people to murder. Even unrequited love . . ." Tidwell's voice trailed off as he took a sip of tea. "Well, you know—"

"No, I don't," said Theodosia. "I really don't."

Long shadows stretched across the sidewalk as Theodosia stepped up to the front door of the three-story redbrick building that Crispin and Weller Auction House called home. Pausing at the front door, Theodosia glanced at the high-tech security camera overhead, wondered if anyone was watching her, then rang the bell. From deep within the old building, she heard a faint chime.

After waiting thirty seconds, Theodosia pressed the bell again. There was a click and a buzz and then a tinny voice announced, "We're closed."

That's Simone's voice, thought Theodosia.

"Please," she called, "this is Theodosia Browning. I need to talk to you for a moment."

There was another annoying click and buzz and then nothing.

Is that it? thought Theodosia. *Simone's just going to leave me standing here?*

But a few moments later, a latch rattled open and the ponderous front door swung back on creaking hinges.

"What?" said an impatient-sounding Simone. Her face appeared in the eight inches of space she'd allowed the door to open.

"I need to talk to you," said Theodosia. "Please, it's important."

Anger was apparent in Simone's patrician face. "I told you, we're *closed*."

"No, you're not," said Theodosia, sticking her foot in the door so Simone couldn't just shut her out. "You can spare five minutes, I know you can." She knew she was acting impulsively, she knew Jory wouldn't approve. But what was she to him now anyway?

Simone's eyebrows shot up. "You're very bold," she said.

"More like persistent," said Theodosia. She knew she had to tread cautiously. To anger Simone would be to end this little exchange permanently.

Simone seemed to relax a bit. The anger that had flared across her face seemed to have dimmed. "You wanted to ask me something? What? What is it?"

"May I come in?" asked Theodosia.

"No. And please hurry. I have an appointment this evening."

Theodosia wondered if Simone's appointment had to do with one of the many boards of directors she sat on. Or the large roster of charity events she attended.

"What did Crispin and Weller donate to the Heritage Society's Spring Auction?" Theodosia asked.

Now Simone just looked perplexed. "To the auction? It was . . . let me think . . . oh yes, a painting by Barnard Parish. Nice, but nothing spectacular."

"Simone," said Theodosia. "May I call you Simone?"

Simone lifted a shoulder imperceptibly.

"How much do you trust Russell Weller?" Theodosia asked, knowing Simone might very well be the one who was not to be trusted. Or even believed, for that matter.

Amazingly, that question served to disarm Simone. She smirked, then gave a short, derisive laugh. "You can't be serious. It doesn't matter whether I trust him or not. Weller has barely ten percent interest in this auction house. In fact, now that I also control Roger's share, I can finally put him out to pasture."

"A power play," said Theodosia. *Motive enough to kill one's husband? Maybe.*

"Why not," said Simone, looking pleased.

"One more question, if I may," said Theodosia. "I understand that Roger drove down to Savannah last Sunday. I'm trying to figure out if that trip was in any way connected to his death."

"Are you kidding?" Simone snapped back. "He was probably with that little tart. I wouldn't trust her as far as I could throw her."

Theodosia thought about this. *Yes, Simone might be right. Roger and Gracie could have been together. Gracie could have lied. And Simone could be getting her revenge by setting Gracie up. Could have also gotten her revenge by murdering Roger.*

"Will you please leave now?" asked Simone.

Theodosia hesitated. "Simone, could I look at Roger's calendar? Would you let me do that without calling your law firm and stirring up a hornet's nest?"

Simone stared back, a disgusted look on her face.

"Come on Simone," urged Theodosia. "Do the right thing

here. It'll take five minutes and then I'll be out of your hair. Permanently."

Simone heaved a gigantic sigh. "You're very persistent, aren't you? Why on earth should I allow you to poke into this firm's personal records?"

"Believe it or not," said Theodosia, "I want exactly what you want."

"And that is . . . ?"

"Justice," said Theodosia, staring Simone directly in the eye. "Call me old-fashioned, but I still adhere to the tried and true notion of justice."

Theodosia's declaration seemed to stop Simone dead in her tracks. Eyes narrowed, she gazed at Theodosia as if weighing the situation. Finally, the door creaked open another foot. Simone was inviting her into the inner sanctum.

"Very well," said Simone. "Just this one thing. But that's it. No more questions, no more snoopy visits."

"Cross my heart," said Theodosia, as she followed Simone down the dark corridor.

Traffic was in a snarl in the antiques district. Friday evening meant tourists were pouring into Charleston, eager to kick off their weekend getaways. A chance to poke in art and antique shops, stroll the magnificent coastal Battery, dine on succulent sweet shrimp and fresh-caught crabs, and drink in the romantic atmosphere that was Charleston.

Which meant Theodosia's mind was half consumed with

carefully negotiating the crowded streets while the other half pondered the words she'd discovered on Roger's calendar.

She'd found only two words scrawled in Roger's loopy handwriting. *Jeanty* and *Barakat.*

What did they refer to? Theodosia wondered. *Restaurants? Antique shops? Or were these just names of friends?*

She'd asked Simone, but the woman just stood there shaking her head. Theodosia didn't know if Simone was being coy or genuinely had no idea what they meant. Either way, she felt she was in no position to do any more pushing.

If she had to venture a guess, Theodosia decided she'd have to go with antique shops. Antiques were Roger's business, so prowling through a couple Savannah antique shops would have been right up his alley.

Just as Theodosia squeaked across Logan on a yellow light, her cell phone rang. She fumbled for it, then hit the receive button.

"Theodosia," said Jory Davis as she put the phone to her ear.

A spark of anger ignited within Theodosia. "Did she call you already?" Theodosia demanded. *Crap. I should have known Simone would be on the phone to Jory two seconds after I left.*

"Did who call me?" was Jory's puzzled response.

Oops, looks like Simone didn't call him after all.

"Sorry," said Theodosia. "I thought you were someone else."

"Really," said Jory. Now he *did* sound suspicious.

"What do you want?" asked Theodosia cautiously.

Jory's words tumbled out at her. "I'm sorry I yelled at you last night, Theo. Really. My frustration got the better of me and I completely lost it, as you probably noticed." He paused. "Listen, I still care deeply about you. We're a team, we're . . ." he fumbled for the right words. "We're soul mates."

I thought we were, too, Theodosia thought to herself.

"I really want you to come to New York with me," continued Jory.

"That's probably not going to happen," said Theodosia slowly. "I think we both know that."

Silence and frustration hung heavy between them. Neither wanted to give up on the other so abruptly. And then Jory said, "Okay, but here's the thing: I'm still going. I don't know for how long, but I pretty much have to go if I want to make senior partner around here." He paused again. "Does that change anything?" His voice softened. "Does that change your mind?"

"No, not really," said Theodosia. Sitting at a stoplight, she stared out the side window of her Jeep. A white-haired couple who had to be in their seventies were standing on the sidewalk, gazing into March Forth Antiques. As the woman pointed to something, her husband put an arm around her and bent his head down to kiss the top of the head. Theodosia's heart ached at the tenderness of the scene.

"I don't want to give up on us," said Jory. "Can we still see each other? I'll be commuting back and forth. Can we stay friends?"

"Of course," said Theodosia, her voice suddenly sounding thick.

"I still love you," said Jory. "You know that, don't you?" He sounded like he was ready about to cry.

"Love you, too," said Theodosia as she clicked off the

phone. She sat there, wondering just what had happened between them. Had Jory's career goals been far stronger than
their relationship? Perhaps. Did he intend to jilt her and this
was the most humane way? Maybe.

Or maybe, she thought, *maybe our relationship just ran its
course. Maybe we just sputtered out. Not with bang but a whimper.
Good friends, just not good candidates for wedded bliss.*

Not thirty seconds later her phone shrilled again.

Jory's calling back? she wondered.

"You know," she said into the phone. "I'm going to need
some time to get my arms around this."

"Take all the time you want," came a voice. Not Jory's.

Whoops. "Oh . . . sorry," said Theodosia. *Who is this? Uh
oh, I think it's . . . Parker Scully?*

"This is Parker," he said, confirming her suspicions.
"Uh . . . are you at home?"

"No," she told him. "Stuck in traffic."

"And where might that be?"

Theodosia squinted at the street sign up ahead. "I'm edging down King Street just crossing Lenwood."

"Excellent," replied Parker. "You can swing by Solstice.
Just hang a left at Legare then a right at Market Street.
We'll turn the homing beacon on for you."

"I can't stop by tonight," she told him.

"I was afraid you'd say that," he said. "But I had to give
it a shot."

Theodosia hesitated. *Should I? Could I?* "No, not tonight," she told him again.

"Okay, suit yourself," said Parker. "But I'm not about to
quit on this."

A few blocks later, Theodosia had a major change of heart. *Wait a minute. I'm going to go home and mope around when I could maybe go over to Solstice and have a drink with a somewhat interesting man?* She thought about that for a few moments. *Am I on the rebound here? Is my head sort of spinning? Yeah, maybe. Would I feel disloyal? Probably. Is that a really awful thing? Mmm . . . maybe not.*

Pulling over to the curb, Theodosia found herself outside the front door of the Funky Bubble, a music club know for its jazz, bluegrass, and rockabilly venues. People were already piling in. And they all looked like they were ready to have a rockin' good time.

She dug inside her Tommy Bahama handbag, hunting for the business card Parker Scully had given her a few days earlier when she'd run into him at the Segrova Gallery.

Finally, at the very bottom of her bag she found his card. It was dog-eared but relatively intact, nestled next to a pack of breath mints and an old ticket stub. Popping a mint in her mouth, Theodosia glanced at the number he'd written on the card, then dialed his cell phone. Yes, she'd tell Parker Scully she was going to stop by after all. Only for a few minutes, of course. But she was for sure going to stop by.

19

Gold mesh bags, cinnamon sticks, paper tubes filled with sugar, truffles wrapped in gold foil, and delicate glassine bags of loose tea lay on the front counter of the Indigo Tea Shop. All tiny treasures that would soon be transformed into tea party favors.

"Hurry it up," Drayton called to Haley as she moved from table to table, putting out small crystal vigil lights with white candles. "We still need to run through the menu and serving order."

"What do you want me to do?" asked Theodosia. She'd just finished folding and arranging white linen napkins and placing tall glass vases filled with fresh-cut red roses and viburnum on all the tables. And even though she was still reeling from the aftereffects of yesterday's strange occurrence at Bow

Geste, her meeting with Simone, and her impromptu date with Parker Scully, Theodosia knew she had to be sharp today. Because today Drayton's long-awaited teacup exchange was taking place.

Drayton held up a single finger as Theodosia watched him glance nervously about the tea shop, and her first smile of the day crept across her face. Drayton was running through his mental checklist. Cups and saucers, check. Fresh flowers, check. Linens folded, silverware placed just so, check.

"It's going to be wonderful," she told him. "But, please, put me to work." She had spent most of the morning in her office, updating their Web site. She'd even glanced through Drayton's auction list for tonight to see if anything might ring a bell in regard to Roger Crispin's murder. Unfortunately, nothing had.

"You, my dear," said Drayton, "can help me ready the tea and teapots." He glanced at the ancient Piaget that circled his wrist and frowned. "We're getting dreadfully tight on time."

"Then I'll finish up the favors," offered Haley.

"I'd feel better if you remained in the kitchen," said Drayton. "Doing what you do best. We'll get Miss Dimple to tackle the favors when she arrives."

"Hey," said Haley, holding her hands up in mock surrender. "No problem. I've got plenty to do."

"Right," said Drayton slowly. He scratched his head, looking even more perplexed.

"What?" said Theodosia. "What's wrong?"

"So we'll serve the maple nut scones first," said Drayton, struggling to keep all his planning straight in his head.

"Maple nut scones with streusel *topping*," corrected Haley. "And we're using the little dishes with three sections because we're pulling out all the stops. Devonshire cream, lemon curd, *and* jelly."

"With a first course like that our guests will think they died and went to heaven," said Theodosia. "It probably doesn't matter what we serve next."

"Don't say that," scolded Drayton. "Because we're serving an incredible lineup of savories and pastries." He ticked each item off on his fingers. "Honey pecan chicken tea sandwiches. Date cream cheese sandwiches. Vinaigrette asparagus wrapped in proscuitto. Tiny fruit compote. Coconut biscuits. Flourless chocolate cake. And apricot tartlets."

"But once the scones are served we're putting everything out on big three-tiered serving trays," Haley explained to Theodosia. "Tea sandwiches, asparagus and ham, and all the biscuits and desserts. Drayton thinks it's simpler that way, since we've got such a large crowd coming in."

"Simplification does lead to efficiency," said Drayton, "but I'm far more concerned with elegant presentation. I want the overall impression to be one of incredible abundance!"

"Absolutely," said Haley, giving Theodosia a surreptitious wink. "Abundance is good and presentation is everything."

Five minutes later Miss Dimple breezed in.

"Sorry I'm late," she called out cheerily.

"You're not late," said Drayton, handing her the mesh bags and all the fixings. "You're actually right on time."

"Thanks for coming in," said Theodosia, as she pulled a dozen or so different teapots down from overhead shelves.

"We really appreciate your giving up your Saturday to help out here."

"No problem," said Miss Dimple, her plump face arranging itself in a wide smile. "Besides, it's *fun* working here. I get such a kick hanging around all of you. And serving tea is so much like old-fashioned visiting and Southern hospitality. You know, being nice to people. Taking care of them." Miss Dimple glanced around the tearoom, taking in the newly created wreaths and garlands, the elegantly set tables, the flickering candles, the extra chairs wedged in around the tables. "You've got a big crowd coming in today for the . . . what is it you're having again?"

"Teacup exchange," explained Drayton. "Everyone is bringing a teacup in a gift bag. We'll arrange them all on the sideboard and, at the appropriate time, numbers will be drawn to determine the order of selection."

"Like a lottery," said Miss Dimple.

Dayton's eyebrows edged up. "I prefer to think of it more as a forum for sharing artistic tastes. Lottery sounds a trifle crass."

"Okay then," said Miss Dimple, staring at Drayton from behind her thick lenses. "Are these going to be new teacups or old teacups?"

"Could be either," answered Drayton. "Obviously some people will bring teacups that are, shall we say, a tad more collectible. Others will dash out and purchase contemporary teacups. But all types and styles of teacups are welcome."

"I guess that's what makes it fun," said Miss Dimple.

"Exactly," said Drayton, reaching for a silver tin of Darjeeling that had arrived only yesterday via Federal Express.

"You're serving how many teas today?" Theodosia asked him.

"Three . . . well, technically four," answered Drayton. "A Formosan oolong, this new Darjeeling called Risheehat, and my own blend of Ceylon black tea with a pear essence. The one we dubbed Ashley River Royal. Then, because it turned out to be such a warm day, I'm also making sweet tea."

Theodosia gave a knowing nod. Sweet tea was what Southerners called iced tea. Only it really was supersweet. You made sweet tea by boiling sugar and water together to get a nice syrupy mixture. Then you added your loose tea or tea bags, covered it up, and let it steep—the longer the better. Once the sweet tea was dark and syrupy, you poured in into a large pitcher, added fresh cold water, and served it up. Delightful!

"*The news is* out!" announced Delaine as she breezed into the tea shop, toting her little gift bag, the very first guest to arrive. "Gracie is disgraced and her shop is closed!"

"Closed!" exclaimed Haley. "Are you sure? I thought Bow Geste would be open today!"

Delaine favored Haley with a knowing smile. "Sweetie, it's highly unlikely Bow Geste will ever reopen. Not after the police came storming in yesterday."

"You make it sound like a SWAT team came tumbling out of black helicopters and assaulted the place," grumped Haley. "It wasn't like that at all."

"But it may as well have been," said Delaine. "From what I observed, everyone was horrified. And, if I were Gracie Venable, I'd be absolutely *mortified*."

"I didn't think people were all that horrified," said Theodosia, noting that Delaine was wearing the hat Gracie had created for her. "Most were curious, to be sure. But I think they'll be back to buy. Gracie's not only got a terrific product, but she's a lovely person and, I think, a survivor."

"You're telling me those women yesterday were merely curious observers?" shrilled Delaine. "You think they found that police assault an amusing diversion? No, my dear, yesterday's fiasco at Bow Geste was all my customers could talk about this morning. I went in to Cotton Duck early because we received a shipment of utterly *adorable* white lace camisoles with matching froufrou skirts. And by the time I left to come over here, almost a half dozen of my customers had mentioned it. They'd either been there or heard tales about it. Believe me, bad news travels fast!"

"Oh dear," said Haley, looking more than a little unhappy.

Theodosia wanted to second Haley's *oh dear,* but refrained from doing so. Negativity was not going to get them anywhere. And worrying about Gracie's hurt feelings was not going to move the murder investigation forward. Even though edging the investigation (at least *her* investigation) one inch forward seemed akin to pushing water uphill.

While Delaine wandered about the tea shop, making the odd comment here and there and pestering Drayton, Theodosia pondered the whole situation. Jester Moody had been angry at Roger Crispin the night of the Poet's Tea. And Gracie and Roger were in the throes of breaking up. She didn't know if Simone Crispin had been in attendance or not and had been a little afraid to ask her last night—Theodosia wasn't a big believer in pushing her luck. As for Weller . . . he wasn't looking much like a suspect, either.

On the other hand, she supposed Gracie *could* have been with Roger that afternoon. Gracie could have lied about her whereabouts. So she'd been . . . what? Busy plotting? Waiting for an opportune moment to kill him? Theodosia chewed on her lip and thought about this. But nothing, absolutely nothing, seemed to come together.

"That's a pretty teapot," Delaine told Drayton. She was lounging at the counter, stretching one leg out to admire her new Manolo Blaniks, while she watched Drayton work his magic with tea.

Since Drayton had a captive audience smack-dab in front of him, he did what he always did when faced with that situation. He lectured. Right now he was explaining to Delaine the importance of using the correct teapot.

"You see," he said, "ceramic teapots absorb the oils and essences of teas and take on what's called a lining. For more delicate teas, such as Darjeeling and oolong, one needs to make sure the flavors are kept separate."

"You mean you use a *different* teapot for each tea?" squawked Delaine.

"Of course," responded Drayton, as he fussed with the CD player. An instant later, a selection by the French composer Claude Debussy, always so complementary to tea drinking, flooded the room. "Doesn't everyone?"

At eleven o'clock, the floodgates seemed to open. Maribo Pratt came rushing in to join Delaine. Angie Congdon from the Featherbed House and Brooke Carter Crocket, who owned Heart's Desire, also showed up, along with Hattie Boatwright from Floradora down the street.

And right on their heels, the big guns arrived.

Pookie Wilkes came sailing in, cutting across the floor of the Indigo Tea Shop like the prow of a great ship. A society matron who headed the Ladies Auxiliary of the Glorious Confederate Reenactment Group, Pookie also chaired the Meeting Street Tea Club, of which there were at least sixty members. Pookie, probably in her late fifties, was married to Duke Wilkes, a frail man thirty years her senior, who for years had claimed to be the last living Confederate soldier. Duke got away with his audacious bragging until, finally, one brave soul ventured the opinion that Duke would have to be a hundred and sixty years old for his claim to be valid. Duke was not amused by the young man's insolence and continued to make his Civil War veteran claim, although now he relegated his tall tales to smaller groups of more intimate acquaintances.

"Drayton!" Pookie Wilkes gushed. "You simply *must* join us when we reenact the Battle of Secessionville this September. We've just placed an order for new uniforms," she told him, "complete with fringe and authentic buttons." Pookie's eye roved across Drayton as though he were a chicken about to be selected for Sunday dinner. "I could pretty much guarantee you'd be awarded a plum part. Maybe even the role of Brigadier General Nathan Evans himself."

As he led Pookie and her group to their tables, pulling out chairs and fussing over them, it was obvious Drayton was intrigued by Pookie's offer. "I've done some acting in community theater," he told her. "And of course there's my work at the Heritage Society."

"Drayton's a *pillar* at the Heritage Society," Pookie announced loudly to the women at her table and the tearoom in general. "Practically *runs* the organization. Oh, for heaven's sake!" she exclaimed. "Will you look at these favors . . . and the floral centerpieces. Everything's so *exquisite*!"

"Isn't Pookie married to that Civil War impostor?" Haley asked, as Drayton hustled back to grab pots of tea.

"It's just a tall tale," said Drayton, waving her off. "Doesn't do anyone any harm. Old Duke is simply a history buff. In fact, he spoke at the Heritage Society once."

"Drayton," yelled Pookie. "Tell us about the origin of tea for two, will you?"

"Yes, tell us!" chimed in another group of ladies. Drayton's grasp of tea lore was well known in the community.

"The phrase, tea for two, originated back in the seventeen hundreds," began Drayton, as he made his way around the tables, pouring steaming cups of tea. "As tea gained in popularity throughout Britain, street vendors offered little pots of the wonderful new brew by crying out *tea for tuppence*. Thus, tea for two was originally about price!"

"While we're on the subject," said Delaine. "Could you please explain to us what high tea really is."

"That," said Drayton, "has become a bit blurred of late. High tea *sounds* very fancy and upscale, but afternoon tea is simply not high tea. Rather, high tea is served late afternoon or early evening at a *high table* using regular place settings. The fare is heartier and often includes sliced meats, custards, salads, and various hot dishes.

"You're a veritable fountain of knowledge!" gushed Pookie as Theodosia and Miss Dimple arrived with giant trays bearing Haley's maple nut scones.

With their guests happily sipping tea and devouring scones, they all congregated in the kitchen, helping Haley arrange the rest of the food on her three-tiered serving trays, putting on the finishing touches. Then it was back out to the tea room where refills were poured, teacups topped off, and dishes cleared away. Finally, Haley's scrumptious selections of savories and sweets were borne to the table amidst appreciative choruses of *oohs* and *aahs*.

"Tell me, Theodosia," said Maribo Pratt, eagerly reaching for a cashew chicken tea sandwich. "What's the distinction between the various courses? Your little printed menu lists scones, savories, and pastries." Maribo laughed. "I know I've got the scone part down, and I think I know what pastries are. But what exactly are savories?"

Theodosia was happy to launch into her standard Tea Shop 101 explanation. Savories, she told them, usually consisted of tiny sandwiches or appetizers. These could be tea sandwiches, cheese puffs, tiny bits of meat wrapped in puff pastry, or even smoked salmon and cream cheese pinwheels. And pastries were pretty much what everyone thought they were—cakes, cookies, shortbread, and petit fours. Pretty much anything that was sweet and sugary and delicious.

Forty minutes later, the clink of teacups hitting saucers intermingled with happy and contented groans. Theodosia grinned to herself as she poured tall glasses of sweet tea for Maribo and Brooke. For some reason, a luncheon tea or cream tea always *looked* like a small amount of food. In fact she'd had some hungry customers express concern that they might not get enough to eat. But the reality of the situation was that six or seven small offerings, usually consisting of rather rich food, ended up being amazingly filling. Of course, three or four cups of fresh-brewed tea also helped fill you up!

"A couple of your guests want to take their sandwiches and cookies home," said Miss Dimple. "Should I go ahead and pack those up?"

"Would you?" said Theodosia. She reached over and grabbed a small stack of indigo-blue boxes which, when folded, became a kind of pillow-shaped box. Perfect for toting home leftover scones and tiny sandwiches in style.

As Miss Dimple packed leftovers and Theodosia shuttled dishes and trays to the kitchen, Drayton began the teacup exchange.

Hattie Boatwright had drawn the number one, so she had first choice. Her eyes were immediately drawn to a silver mylar gift bag accented with a hot pink silk flower—really a pin that could be used to adorn a sweater or jacket. Enticing and showy, it was naturally the bag Delaine had brought in.

"Oh my goodness!" exclaimed Hattie when she pulled out a teacup and saucer decorated in a dainty Chinese-style floral motif.

"Lovely," said Drayton. "The Queen Victoria pattern by Herend."

As the teacup exchange continued, Theodosia popped in and out of the tearoom, cleaning up, fussing, putting on a new CD—*The Lark Ascending,* by Ralph Vaughn Williams.

Pookie found a wonderfully contemporary Fitz and Floyd teacup in the bag she chose, Delaine ended up with a Shelley

Primrose Chintz teacup, while other guests exclaimed over pieces by Spode, Wedgewood, Royal Dalton, and Minton.

All in all, Theodosia decided, Drayton's teacup exchange was turning out to be a grand success.

"Theo, dear," said Delaine.

Theodosia whirled about. She hadn't heard Delaine come up to the counter.

"Could I get a glass of sweet tea?" she asked. "It's gettin' kind of warm in here, and I'm not sure I can handle another cup of hot tea."

Pulling out a tall glass, Theodosia filled it to the brim with ice, then trickled in the sweet tea. "Lemon?" she asked.

"Please," said Delaine.

"Delaine," said Theodosia slowly, as she handed the glass of sweet tea to her. "When did you pick up your hat from Gracie?"

Delaine put her fingers to her lips. "*Ssh,* don't tell anybody I got it from her, okay?"

"As you wish," said Theodosia, deciding Delaine was being overly paranoid.

"I picked it up Sunday afternoon," said Delaine.

"Sunday afternoon," said Theodosia. "The day of the Poet's Tea?"

"Yes," said Delaine. "Isn't that what I just said?"

"And Gracie was working on it," said Theodosia, wanting to be very clear on the matter. "She was in her shop."

"Right," said Delaine, taking a quick sip of tea. "Gracie was just finishing up. Putting on little sprigs of flowers." She stopped abruptly and stared at Theodosia. "As I mentioned before, it was a *custom* order."

A custom order, thought Theodosia as she went back to work. *So Roger went down to Savannah alone, after all. Gracie wasn't with him. So what did Roger do down there?*

She tried to sort out what she knew. Gracie's reputation was in shreds, thanks to various machinations. The feather she'd found wasn't really a feather at all, but some weird bit of elk fur. Simone Crispin had pretty much gone mum—she wouldn't be coughing up more information any time soon. And Jester Moody seemed like he might be out of the running as prime suspect. Just having a nasty temper didn't necessarily mean a person was a cold-blooded killer.

So, thought Theodosia, *who's left? And what, if any, clues do I have?*

Pulling a sheet of paper from her pocket, she stared at the two words she'd scribbled down yesterday. *Jeanty* and *Barakat.*

"*Drayton,*" *said Theodosia.* "If I ducked out right now could you hold down the fort?" She stood at the counter, watching him measure out Darjeeling, thinking again that fresh tea leaves made for wonderful aromatherapy.

"Yes, of course," he answered, peering at her over his tortoiseshell glasses. "The teacup exchange is nearly over, I'm just brewing a couple final pots of tea. But where on earth are you off to?"

"Believe it or not, I'm going to make a fast trip down to Savannah," she told him, keeping her voice low.

Drayton's eyebrows shot up. "You're going to Savannah? *Now?* What on earth in Savannah demands your immediate attention?"

Theodosia sighed. Drayton asked a fine passel of questions for which she had no answer. "Actually, Drayton, I'm not even sure. Let's just call it another wild and crazy hunch."

"Oh dear," said Drayton. "These hunches of yours seem to be occurring with greater and greater frequency."

"Maybe I'm just going through a phase," said Theodosia.

"In my estimation," Drayton warned, "your hunches often lead to trouble."

"They sometimes lead to answers, too," she told him.

"Just be careful," was Drayton's stern warning.

"*Where are you* off to, dear?" asked Delaine. She'd been buzzing about the tearoom like a social butterfly, gabbing with everyone, exchanging bits of gossip. But when Delaine saw Theodosia pull off her apron, she rushed over to the counter, convinced something was up.

"Just running an errand," Theodosia told her. *Stay cool, Delaine may be a little paranoid, but she can also be highly perceptive.*

"But you're coming back?" asked Delaine. "I so wanted to talk to you about helping me stage a French tea for my very special customers. The really special ladies who spend *oodles*."

"I'll see you later, Delaine," said Theodosia, putting a note of finality in her voice. *In fact, I'll probably see you tonight. At the Heritage Society's auction. An event for which I no longer have a date.*

"A moment, Theo," said Drayton, as she started to duck between the green velvet curtains.

Theodosia stopped and turned, only to have Drayton hand her a silver thermos bottle.

"A bit of refreshment," he told her.

Theodosia grinned. "Sweet tea?" Trust Drayton to always remember the little niceties.

Drayton nodded. "Of course. The day is warm and the drive a lengthy one."

She reached out and grasped his arm. "Bless you," she told him. "You're always such a lifesaver."

20

Even though Savannah, Georgia, was laid out in an orderly, compact grid, this grande dame city could easily be construed as Charleston's sister city. Savannah enjoyed the same languid pace, spectacular architecture, and ethereal, highly atmospheric environs. A pastiche of pocket-sized parks, narrow lanes with enormous Regency-style homes, and live oaks dripping with Spanish moss, Savannah also boasted gingerbread bungalows and the Gothic grandeur of Bonaventure Cemetery.

Savannah also enjoyed its fair share of ghosts, scandals, and colorful characters. Why, just crack open John Berendt's best-selling book, *Midnight in the Garden of Good and Evil*, and one soon becomes well aware that Savannah fairly shimmers with intrigue.

The one hundred and fifty mile drive from Charleston to Savannah had flown by quickly for Theodosia. She had cruised down Highway 17 through Parkers Ferry and Ashepoo, crossing over countless rivers, bayous, swamps, creeks, inlets, and fishing holes. And even though she'd pressed the pace, keeping the speedometer needle well past sixty, she had reveled in the beauty of the countryside. Here, in this southernmost part of the low country, were heroic stands of pine and fields lined with enormous live oaks. She'd caught glimpses of old plantations and praise houses, too. And had been charmed by the many roadside stands. Stolid little wooden shacks where sweetgrass baskets, tiny creek shrimp, and tomatoes were sold, as well as shad roe from the Edisto River, soft-shell crabs, and fresh-picked strawberries.

Two-thirds of the way down, Theodosia had turned east toward the city of Beaufort. Here was a Southern town that had retained its charm, preserved its architecture, and been immortalized in films such as *The Big Chill, Prince of Tides,* and *Forrest Gump.*

From Beaufort to Savannah was an easy run. Across the Port Royal Sound, skirting the Savannah National Wildlife Refuge, then on into Savannah proper.

Because Theodosia was most familiar with the Old City Market area, just a few blocks from the Savannah River, she drove there first. This was an area where splendid old buildings had been transformed into quaint shops, galleries, restaurants, and clubs.

Theodosia went into the Persian Cat, a combination gift shop and gallery that she'd visited a year or so ago. She nosed about, picked up a tin of Savannah butter cookies for

Drayton and a delightful necklace, a silver dragonfly on a matching chain, for herself.

Then Theodosia asked to borrow their phone book. She hit pay dirt immediately. Barakat, whatever it was, was located just a few blocks away at one twenty-two East Congress Street. Jeanty, however, didn't seem to be listed. Either as a business or a residential number.

Parking near Warren Square, Theodosia checked street addresses as she walked along East Congress and found that she didn't have far to go. Barakat turned out to be an elegant-looking restaurant housed in an old yellow brick building that had been enhanced with dark green awnings and wrought-iron decor.

But on this fine Saturday afternoon, it also appeared to be closed.

Two hours down for this? Now what? Theodosia wondered.

Walking up to the door, Theodosia peered through the glass panes of the handsome double doors into the dim interior. Dark wood, fresh-cut flowers, and a chandelier were visible, and Theodosia could just imagine the dining room with its damask linens, tall flickering tapers, gold chargers, and elegant stemmed wineglasses. A woman, possibly the hostess or manager, was talking on the phone behind a desk in the small reception area.

Knocking on the glass, Theodosia gestured to her. The woman held up a finger as she continued to talk on the phone while jotting something down.

Probably taking a reservation, Theodosia decided.

Then, a smile lighting her face, the woman came out to greet Theodosia. "I'm sorry, we don't open till five," she began as she unlatched the door. "But if you'd like to make a reservation . . ."

"No," said Theodosia, "I'm just doing a little sightseeing in the area. You say the restaurant opens at five every day?"

"Except on Sundays," the woman said. "Then we serve brunch from ten to three. It's really quite a lovely affair. Tomorrow, Chef Joseph is preparing salmon-crusted grouper and venison medallions as our two main entrees. Of course Barakat always offers at least two dozen additional side dishes. Sweet potato cakes, red beans and rice, fried plantains . . . well, you get the idea."

"Sounds fabulous," said Theodosia, who'd begun to feel a little ragged. She'd had breakfast but foregone lunch. "Your restaurant comes highly recommended by a friend of mine," she told the woman. "Roger Crispin. Perhaps you know him?"

The woman's smile never wavered as she shook her head. "Sorry, I don't. But I'm fairly new. I've only been hostessing here for about five weeks."

No answers to be found here, thought Theodosia.

"Okay, thanks anyway," said Theodosia. She hesitated. "Excuse me, but does the word Jeanty mean anything to you?"

This time the hostess looked a little startled. "Are you talking about the Jeanty Gallery?"

"Yes, that's it," said Theodosia.

"It's two doors down."

Bingo! thought Theodosia. "Thanks so much," she told the hostess. "And I really will be back to try that brunch sometime."

* * *

Rod Stewart was crooning the lyrics to Jerome Kern's "The Way You Look Tonight" as Theodosia stepped into the Jeanty Gallery. She recognized the tune as being one of the songs on Stewart's *Great American Songbook,* still one of her all-time favorite CDs.

Colorful paintings as well as black-and-white photographs hung on the gallery's pristine white walls. Gray industrial carpeting and pinpoint spotlights set in high ceilings ensured the artwork took center stage. In the middle of the space, white Formica blocks showcased bronze sculptures, a few pieces of ceramic, and some multicolored hand-blown glass vases.

Against the wall, at the midpoint of the space, sat a large wooden counter with a bookshelf tucked underneath.

"Hello there!" called a young woman as she hurried from the back room to greet Theodosia.

"Hi," said Theodosia, figuring she must have tripped some sort of buzzer. Or maybe there was a camera in back.

"I'm Elizabeth Jeanty," said the young woman who was clad head to toe in black. Black T-shirt, black skirt, black ballet slippers.

"You're the owner," said Theodosia, shaking hands with the woman, who also had a goodly amount of long auburn hair. "I like your hair."

Elizabeth Jeanty brushed at her hair and gave a slightly embarrassed smile. "Clairol. Number 108, Natural Reddish Blond."

"Looks natural," said Theodosia. "You could have fooled me."

"No," laughed the young woman. "*Your* hair looks natural."

"This is a lovely gallery," said Theodosia. "Is it fairly new?"

Elizabeth Jeanty squinted, thinking. "Five months and counting. Pretty new."

"I hope business is brisk," said Theodosia, knowing the art business was a fickle thing. Gallery owners seemed to either make it big or politely starve to death.

Elizabeth Jeanty shrugged. "Business has been building steadily, but it's still tricky coming up with the right artists to showcase as well as the perfect mix of objects. Obviously, we try to appeal to several different markets. Some of our customers are true connoisseurs who buy art because they fall in love with it." She laughed. "Those are the best kind. Of course, others are collectors looking for the hot new thing. And then we get the occasional customer who just wants something colorful to hang over their sofa."

"I'm an art lover," said Theodosia, "who's just shopping around to see what's out there."

"Nothing wrong with that," said Elizabeth. "In fact, most people don't take enough time to look around. Savannah's an up-and-coming art market. We've got photographers and watercolorists who do a spectacular job capturing the haunting beauty of our coastal waters. And wonderful potters and ceramists who draw inspiration from our history and architecture."

"Plus," said a young man, as he emerged from the back of the gallery, balancing a huge stack of prints and posters, "Savannah has a thriving antique market that also deals in old maps, antique prints, and fine oil paintings. So there's really something here for everyone."

"Thank you, Charles," said Elizabeth in a dry tone. "Your input is always appreciated."

"Your husband?" asked a bemused Theodosia. The young man was also dressed completely in black and bore a resemblance to Elizabeth Jeanty, except for the reddish hair.

"My brother," said Elizabeth, making a slight face.

"Do you ever work with dealers in Charleston?" Theodosia asked them. "Or auction houses?"

"Sure," said Elizabeth. "Sometimes. Is that where you're from?"

"Yes," said Theodosia. "Do you by any chance know Roger Crispin?"

Elizabeth Jeanty's face immediately registered the name. "Oh sure. In fact, Mr. Crispin was in a week or so ago. I take it he's a friend of yours."

"Was a friend," said Theodosia. "He's dead."

Her announcement came as shocking news to both of them.

"What!" exclaimed Charles Jeanty, putting a hand to his face. "I had no *idea* Roger Crispin passed away. How *awful*. How *sudden*."

Elizabeth, too, was badly shaken. "What on earth happened?" she asked.

"He was shot," said Theodosia. "The police are still investigating."

"Oh, my *lord*," exclaimed Charles. "What an insane world we live in!"

"How terrible," murmured Elizabeth.

Now that Theodosia had their complete and undivided attention, she decided to press the issue. "You were doing business with him?" she asked.

"Not exactly business," said a stricken Elizabeth. "But, like I said, he stopped in just last week. We talked, exchanged business cards, that kind of thing." She shook her head as if to clear her thoughts. "Wow."

"Mr. Crispin was in on Sunday," said Charles, looking pensive. "I remember because we were having a gallery opening for a wonderful new painter, Flannery Fowler."

"Has there been a funeral?" asked Elizabeth. "Is there somewhere we could send a memorial?"

"I think all memorials are going to the Heritage Society in Charleston," said Theodosia.

"Goodness," said Charles. "What a nasty shock. So the police are . . ."

"Still looking at suspects," said Theodosia. "Sorry to be the bearer of such awful news."

"I'm just glad you told us," said Elizabeth. "Sometimes you don't hear about these things for months and then when you do, you just feel terrible."

"Are these the paintings by Flannery Fowler?" asked Theodosia, turning to inspect a series of impressionist seascapes. Thick swirls of moody blue and dark red tempera paint had been laid on with a palette knife.

"Yes," replied Elizabeth. "We've sold three pieces so far and have six remaining. They're really quite powerful, don't you think?"

Theodosia continued to stare at the paintings, wondering

just what had occurred down here in Savannah last Sunday. She figured maybe Roger Crispin had driven down to meet someone for lunch. But who? Another dealer? A client who wanted Crispin and Weller to handle an auction? Maybe. Probably. And then what? Roger Crispin had wandered over here to the Jeanty Gallery and . . . ?

Theodosia frowned. There didn't seem to be anything here that connected to Roger's death, though. Maybe . . . maybe if she knew who it was Roger had met for brunch. But she didn't think Barakat was about to turn over their reservation book to her. Perhaps she could convince Tidwell to procure a court order.

"Fowler's a terrific painter," she told Elizabeth and Charles, pulling herself out of her musings. "I'm sure you'll do extremely well if you continue to handle this caliber of artist."

"We're trying to," said Charles. "But it is a competitive market."

"I'm sure," said Theodosia, edging toward the door.

"Thanks for stopping by," Elizabeth said, handing her one of the gallery's promotional pieces. "Nice to meet you," she said, looking a little forlorn.

"Sorry about the bad news," responded Theodosia.

Elizabeth nodded. "Come back again, please."

"I will," Theodosia promised.

"You know," murmured Charles, thinking out loud, "the Fowler wasn't what caught his eye."

Theodosia hesitated, then turned. She almost hadn't heard Charles's words. "Pardon?"

Charles was staring at the grouping of sculptures in the center of the room, seemingly in the throes of trying to recall something. "Mr. Crispin was more taken by a painting we had in storage," Charles said slowly. "Well, not really storage . . ."

"That's right," said Elizabeth. "That little landscape we had stashed in our back room. We don't let the general public back there, but dealers . . ." Her voice trickled off.

"Anyway," said Charles, removing one of the glass vases from its pedestal, "Mr. Crispin was quite taken with that particular painting. All I remember is that he wanted to know more about the artist." Charles shrugged, then held up the vase to Elizabeth. "I'm going to exchange this for the green one."

A low hum had suddenly insinuated itself inside Theodosia's brain. *Was there a connection here after all? Albeit a tiny one?*

"Do you still have that painting?" Theodosia asked Elizabeth. "The one Roger was interested in?"

"No," said Elizabeth. "It actually sold a couple days later, right after we moved it out here to the main gallery. One of our regular customers, a woman who lives over near Forsyth Park in the Victorian District, purchased it."

"Too bad," mused Theodosia. She stopped, couldn't think of anything else to ask. Or say. She was about to make her exit for the second time when a thought struck her. "By any chance, do you have a photo?" she asked. "Of the painting Roger was interested in?"

Elizabeth thought for a moment. "We might. It would probably be a black-and-white, though. Not terribly good on detail."

"That's okay," said Theodosia, edging back toward their desk.

Kneeling down, Elizabeth slid out a file drawer, then her fingers walked down the row of folders. "Here it is." She pulled out a manila file folder, flipped it opened. "Oops, not much here."

"Let me see," said Theodosia.

Elizabeth handed her a sheet of paper. But it was text only, no photos.

"But no photo," said Theodosia, disappointed.

"Guess not," said Elizabeth, looking confused. "I thought we had one."

"We did," said Charles, returning with the green vase. "I gave it to Mr. Crispin."

"You gave it to Roger?" asked Theodosia.

Charles nodded. "I kind of forgot about that until now. He seemed so taken with the painting and I thought he was probably going to purchase it."

Theodosia squinted at the page with the bio. "Dan'l Oates," she said. "The artist's first name is Dan'l?"

"That's right," said Elizabeth. "As in Dan'l rhymes with flannel."

"This Dan'l Oates," said Theodosia. "He's a local artist? He lives around here?"

Charles shrugged. "Yes," he said, and his eyes slid over to Elizabeth. "But it's extremely difficult to obtain any of his pieces. I understand Mr. Oates takes his own sweet time with each painting he produces. And last time he stopped in, I pretty much got the impression he was working with one gallery exclusively. It was really just a fluke for us to get the one."

"But you could give me the address of this artist," persisted Theodosia. She didn't know why she was pursuing this, probably shouldn't, except for that tiny vibe that pinged inside her.

This time Charles Jeanty looked downright disappointed by her request, and Theodosia knew he was imagining a lost commission. A client going directly to the artist, cutting out the middle man. Then Charles relented and scrawled an address on a piece of paper.

"Here," he said, all business now. "Good luck to you."

21

❧

Heat and humidity were building as Theodosia drove back down Congress Street. At Bull Street she hung a right, then motored slowly through Savannah proper, admiring the mansions and row houses that offered spectacular examples of Italianate, Regency, Victorian, Gothic Revival, and Second Empire–style architecture. With more than twelve hundred buildings that were of architectural significance, Savannah boasted the nation's largest registered Urban Historic District.

At four twenty-nine Bull Street, Theodosia stopped to admire the Mercer House, a redbrick Italianate mansion that had been the former home of Jim Williams, the notorious bon vivant and antique dealer immortalized in *Midnight in the Garden of Good and Evil*.

Five years ago, Sotheby's had conducted an auction of Williams's most prized possessions, and his paintings, furniture, and collectibles had all sold for hefty amounts. Theodosia remembered Drayton telling her that a silver-and-turquoise dagger, reputedly used in the murder of Rasputin, had fetched a record sum of twenty thousand dollars.

Sitting in her Jeep, air conditioner blowing a cool breeze upon her face, Theodosia wondered what to do. Take a quick drive to the famed Bonaventure Cemetery for a dose of historical sightseeing and then head home? Or try to locate Dan'l Oates? She reached down, grabbed the silver thermos bottle Drayton had given her. Unscrewing the top, she poured out a half cup of sweet tea, sat there enjoying the welcome refreshment, thinking about what her next move should be.

Is this Dan'l Oates thing even worth pursuing? she wondered.

Theodosia watched as a horse draw carriage *clip-clopped* its way down Bull Street, then stopped in front of the Mercer House to disgorge its passengers.

The fact remains, she decided, *that Roger Crispin was down here the same day he was murdered. He must have had brunch with someone, then wandered into the Jeanty Gallery. And I know that he definitely took notice of the Dan'l Oates painting.*

Theodosia frowned. Of course he did. Roger had been an art lover and gallery owner. Or maybe he was just being polite to Elizabeth and Charles Jeanty. Schmoozing them in case they ever wanted to put some art up for auction.

Still . . . there could be a connection.

Digging in her handbag, Theodosia pulled out her sunglasses. The day had been overcast, but now the haze had burned off and the sun was shining with force. And Savannah, jewel that she was, sparkled brilliantly.

Theodosia reached back into her handbag and brought out the crumpled piece of paper Charles Jeanty had given her. Dan'l Oates lived somewhere over near the small town of Bluffton. Off Highway 46 on a backwoods road by the name of—she scanned the paper—Shoals Trail. It was *sort of* on her way home, she surmised. Not too much out of the way, just a small detour.

Even though it seemed like a long shot, her gut feeling told her to check it out.

"Okay," Theodosia said out loud, more to convince herself than anything else. "Then that's what I'm going to do."

At Beaufort, Theodosia swung east, hit Highway 170, and crossed the Broad River Bridge. Watching for her next intersection, charmed by the way the sunlight danced on the saltwater sloughs, she had a sudden flash of inspiration.

The Rembrandt Peale that Timothy was counting on to fetch big bucks tonight came from somewhere down here. Could there be a connection?

Theodosia knew that Roger Crispin had been asked to authenticate the Peale. And she also knew that he'd never really given Timothy Neville a definitive answer. He'd been killed before he could do that. So . . . what?

Had the Rembrandt Peale been stolen? she wondered. *Was it not the genuine article? Is there some weird connection to the piece that was just sold by the Jeanty Gallery?*

Now the jazzed-up feeling that pulsed through her veins

felt even more intense. She pressed forward. Taking what turned out to be a wrong turn, Theodosia looped back and made her correction. Checking directions on the map she kept stashed in her Jeep, Theodosia turned right onto Highway 46 and proceeded more cautiously. Shoals Trail had to be somewhere close by.

The tiny sign for Shoals Trail loomed up out of a clump of mangroves, and Theodosia had to brake fast to make the hard right. Then she was bumping down a rutted dirt road. On either side, marshes and tidal flats shimmered in the late afternoon sun. Cypress and waterlogged pines poked up out of the water. This was the domain of blue crabs and diamondback turtles. Heron and ibises and kingfishers thrived here, too. Probably, she decided, if you were skillful enough, you could bring a *bateau* in here. A small, flat-bottomed boat that could be poled through swamps. South Carolina had one hundred thousand acres of these tidal swamps. Places of great beauty with stands of red maples, tupelo, and gum trees. Where a dip net and a bucket could score you a tasty catch. But these swamps could be treacherous places, as well. Populated by cottonmouths and alligators, riddled with pockets of ravenous quicksand.

A good seven or eight miles down the trail, a clearing opened up and Theodosia turned in. A wooden camp house squatted in the dust, weathered gray and smooth as only cypress can get, paint worn off by years of rain, heat, and humidity. Adjoining the camp house were two small, run-down buildings.

Jumping out of her Jeep, the acrid smell of wood smoke hit Theodosia's nostrils and jerked her back more than a quarter of a century. Back to when she'd been a kid, bold and curious. Charging bareback on an old paint pony across fields and through woods, jumping old rice dikes. Her only mission in life the exploration of the old rice fields, trails, and shacks that were hidden and sheltered in the lands surrounding Cane Ridge Plantation.

A dog, grayish-blue, the kind folks usually called an old tick hound, came loping up to Theodosia. Alert but cautious, the mild-mannered dog stretched his neck out to give an inquisitive sniff.

Theodosia held out her hand, letting the dog take his time.

"B.J. won't hurt you," called a voice. A man, presumably Dan'l Oates, stood in the doorway of one of the small shacks. With the sun at a lower angle now, Theodosia could just make out his outline.

"I'm not all that worried," said Theodosia, as the dog edged closer. The hound delicately raised a front paw, then allowed her to scratch its stubbly chin.

Gazing about, Theodosia took in the junky yard. The debris that was strewn about looked like the dismantled midway of a county carnival. Colorful wooden boards were painted with winged skulls that wore jaunty porkpie hats. Pieces of tin had been adorned with primitive-looking flying birds. There were a half dozen sideshow-type posters that integrated cartoon drawings with words and numbers. And an oval piece of scrap metal was festooned with a painting of a grinning blue dog that had an oversized head.

Dan'l Oates, Theodosia decided, produced the kind of art that was termed "outsider art" by the traditional art community. Art that a few decades earlier had been labeled primitive.

This was strange stuff, she decided. Bizarre subjects, unusual techniques. But these pieces were also wonderfully enchanting and extremely powerful.

"How do," said the man. Walking toward her, he touched his cap in greeting. "You lost?"

"I hope not," said Theodosia. "Are you Dan'l Oates?"

The man gave a slow nod. "That's me."

Dan'l Oates was tall, lanky, dressed in faded denim. Probably forty-five years old, but a hard forty-five. Like he'd probably worked outdoors as a laborer most of his life.

"I understand you have some paintings for sale," said Theodosia.

Dan'l Oates scrutinized her for a moment, then cocked his head a couple degrees. "A few," he drawled slowly.

"Is this your work here?" Theodosia asked. She gestured around at the strangely compelling pieces of painted tin and wood.

"Some of it," said Dan'l Oates. "But I got newer pieces. Better pieces."

"May I see them?" she asked.

Dan'l didn't budge. "You from some sort of gallery?" he asked.

Theodosia knew she had to play it straight. "The Jeanty Gallery in Savannah gave me your name and address," she told him. "You used to have a painting on display there?"

A small smile flickered across his weatherbeaten face. "Used to?" he asked. "Guess that means it sold. It was there for a while, though."

"It did sell," said Theodosia. "That's why I'm here. I missed out."

"Well, come on then," said Dan'l. He led her across the dusty yard toward one of the small buildings, B.J. trailing behind them. "Most of my stuff's in here."

Stepping into the shed, it took Theodosia's eyes a few moments to adjust to the low level of light. Then she gazed about, taking in the dozen or so large-scale canvases that hung on the bare walls.

"Good lord," said Theodosia, putting a hand to her heart.

"You like 'em?" Dan'l Oates asked. He seemed pleased by her stunned reaction.

Theodosia stared in amazement at the paintings. They all had the same light-dark chiaroscuro effect, all portrayed the same haunting subject matter—the saints, the forlorn landscapes, the Russian peasants—as the paintings that hung in Maribo Pratt's Segrova Gallery.

"They're forgeries," breathed Theodosia in a shocked whisper. Her words were meant only for herself, but Dan'l Oates had keen hearing.

"No, ma'am," he said with complete conviction. "These are what you'd call *commissioned* works." He pronounced the phrase like it was foreign to him, but he'd been carefully schooled to say it. "I'm just painting what this one dealer asked me to." He shrugged. "I never had no formal art school training. Most of my life I just painted what I felt in my head. Now I do these."

As Theodosia gazed around, her eyes landed on a clutter of books spread out on a chipped wooden table. Books on Russian landscape painting, contemporary Russian art,

magazines that included *Art and Antiques* and *ARTnews.*
"You use those books for reference?" Theodosia asked him.

"Source materials," said Dan'l Oates, following her gaze.
"That's what they call that stuff."

Theodosia was still stunned. "All these pieces were painted
for one buyer?" she croaked.

Dan'l Oates nodded eagerly. "A lady from Charleston."

"A lady from Charleston," repeated Theodosia. *Maribo.*
Maribo doesn't really import paintings from Russia and the Balkans
at all. She has Dan'l Oates create them for her.

"Maribo Pratt," said Theodosia, spitting out the name.

Dan'l bobbed his head happily. "Sounds like you know
her. The one who drives a big fancy car like the old movie
stars used to drive?"

"A Rolls Royce," whispered Theodosia. "Yes, I know her
quite well. You say she buys *all* your paintings?" Theodosia
knew she was stumbling around with her questions. But
never, in her wildest dreams, had she thought she'd uncover
such a forger's nest.

"First she tells me what she's interested in and then I
paint it," Dan'l explained. "Like I said, a commission."

"But Maribo selects the subject matter," said Theodosia.
This is beyond bizarre, she told herself.

Dan'l squinted at her. "That's pretty much how it works.
Sometimes she brings me a book and asks me to come close
to what's already in there."

"And she pays you well?" asked Theodosia.

Dan'l nodded safely. "Usually a couple hundred dollars
per painting. Sometimes more."

"A couple hundred dollars," said Theodosia, thinking of

the twenty and thirty thousand dollar price tags Maribo had placed on some of this man's paintings. "Imagine that."

"It's good money," Dan'l Oates assured her.

"It certainly is," replied Theodosia. *Maribo . . . the lousy fraud. The cheat.*

"But you don't sign these paintings," said Theodosia.

Dan'l shook his head. "Not with my real name. Miss Maribo wants me to use what they call a pseudonym. Writers do the same thing, you know? Like Samuel Clemens was Mark Twain. She says it's done all the time."

"And you chose the name Draco Vidak," said Theodosia.

"She chose that one," said Dan'l. "Of course, six months ago she wanted me to sign everything Serge Tarak. Funny, ain't it?"

"Hilarious," replied Theodosia. "So these are all headed for Maribo's gallery," said Theodosia.

"Oh, I have a few I painted for myself," replied Dan'l.

"Can I see them?" Theodosia asked. *Holy cow, there's more?*

"Those are in my other place," said Dan'l Oates, gesturing.

He led Theodosia back outside and into the other small building. This shack wasn't quite as dark and had long workbenches running around three interior walls. A half dozen smaller canvases leaned up against one wall.

"These are my own," said Dan'l Oates proudly.

Theodosia crossed the floor, picked up one of the unframed canvases, and studied it. Dan'l Oates, when he wasn't forging or doing outsider art, was a remarkably gifted painter. This painting, a depiction of two shrimp boats pulling into port, was startling in its reality and depth of feeling.

"You're developing your own style," said Theodosia.

Despite his forging—and Theodosia knew that probably hadn't really been his intended path in becoming an artist—she was beginning to like this quiet, seemingly guileless man.

Dan'l Oates scrunched up his face. "I've been working mostly on realistic stuff. Portraits. Landscapes. I've been studying art magazines, and they seem to say that's the stuff that sells best."

"And you took one of your more realistic paintings to the Jeanty Gallery in Savannah?" asked Theodosia.

Dan'l Oates suddenly looked nervous. "No," he said slowly. "It was one of the Russian-style ones. But a smaller piece. Miss Maribo only wanted big paintings, so I didn't think she'd care."

"Does she know you took one to the Jeanty Gallery?" asked Theodosia.

"Probably not," said Dan'l Oates.

"But you signed your real name," said Theodosia, seeing the inevitable scenario spin sickeningly out in front of her.

"Sure," said Dan'l. "Why not? I painted it."

There it was, she thought. Curiosity had probably killed Roger Crispin. He'd seen Dan'l Oates's painting and immediately made the connection. He'd served on a board with Maribo, was familiar with the work in her gallery. Roger must have called her, told her that he was on to her.

Theodosia gently laid the painting down, turned to leave. *Tidwell,* she thought. *I have to talk to Tidwell.*

It was only then that she saw the corkboard crawling with tiny, furry insects.

"What's that?" she asked.

"That's my other business," said Dan'l, brightening. "Besides making paintings, I also tie flies."

"Explain please," said Theodosia.

"Flies like fisherman use," Dan'l told her. "You know, wet flies, dry flies, nymphs, streamers . . . like that. I sell 'em at Del's Fishing Shack over in Beaufort."

The sick feeling in the pit of Theodosia's stomach was spreading by the second.

But Dan'l Oates was on a roll. He obviously didn't get a lot of visitors and was thrilled to pour out a stream of consciousness to anyone who'd listen.

"My specialty is dry fly caddis," said Dan'l, unzipping a leather case where a dozen or so flies rested on piece of white nubby wool. He unhooked one of the tiny flies and carefully placed it in Theodosia's palm. "What fishermen call your top dropper. You just pop that baby down onto a stream, let it float around, and wait for the fish to take it."

"What's that made from?" asked Theodosia. "The . . . what did you call it? Caddis?"

"I use synthetic dubbing for the body and elk hair for the wings," explained Dan'l.

"Elk hair," repeated Theodosia.

"It comes in these little packets," he explained, pulling a couple packets off a shelf to show her. "You have to be real careful 'cause it's expensive stuff and the little hairs get all over the place. I think that is one of the reasons Miss Pratt and I hit it off so well. She's kind of an amateur fisherman herself. Or fisherwoman, I guess you'd say."

The last piece of the puzzle clicked into place for Theodosia.

Maribo spoon-fed us a pack of lies, she thought. *And we all stood around at her gallery eating it up. Not knowing she'd probably murdered Roger.* Theodosia shook her head angrily. *Maribo fooled us with her packed house, her PR, and her twenty cases of mediocre champagne.*

"Stick around," said Dan'l, "and you can say hi to her."

Panic suddenly struck hard in Theodosia's breast. "Stick around?" she whispered.

"Yup," said Dan'l, glancing at his watch. "Miss Maribo's supposed to be here around five. First she told me she didn't need more paintings until next week, then she called . . . oh, maybe two days ago, all excited and yellin' about how she needed 'em right away. Said I had to pull out all the stops."

Two days ago, thought Theodosia. *Maribo called Dan'l Oates the morning after her big opening and told him to have the rest of the paintings ready. Told him to get cracking.*

"And she's coming here today," said Theodosia. *Stick around and run into her? No thanks. No way.* "Sorry," said Theodosia, edging nervously toward the door, "but I'm supposed to be somewhere else."

"Want me to tell her . . . ?" began Dan'l.

"No!" said Theodosia. "I'll be seeing Maribo . . . uh, later tonight. I'd rather surprise her." *Oh yes I would! Would I ever.* "Please don't mention I was here, okay?"

"Sure," said Dan'l. "No problem."

22

❧

Shadows were lengthening, the sun beginning to dip in the western sky as Theodosia revved her Jeep and headed back up Shoals Trail. Plumes of dust rose behind her and she wondered if, tired as she was, she could push it a little harder. If she could make the drive back to Charleston in record time, she could alert Tidwell, assure Gracie Venable she wasn't going to be falsely accused, and still, hopefully, take part in the apprehension of Maribo Pratt.

Much to deal with, she told herself as she eased to a stop at the blind turn onto Highway 46. Just as she turned, another car also slowed to make its turn down the narrow trail Theodosia had just traveled.

Glancing quickly as she gunned her engine, Theodosia gazed into the inquisitive face of Maribo Pratt. Maribo seemed not to register her presence for a split-second, then her eyes widened in recognition.

Oh rats! thought Theodosia as she tromped down on the accelerator and took off fast. *Now I really have to get out of here! For sure Maribo's going to ask Dan'l Oates about me and then she's going to . . .*

Theodosia's eyes sought out the rearview mirror, watching as Maribo's big car negotiated the turn. It was only when she saw the quick red flare of the Corniche's taillights that Theodosia realized their little encounter wasn't over. Not by a long shot.

Theodosia watched in horror as the Corniche swept around in a wide U-turn and came barreling down the highway after her.

She's coming after me? Maribo's coming after me? To do what? Tailgate me all the way back to Charleston? All the way to the Heritage Society? Or Detective Tidwell's office?

But Maribo was rapidly picking up speed, not satisfied with merely tailgating. Ten seconds later the big Corniche roared ahead and slammed its massive front bumper into the rear end of Theodosia's Jeep!

Holy smokes!

Stunned by the force of the impact, thrust forward onto her steering wheel, Theodosia momentarily lost control of her Jeep. Fishtailing down the middle of the narrow road, she fought to regain control.

Gotta get out of here, Theodosia told herself, stunned that she was being so aggressively pursued. *Have to put some distance between us.*

Theodosia snuck a peek at her speedometer as she flew

down the road. Fifty miles an hour, sixty, approaching seventy.

Way too fast! her brain screamed. *This is a tiny little country road with dangerous twists and turns. Gotta slow it down!*

Theodosia's foot edged onto the brake. But at the same time she tapped the brakes, Maribo sent her Rolls Royce rocketing forward and slammed into the back of the Jeep a second time. This time Theodosia swerved dangerously onto the shoulder and heard the *whap whap whap* of nearby low-hanging branches swatting the sides of her Jeep.

As she caromed down the road, gravel flew out from beneath the Jeep's wheels, hammering and pinging at the front grill of the Rolls. Theodosia managed to straighten out, then quickly stomped down on the accelerator again. She was flying along at seventy-five, eighty miles an hour. But another quick peek in her rearview mirror told her the Rolls Royce Corniche was gamely keeping up.

Theodosia gritted her teeth as the road straightened. Even with her small lead, she knew that on the straightaway her Jeep was no match for the powerful Rolls Royce Corniche.

Theodosia had a certain familiarity with Rolls Royce engines. Her dad had served in the Korean War and had landed on a PT Boat. He'd entertained her with bedtime stories about the powerful little mosquito boats with their amazing Rolls Royce engines that literally propelled them across the top of the water. There wasn't anything built that could catch one, he'd told her, except maybe the old P-51 Mustang fighter planes that had also been powered by the same monster engines.

What about on corners? Theodosia fretted, as she swept

into a series of turns. *My Jeep's not good at cornering, so maybe this is where she'll catch me! Then what?*

Theodosia knew exactly what Maribo would do. She'd creep up next to her and run her right off the road. Send her flying into a stand of immovable hardwood trees at seventy miles an hour.

Theodosia decided she had one chance. Off road. *A Jeep is built to bump across rough terrain, even ford a stream or two,* she reasoned. *And that big old Rolls Royce is not. If I can find a side trail to head down, I just might be able to lose Maribo.*

Flying down the road, Theodosia's eyes searched ahead for some sort of path or trail. Something unpaved that her Jeep with its four-wheel drive and heavy-duty tires could eat up.

A little white church, a praise house, loomed ahead. And as Theodosia swept past it, she noticed an indentation just beyond. A grassy, rutted trail, almost but not quite a road, that lead into a thicket of woods and swamp.

Cranking her steering wheel hard to the left, Theodosia aimed for the little trail, knowing this was going to be her ultimate off-road test!

There was a crunch and a thud as her Jeep bounced over the shoulder, dug through gravel, and then jounced down the rutted trail.

Maribo, no slouch in the courage department, hesitated briefly, then headed gamely after her.

She's following me? thought Theodosia. *I never in a million years thought she'd do that!*

Branches slapped her windshield as Theodosia bumped down the twisting trail. The tin of cookies she'd bought for

Drayton went flying off the passenger seat and crashed to the floor. *Crumbs,* she thought. *There'll just be crumbs left.*

Mud and wet grasses turned to spongy, soggy swampland, yet still Theodosia continued to jostle along, dodging trees, rolling over entire bushes.

What if I bog down? Dear lord, don't let me bog down!

She turned to steal a glance, wondering if Maribo was following, but didn't see her. Plunging from side to side as the road got rougher and soggier, Theodosia found herself negotiating pure swampland. It would be just a matter of time before she finally ran out of terra firma.

The trail that she'd followed in had basically disintegrated as Theodosia plowed ahead, zigzagging, searching for a hint of solid ground that would give her wheels slightly better purchase.

Fifty more yards, a hundred more yards in, she wondered if she'd maybe lost Maribo. Slowing, she hit the button to lower the driver's-side window, then listened carefully.

Behind her, branches snapped and an engine whined as Maribo continued to barrel through the swamp after her.

Panic rising now, Theodosia downshifted, steering left then right, doing whatever she could to keep advancing forward.

Suddenly, directly in her path, she spotted a giant puddle of brown ooze!

Veering hard right, hoping to skirt this new water hazard, Theodosia felt her wheels spin sickeningly for a few moments. She eased off the gas, paused, and began to gently rock her way forward. Then, at just the right moment, she gunned it. Her Jeep rocketed ahead just as the giant Rolls Royce lurched into view behind her. And Maribo, and all three thousand pounds of her British behemoth, dove nose first into the ooze.

That's it, thought Theodosia. *That muck just stopped her for good!*

Theodosia bumped along another hundred yards, then gently eased off the gas and rolled to a stop.

Wary, she cranked open the door, stuck her head out, and looked back.

Mangroves and Spanish moss hung in a tangle, but Theodosia could see a glint of silver. Maribo's car had been stopped dead in its tracks.

Climbing out of her Jeep, Theodosia was dismayed to find herself sinking up to her ankles in wet, boggy muck. *Thank goodness I put oversized tires on my Jeep,* she decided. *Good Jeep. Good tires.*

Carefully, quietly, Theodosia crept back twenty feet or so. Her curiosity was at a fever pitch, and she wanted to see for herself that her pursuer had been halted.

As she got closer, Theodosia could see that Maribo's big car had indeed sunk up to its wheel rims in brown ooze. *Good,* she thought. *That puddle of muck must be a lot deeper than I thought.*

A faint noise made her instantly alert.

What was that?

Theodosia listened again.

"Help!" came a small cry. "Help me!"

It was Maribo.

"Help me!" came her keening cry again.

Is Maribo crying wolf? Theodosia wondered. *Trying to lure me in?*

Theodosia slogged a more few steps through the swamp, trying to stay in the tracks she'd created. And she had to admit, Maribo's calls sounded decidedly more frantic now. Like the woman truly needed help.

When she got within ten feet of Maribo's Rolls Royce, Theodosia hesitated, peering tentatively through the tangle of swamp grass and trees.

Maribo's behemoth of a car had sunk even deeper! In fact, it seemed to be sinking right before Theodosia's eyes!

Oh no, thought Theodosia. *Quicksand.*

She'd grown up hearing horror stories about quicksand. How the slimy, waterlogged sand could swallow farm animals whole in a few minutes' time. How the more a person struggled in quicksand, the faster they sank.

Now the front bumper was beginning to disapear and Theodosia had to think fast.

Ohmygod, it's a heavy car and sinking fast, she thought. *But what do I do? Try to save her? Or run and get help?*

Her brain told her there wasn't time to find help. She had to make a stand here and now, not just sit idly by and watch Maribo disappear into a bottomless morass!

The irony that Maribo had been chasing her, intending her real harm, was not lost on Theodosia.

"Help!" came Maribo's piteous cry. "Help me!"

Theodosia approached the car tentatively. The engine was still on, the wheels, what she could see of them, rotating slowly in the roiling quicksand. Theodosia figured there wasn't much time.

Still in the driver's seat, Maribo squirmed about, pounding on the glass, gripped by fear, overwhelmed with panic.

Theodosia worried that Maribo's thrashing might even be making the car sink faster.

"Sit still!" yelled Theodosia as she watched Maribo scratch frantically at the side window. "Try to open the door!"

"I can't!" Maribo screeched. "It's stuck! The car's sinking!"

"Try to put your window down," urged Theodosia. "If you can get it down, you can squirm your way out."

Maribo fumbled for the controls and then, miraculously, the driver's-side window slid down.

Good car, thought Theodosia. They could probably do an ad campaign based on this. Sunk in a hole but continued to roll.

Now Maribo's screams increased dramatically in volume. "Get me out of here!" she demanded.

"Hang on, Maribo," yelled Theodosia. "Sit tight for a couple seconds and I'll be right back."

"Don't leave me!" Maribo pleaded pathetically as Theodosia dashed back to her Jeep. Popping open the back hatch, she fumbled about, searching for something—anything—she could use to help pull Maribo to safety.

Finally she found it. Earl Grey's flexi-leash!

Sprinting back to where Maribo was stuck, Theodosia clung to the flexi-leash. Made of durable nylon and a good twenty feet long, Theodosia knew Maribo could loop it around her waist and then, hopefully, let herself be pulled to safety. Hopefully.

Theodosia spun out the leash as fast as she could, then tossed the molded plastic end to Maribo.

"Wrap it around your waist!" Theodosia instructed her. "Take it around a couple times and then tie a knot. When you come through that window, I'll take up the slack and pull you out!"

Frantically, Maribo worked to tie the red vinyl leash around her waist. As she did so, Theodosia snugged the opposing end around a cypress tree.

There, she thought, *this should work. This should do the trick.*

"I can't do it!" screamed Maribo. "Go get help. Get the fire department or something! A rescue crew!"

"No time!" Theodosia screamed back, noting the car had sunk at least another foot in the time she'd been gone. "The entire car is sinking! You have to jump, it's the only way!"

Maribo tentatively stuck a leg out the window.

"Come on," urged Theodosia. "Jump! Take the plunge and I'll reel you in!"

There was a long moment when Maribo was poised, scrunched in the window, then she pushed through the window and threw herself out.

Splat!

Maribo began to thrash frantically even as she hit the muck.

"I'm being sucked down," she cried piteously. "Help me, please!"

Theodosia cranked the flexi-leash another notch around the tree, taking up the slack. "I've got you!" she called to Maribo.

"Pull!" screamed Maribo.

"Swim!" yelled Theodosia. She knew that quicksand was more water than sand and that swimming was probably the best way to work your way to the surface and to safety.

Moments later, Maribo emerged, smeared in brown

slime, hissing like an angry snapping turtle. Still clutching her handbag, she had one shoe on, the other shoe lost forever to the muck.

"Are you *insane*?" Maribo screamed as she scrabbled to her feet. She slipped, went down hard, fought to pull herself up again. "Are you *daft*?" she continued once she'd righted herself. "Leading me down a stupid trail like this? You ought to be *horse-whipped*. What were you *thinking*?"

"I was trying to get away from you!" Theodosia screamed back.

Maribo suddenly halted her hysterics, trying frantically to wipe a patch of bright green algae from her face. Then she noticed her car had almost disappeared. Only the top few inches were visible.

"My car, my beautiful car!" she wailed. "You're going to *pay* for this," she said, challenging Theodosia. "You're to *blame*!"

"You're nuts," said a disgusted Theodosia. "Besides, where you're going, lady, you're not going to be doing a whole lot of driving."

"What are you talking about?" demanded Maribo.

Theodosia was tired and running out of steam. She'd had enough of this madness. "I'm talking about Roger Crispin," she said. "I know what you did."

"You don't know, you don't know," stammered Maribo. "How could you?"

But Maribo's eyes told Theodosia all she needed to know. Maribo knew she'd been caught.

Now tears streamed down Maribo's face. "Roger called me," she explained in a rush. "He threatened to expose me!"

"Right," said Theodosia. "So you stalked him. You knew he'd be at the Poet's Tea and you went after him. Shot him in cold blood."

"Theodosia!" she cried, her face crumpling. "You don't get it! I would have been *ruined*! My reputation left in shreds! Everything I worked for gone!"

Theodosia put a hand up as if to fend Maribo off, diffuse the rage and negative energy. She was tired. Exhausted. The only thing to do now was to call the authorities. Get the police or sheriff out here. Maybe a tow truck, too.

Theodosia turned, headed back toward her Jeep in disgust. Maribo was, after all, a murderer. A cold-blooded killer. There was no need to be polite, the cards were all on the table.

Theodosia was almost at her Jeep when a slug thwacked into a tupelo tree not more than a foot from her head.

Theodosia's initial reaction was, *She's shooting at me? She's trying to kill me after I saved her life?*

Diving for cover, Theodosia suddenly had a mental picture of Maribo being dragged out of the quicksand. Her handbag hanging intact on her arm.

Must have had a gun stashed in there, Theodosia told herself. There was a fast rustle behind her and then Maribo came crashing through the brush after her.

Theodosia did the only thing she could do. Picked herself up and ran like crazy, making a final mad dash, crouching and zigzagging so she'd be less of a target. Then, just as she put a hand on the door of her Jeep, Theodosia's left shoulder exploded with hot, searing pain!

Owwww!

Looking down, Theodosia was shocked to see a bloom of red across the front of her blouse, was startled by the sheer intensity of pain. On a scale of one to ten, it definitely registered eleven!

I'm shot! Maribo shot me!

Turning, staggering the last half-step, biting her lip to keep from fainting, Theodosia tried to pull herself inside.

Gotta get inside . . . lock the door . . .

She almost made it, was starting to clamber in when she heard the sucking sound of mud as Maribo plodded toward her, was just steps behind her. Terrified, knowing she had only one chance to act, Theodosia reached inside her Jeep and grabbed the first thing her flailing fingers touched. Her thermos full of sweet tea. With all the strength she could muster, Theodosia swung the heavy metal thermos with her good arm, following through like a home run hitter, and connected squarely with the side of Maribo's head. There was a loud, sickening *thwack* as metal hit bone, followed by a fine spray of blood. Then Theodosia watched, horrified, as Maribo's eyes rolled back in her head and she crumpled to the ground, a slow hiss of breath escaping her lips as she went down.

"I've killed her!" exclaimed Theodosia. "Dear Lord, forgive me!"

Theodosia fumbled for her cell phone, but her left arm didn't seem to be working. Gazing down, she was appalled to see that the bloom of red on her blouse was expanding.

Oh man, is this it? Am I going to die out here?

Theodosia struggled to make her fingers work, but the cell phone kept slipping away, her memory kept failing.

Going into shock, she told herself.

Vision already blurry around the edges, she gripped the phone and stabbed viciously at the redial button. *Who am I calling?* she wondered. *No matter.* When she heard a faint answer, she identified herself immediately and began babbling. *Hurt bad. Stuck in the swamp. Off Highway . . . uh . . . 46.* She momentarily lost track of what she was saying. *By the white church. Please . . . send help!*

She wanted to say more, knew she should have given better instructions, but she was fading fast.

Fade to black, was Theodosia's final, giddy thought as she slipped into the dark recess of unconsciousness. *Exactly what I used to tell my film editors when I produced TV commercials. Fade to black.*

23

❧

Somebody was kissing her. A tiny, nibbley kiss that tickled like crazy.

Who's kissing me? was Theodosia's murky thought as she tried to swim toward consciousness. *A man with a beard? Or a mustache?*

Working up considerable energy to cock one eye open, Theodosia gazed into a pair of limpid brown eyes.

Earl Grey? she thought. *Here in the hospital? At least I'm having a decent dream.*

She closed her eyes again, tried to move her left arm, discovered it had become a lead weight.

Or maybe I died and went to heaven, she mused to herself. *A wonderful, equal-opportunity heaven where all the dogs and kitties*

*you've loved and lost throughout the years come bounding up to greet
you. Wouldn't that be some kind of paradise?*

"She's waking up," came Haley's soft voice.

"Of course she is," whispered Drayton. "Did you think
you smuggled that dog in here for nothing?"

"Earl Grey's a service dog," said Haley. "He's *allowed*."

"Haley? Drayton?" Theodosia's voice was a hoarse whisper.

"Don't try to move," said Drayton.

"She should try to sit up," argued Haley. "Gather her
wits about her."

"Now I know I'm going to be okay," croaked Theodosia.
"If they let you two in to see me."

"You were shot," said Drayton. "Poor thing, you're still
in shock."

"Did they get—?" began Theodosia.

"Maribo?" said Drayton, jumping in to complete her
question. "Yes, absolutely. She's been apprehended and
hauled off to jail. I truly hope the authorities manage to lose
the key to her cell for a good long while."

"What about my—?" started Theodosia.

"Shoulder?" said Haley. "Just a flesh wound. The doctor
says you'll be bruised and sore for a while, but you sustained
no permanent damage."

Theodosia favored them with a faint smile. "Are we playing twenty questions?" she asked. "Because you two keep
jumping in and finishing every—"

"Sentence," said Drayton. "Oops, sorry," he added, realiz-
ing he'd just done it again. Rolling his eyes, Drayton fid-
geted with his bow tie, obviously uncomfortable at seeing
Theodosia in such a helpless state.

"How did . . . ?" Theodosia hesitated, expecting one of them to jump in again. But they didn't. "How did you find me?" she asked.

"Apparently you made a rather cryptic phone call to Parker Scully," Drayton told her. "Smart fellow that he is, our Mr. Scully immediately alerted the sheriff down in Bluffton. They went out and found you. Three patrol cars, two search dogs, and an ambulance." Drayton sounded pleased. As though Theodosia had gotten the royal treatment.

"You must have hit the redial button," said Haley. "Apparently your cell phone was still clutched in your hand when they found you."

"Indeed, the phone had to be *pried* from her hot little hand," came Burt Tidwell's gruff voice. He'd been standing in the darkness of the doorway for a minute or so.

"Detective Tidwell?" called Theodosia's soft voice. "How do you know about that?" Somewhere in the recess of her mind, Theodosia remembered a kindly EMT gently removing the cell phone from her hand and laying her down on a stretcher. Covering her with a blanket, the EMT had assured her she was going to be just fine. Theodosia remembered thinking she would have married him then and there.

"Because I was down there," said Tidwell, walking slowly toward her bed, carrying an enormous bouquet of roses. "Though you were rather incapacitated at the time, I was at the scene of the accident. Oh, by the way, we *are* calling it an accident for now and not a crime. The technicalities will probably be resolved later."

"You drove down and back already?" asked a confused Theodosia. "To Beaufort or Bluffton or wherever I ended up?"

Tidwell raised a hand and made an upward zooming motion. "I commandeered a helicopter," he told her grandly. "Stole it right from under the nose of a young ATF officer. Told him it was priority one."

Theodosia managed a faint laugh. "Wow. Priority one. All that for me?" She looked around. "How did I get here?" she asked. "To Charleston. I am in Charleston, right?"

"You were my passenger," Tidwell told her. "From the swamps of Bluffton to Charleston Memorial Hospital. We set down right atop their roof."

"Sounds like first-class service," she said, her voice still sounding croaky.

"You broke the case, my dear girl," said an exuberant Tidwell. He set the enormous bouquet down on the table next to Theodosia's bed. "And Maribo Pratt was only too happy to confess. Once she regained consciousness, that is." Tidwell peered down, suddenly aware of Earl Grey. "Good heavens!" he exclaimed. "Even your canine has come bearing good wishes."

"*Ssh,*" said Haley, putting a finger to her lips. "Earl Grey's traveling incognito tonight. The lady at the front desk thinks we're here on official dog therapy business."

"As well you are," laughed Tidwell.

"What time is it?" asked Theodosia, struggling to sit up in bed. "Ouch."

Drayton checked his watch. "Nine o'clock."

"At night or in the morning?" asked Theodosia.

"It's nighttime," said a nurse, bustling into the room. "Time for your guests to take their leave."

"Drayton, you're missing the auction!" exclaimed Theodosia. "At the Heritage Society."

"I'm sure it's proceeding as planned," said Drayton. "In fact, we'll probably head over there now. But your nurse is quite correct. We should leave you alone so you can get some much-needed rest."

"But you'll be back tomorrow?" asked Theodosia. Now that she was safe and well cared for, she hated to see everyone leave.

"We'll be back," said Haley. "And Parker Scully's coming, too. He wanted to come by tonight, but we told him you'd probably be too tired."

"I am tired," Theodosia admitted. "Dead tired." She thought about what she'd just said for a couple seconds, then said, "Maybe I'll amend that to bone tired."

"Better choice of words," murmured Tidwell.

"Are you hungry?" the nurse asked Theodosia as she plumped up her pillows. "Can I fetch you something to eat?"

"I'm starving," said Theodosia. She'd skipped lunch, obviously slept through dinner.

"It would have to be something very light," warned the nurse. "You've sustained quite a shock to your nervous system. The most we could probably allow you is some tea and toast."

Theodosia waved good-bye to Drayton, Haley, and Tidwell as she settled back on soft pillows. "Tea and toast," she said with a yawn. "I think that would be an altogether fitting way to end this crazy day."

FAVORITE RECIPES FROM
The Indigo Tea Shop

Almond Cake To Die For

1 cup butter
1 cup sugar
3 eggs
1 jar almond filling
1 tsp vanilla extract
2¼ cups all-purpose flour
2 tsp baking powder
½ tsp salt
¼ cup milk
2 Tbsp orange zest

BEAT butter and sugar in large bowl until fluffy. Add eggs, one at a time, beating well in between. Beat in almond filling and vanilla extract until blended. In separate bowl, mix together flour, baking powder, and salt. Add to almond mixture, a little at a time, also adding milk in slowly. Add orange zest and beat until batter is blended. Spread batter evenly in a greased and floured 10" tube pan or large Bundt pan. Bake 55 minutes or until center is springy and the sides begin to pull away from the pan. Remove cake from pan and let cool on rack. Top with your favorite frosting or fruit glaze.

Cashew Chicken Salad

4 skinless, boneless chicken breasts (cooked and diced)

½ cup mayonnaise

2 Tbsp orange juice

¼ cup minced green onions

½ cup finely chopped cashews

¾ cup champagne grapes (removed from stem)

Salt and pepper

COMBINE the chicken, mayonnaise, orange juice, onions, and cashews and mix well. Add the grapes, then salt and pepper to taste. Serve on a tulip tomato, bed of field greens, or avocado half. Or you can cut out rounds of bread using a biscuit cutter and top with the cashew chicken salad to create tea sandwiches.

Haley's Strawberry Biscuits

    1 cup diced strawberries
    3 Tbsp sugar
    2 cups flour
    1 Tbsp baking powder
    ¼ tsp baking soda
    ¼ tsp salt
    6 Tbsp cold butter
    ⅔ cup buttermilk

TOSS strawberries with 2 Tbsp sugar and set aside. Sift together flour, remaining sugar, baking powder, baking soda, and salt, then cut in the butter (a few chunks are okay). Stir in strawberries, coating them with flour. Stir in buttermilk until flour mixture is moist. Gently knead the dough on a floured work surface. Pat to about ¾" thick, then use a 2" biscuit cutter to stamp out rounds (you should get about 16 biscuits). Place biscuits on a baking sheet lined with parchment and bake in 450 degree oven until light brown, about 15 to 20 minutes.

Cranberry-Orange Bread

    2 cups flour
    1 cup sugar
    1½ tsp baking powder

¾ tsp salt

2 Tbsp shortening

1 egg, beaten

¾ cup orange juice

Grated rind of 1 orange

1 cup raw cranberries, sliced in half

½ cup broken pecans

MIX together flour, sugar, baking powder, and salt. Cream in shortening, egg, orange juice, and orange rind. Fold in cranberries and nuts. Bake in greased bread pan or two tea-sized bread pans at 350 degrees for 50 minutes to 1 hour. Let cool before slicing.

She-Crab Soup

6 Tbsp butter

1 small onion, finely diced

½ cup celery, finely diced

2 tsp flour

1 pt milk

½ lb crabmeat

½ pint cream

2 Tbsp sherry

1 tsp Worcestershire sauce

Paprika

Salt and pepper

MELT butter in large saucepan, then sauté onion and celery until lightly browned. Add flour, stir to make a roux. Stir in milk gradually until thoroughly mixed. Gradually add in cream, then add crabmeat and simmer over low heat for 30 minutes. Add sherry and Worcestershire sauce, plus paprika, salt, and pepper to taste. Simmer for an additional 15 minutes. Yields 4 servings.

NOTE: "She-crabs" have much more flavor than male crabs, but are often difficult to find. So other crabmeat can certainly be used.

Theodosia's Coconut Macaroons

3 egg whites
½ cup sugar
¼ tsp vanilla extract
5 cups flake coconut

BEAT eggs whites until stiff, then fold in the rest of the ingredients until nicely mixed. Drop rounded spoonfuls onto a cookie sheet lined with parchment paper. Bake for 15 minutes in a 300 degree oven. Yields 3 dozen cookies.

Raspberry Chocolate Chip Muffins

½ cup butter

¾ cup sugar

1 tsp vanilla

1 tsp orange zest

1 cup miniature chocolate chips

2 cups flour

2 tsp baking powder

½ cup milk

2 cups unsweetened raspberries (fresh or frozen)

CREAM butter and sugar together, then add vanilla and orange zest. Mix together chocolate chips, 2 cups flour, and baking powder in a separate bowl. Now add these dry ingredients, a little at a time, to the creamed mixture. Slowly add in the milk, then fold in raspberries. Spoon into muffin tins and bake at 375 degrees for 20 to 30 minutes. Yields 8 to 10 muffins.

Cinnamon Apple Scones

6 Tbsp butter

2 cups chopped apples

2 cups all-purpose flour

⅓ cup sugar

1 Tbsp baking powder

½ tsp salt

½ cup whipping cream

1 tsp ground cinnamon

2 Tbsp granulated sugar

MELT 3 Tbsp butter in pan, add in apples and cook over medium heat. Stir frequently until tender. Stir together flour, sugar, baking powder, and salt in mixing bowl then cut in remaining 3 Tbsp of butter until mixture is coarse. Add whipping cream and apples and mix by hand until dough forms a ball. Put dough on floured surface and knead five or six times. Flatten dough to form an 8" circle, sprinkle with the cinnamon and sugar mixture, and cut into 12 wedges. Transfer wedges to cookie sheet and bake at 400 degrees for 20 to 25 minutes until golden. Serve warm with Devonshire cream, whipped cream, or jam.

Blueberry Sour Cream Muffins

¼ cup applesauce

¾ cup sugar

2 eggs

1¼ cups flour

½ tsp baking soda

¾ cup sour cream

1 cup fresh blueberries

STIR together applesauce, sugar, and eggs. Combine flour and baking soda, then add to wet mixture and mix well. Stir in sour cream, then fold in blueberries. Spoon the batter into muffin tin (use paper liners) making sure cups are about ¾ full. Bake at 400 degrees for 12 to 15 minutes.

Marmalade and Cream Cheese Tea Sandwiches

MIX 2 to 3 Tbsp of orange marmalade and approximately ¼ cup of chopped pecans into a small package of softened cream cheese. Spread this mixture on lightly buttered thin-sliced white bread. Cut off the crusts, then cut again into long, narrow sandwiches.

Strawberry-Banana Green Tea Cooler

POUR approximately 1 cup of cooled green tea over ice cubes, then fill with strawberry-banana juice. Mix and enjoy.

Flourless Chocolate Tea Cake

12 oz semisweet chocolate (baking chocolate or chocolate chips)
½ cup butter
¼ cup sugar
¼ cup water
1 tea bag (citrus-flavored, rose hips, or peppermint)
3 eggs
Whipped cream for topping

MELT chocolate chips, butter, sugar, water, and contents of 1 tea bag over medium heat, stirring for 3 to 4 minutes. Remove from heat and fold in eggs until mixture is smooth. Pour into a 9" pie plate lined with waxed paper. Bake for 12 minutes at 425 degrees. Cool, cover loosely, then chill in refrigerator for approximately 8 hours (or overnight) until cake sets. To serve, remove from refrigerator and allow cake to sit for 15 minutes. Invert cake on serving dish, remove waxed paper, and top with whipped cream.

Lifesaving Sweet Tea

5 cups sugar
3 cups cold water
4 sliced lemons
Fresh mint

1 oz loose black tea leaves
1 qt hot water
1 qt room temperature water

MAKE syrup by combining 5 cups sugar with 3 cups cold water and slowly bringing to a boil. Add sliced lemons and mint sprigs and allow to cool for 15 minutes. Strain syrup and reserve liquid. Now infuse tea leaves in quart of hot water for 5 minutes, then strain finished tea into large pitcher half-filled with room-temperature water. Add syrup to taste, stir, and serve over ice in tall glasses.

Theodosia's Secret for Drying Hydrangeas

CUT flowers at the peak of maturity when they are starting to become slightly papery. Make sure blooms are completely dry. Strip off all leaves, then tie 5 or 6 stems together using string or a rubber band. Hang the bundles upside down in a hot, dry place that is out of the sun. Take care that there is good air circulation so flowers don't begin to mold! Let dry for about two weeks.

GRACIE'S CUSTOM
HAT TRICKS

A tea party is even more special when you're sporting an elegant *chapeau*. Just start with a plain straw or felt hat, then hold it over a steaming tea kettle to steam and work the crown and brim into the shape you want. When hat is set, create a hatband by tying a snippet of silk ribbon or a strip of velvet around the base of the crown. You can even get creative and embellish the hat band by stamping designs on it or sewing on antique buttons. When it comes to adding decoration, think about items you might already have—bits of feather, silk flowers, lace, or tiny jeweled pins. You can also pinch-pleat your own flowers out of ribbon, add tiny charms, or grab a peacock feather and set it at a jaunty angle. Whatever miniature still life you create, simply tack it in place with thread or use hot glue!

You can also turn a so-so straw hat into a stunner by

covering it with thin netting or fine lace. Get a large piece from a fabric store, then stretch it over the crown of the hat. Pleat and fold wherever necessary, then tack your fabric with thread or glue where the hatband would go. Then continue to fold the fabric over and under the brim (more pleating required) and tack to the inside of the hat. Add a pretty hat band to keep your fabric in place and decorate your new hat with a few flowers.

TEA TIME
ENTERTAINING IDEAS

from Laura Childs

There are so many exciting themes that will make your at-home tea party a memorable event.

Chocolate Tea

Your chocolate-loving friends are sure to adore chocolate nut breads iced with cream cheese, chocolate-filled croissants, strawberries dipped in chocolate, and miniature banana muffins with chocolate bits. Be sure to try some of the wonderful chocolate teas that are readily available on the Internet or at tea stores. Or indulge in teas flavored with orange bits, rose hips, or peppermint that will subtly compliment your chocolate-inspired menu. Chocolate truffles for dessert? But of course!

Fireside Tea

Pull all your plump, upholstered chairs up to a crackling fire, lay out your tea tray on the coffee table, and never move again! Fill your three-tiered trays with scones on top, savories in the middle, and pastries on the bottom. This might be the time to serve maraschino cherry scones and Keemun tea—a rich, full-bodied tea often called the Burgundy of teas.

Sophisticated Lady Tea

Elegance reigns with caviar and dollops of crème fraîche on toast points or blinis with sour cream and exquisite tea sandwiches. Set the mood with symphonic music, sparkling china, damask napkins, and lots of candles. Ceylon tea in martini glasses, anyone?

Romantic Tea

Lay down a couple mirrored tiles on your white tablecloth, scatter a few rose petals, then add place cards, roses in cut-glass vases, and lovely tea ware. Serve crab salad tea sandwiches, salmon mousse canapés, and pear and stilton tea sandwiches. Your desert tray could include chocolate truffles, poached pears, and shortbread cookies. Don't forget the romantic music—Debussy or Vivaldi would be perfect.

Solo Tea

Treat yourself royally and fix a tea tray just for yourself. Include cream scones, a mini quiche, and cucumber tea sandwiches. Select an unusual black tea blend. There are wonderful blends of Chinese and Indian teas, some blends that offer a combination of black tea, green tea, and jasmine. Put on your favorite music, wear a hat if you please, or relax in your favorite lounging pajamas. This is your time. Be aware that the very act of sipping tea inspires calm and relaxation. Be sure to treat yourself with a few well-chosen truffles from a fine chocolatier.

Taste of India Tea

Let the flavors of India inspire your menu. Perhaps gingered pineapple and Sultana raisin scones to begin, then curried chicken tea sandwiches or datenut bread spread with cream cheese and chutney. Put out your Indian paisley tablecloth or paisley napkins and accessorize with gleaming brass candlesticks and small Asian tea cups without handles. Darjeeling, the champagne of teas, or Nilgiri tea from India's Blue Mountains, would be lovely.

Scottish Tea

There is a wealth of "Scottish tea blends" on the market, and most tend to be delicious blends of Assam and Ceylonese teas. Start with scones and clotted cream, then get hearty with cheese and chutney sandwiches, crusty bread topped with ham and spread with Scottish mustard, maybe even pinwheels of Scottish smoked salmon and cream cheese. Don't forget the Scottish shortbread cookies for dessert.

DON'T MISS THE NEXT
INDIGO TEA SHOP MYSTERY!

Blood Orange Brewing

Candles flicker and shadows dance on the walls of a historic old home as guests at a Candlelight Concert sip sweet blood orange tea. But when one poor guest suddenly collapses and *real* blood begins to spurt, tea and trouble are brewing for Theodosia and company.

Find out more about the author,
her Tea Shop Mystery series,
and her Scrapbook Mystery series
at www.laurachilds.com

The *Tea Shop* mystery series by

LAURA CHILDS

DEATH BY DARJEELING
0-425-17945-1
Meet Theodosia Browning, owner of Charleston's beloved
Indigo Tea Shop. Theo enjoys the full-bodied flavor of a town
steeped in history—and mystery.

GUNPOWDER GREEN
0-425-18405-6
Shop owner Theodosia Browning knows that something's
brewing in the high society of Charleston—murder.

SHADES OF EARL GREY
0-425-18821-3
Theo is finally invited to a social event that she
doesn't have to cater—but trouble is brewing at the
engagement soiree of the season.

THE ENGLISH BREAKFAST MURDER
0-425-19129-X
Just as she's about to celebrate her work to help protect
the sea turtles of Charleston, Theo spots a dead body
bobbing in the waves.

THE JASMINE MOON MURDER
0-425-19986-X
Theo is catering a Charleston benefit, a "Ghost Crawl"
through Jasmine Cemetery, when the organizer drops dead—
and it looks like foul play.